Gilbert S. Swing

Biographical Sketches of Eminent Men

Events in the Life and History of the Swing Family

Gilbert S. Swing

Biographical Sketches of Eminent Men
Events in the Life and History of the Swing Family

ISBN/EAN: 9783337098568

Printed in Europe, USA, Canada, Australia, Japan

Cover: Foto ©Raphael Reischuk / pixelio.de

More available books at **www.hansebooks.com**

EVENTS IN THE LIFE AND HISTORY

OF

THE SWING FAMILY.

EXAMPLES OF INDOMITABLE ENERGY AND PERSEVERANCE.

PORTRAITS OF A FEW PROMINENT PERSONS WHO SETTLED IN EARLY TIMES IN THE COUNTIES OF SALEM AND CUMBERLAND, N. J.

BRIEF MEMORIALS OF THEIR LIVES.

WRITTEN BY

GILBERT S. SWING.

CAMDEN, N. J.:
GRAW, GARRIGUES & GRAW, PRINTERS,
No. 131 FEDERAL STREET.
1889.

CONTENTS.

CHAPTER III.

MY GRANDFATHER.

Another of the prominent men whose birthplace and home were here was Abraham Swing, the son of Samuel, the hardy emigrant who had braved the storms and danger of mid ocean. Names of his descendants. The war of 1812. Stationed at Billingsport. Brigadier General Jeremiah DuBois, Major General Bloomfield and Lieutenant Stewart. Visit of army officers at the farm of my grandfather, who was first lieutenant in the heavy artillery. Recollections of Leonard Swing. Opening the apple and the turnip caves, while my grandfather treated the soldiers. Encampment at Pole Tavern, where the arsenal was then located. Recollections of my grandmother. The dream of a Quaker lady.

CHAPTER IV.

HISTORY OF THE ARSENAL AT POLE TAVERN.

Military organizations in Salem county. Recollections of Majors Judah Foster and Nathaniel G. Swing. Incidents connected with our Revolutionary struggle in 1776. The arsenal at Pole Tavern. Military training days. Names of the field and staff officers. Soldiers trained for duty by Brigadier General DuBois, Major Bloomfield and Lieutenant Abraham Swing. A post office established here in 1802 called Pittsgrove. The first band of music organized in Salem county. Names of the original members. Description of the guns used in the heavy artillery. Muskets changed from flint to percussion, and used during the late war.

CHAPTER V.

JEREMIAH SWING.

Removal from Pittsgrove, N. J., to York, Pa., in 1764, on the borders of the Susquehanna river. Among the large and stately hemlock, the ash, the elm, and the pine, he saw an extensive field of labor. With three hired men he made a clearing and built his cabin. Floating rafts of logs down the Susquehanna river to Baltimore. Immense tracts of timber land, as yet undisturbed by the approach of civilization or the sound of the woodman's axe. In this wild and romantic locality his marriage is celebrated, and they commenced housekeeping. They were blessed with abundant health and strength, and the providence of God seemed to smile upon their labors and crown their life with success.

CHAPTER VI.

TWO SONS OF JEREMIAH.

Traveling on horseback from York, Pa., to Salem county, N. J. Marriage of Michael Swing to Sarah Murphy, of Pittsgrove, in 1789. Rev. John Murphy, founder of the first M. E. church in Pittsgrove township. Settlement of Michael Swing at Fairfield in 1790. Licensed to preach the Gospel. Extract from the record of the New Jersey Conference of 1792. Building a church at New Englandtown cross-roads, long known as Swing's Meeting House. Names of his children. Description of his farm and residence on the south side of Cohansey river. A never-failing spring of water. Following the stream the road led down to the beach. The rising and the falling tide washes the white sand and pebbles upon the shore. The song of the fisherman, the shrill whistle of a steamboat or a tug, breaks the stillness of the morning air.

CHAPTER VII.

MICHAEL SWING.

The first son born in the family was a bright, intelligent lad, and in his youthful days exhibited tokens of cheerfulness, energy, and ability. In early life he became a student of medicine in the Department of Arts at the University of Pennsylvania, and graduated M. D. Visit of Dr. Charles Swing to Ohio in 1815. Rates of letter postage. No railroads were then built in the United States. Ox teams met on the road hopelessly mired in the mud ; few bridges were then built in Ohio, and the streams of water were difficult to cross. Arrival in Clermont county. Location of Uncle George. Teaching school in Ohio. After the expiration of one year he purchased a horse and saddle, and started for home, taking the old stage road up the west side of the Ohio river to Fort Pitt. Return to New Jersey on horseback. Visit of George M. and his father, Rev. Michael Swing, at York, Pa., in 1816. A two-wheeled gig. First night on the road. The farmhouse of Abraham Swing. Crossing the Delaware in boats propelled by horses. The price of dinner and supper at Lancaster. Arrival at York. The home of our childhood ; the only sister of my father. Arrival of the Doctor from the West ; we missed seeing him on the road. Crossing the Delaware river at Port Penn. Cold winter and summer of 1816. Did you ever ride on a stage coach?

CHAPTER VIII.

The first Methodist Society in Bridgeton organized in 1804, by Rev. John Murphy and his son-in-law, Michael Swing. A plain house of worship was erected here in 1807, and soon after this society was admitted within the bounds of " Salem Circuit." With the exception of Bishop Asbury, who had previously traveled through New Jersey, John Murphy

---

CHAPTER IX.

MICHAEL SWING—CONTINUED.

CHAPTER X.

SARAH S. ATWOOD.

CHAPTER XI.

NATHANIEL G. SWING.

of industry. Teacher of the military drill. Assistant commander of the arsenal. Appointed to the office of major. Loved peace rather than war. Collector of taxes. Superintendent of public instruction. Examination and license of teachers. Member of the New Jersey Legislature. Familiar with the political and religious history of the past half century. The family circle. Recollection of a friend, &c. Tough of fiber and stout of heart, he celebrates his ninety-first birthday, March 30th, 1889.

CHAPTER XII.

CHAPTER XIII.

JONATHAN L. SWING.

nfluence of early habits. Religious impressions. The love of music. Intelligent in conversation and wonderfully gifted in song. Celebrating his marriage. Interesting family of children. By trade and occupation a farmer and mechanic. Earnest and devoted in his work. A Sunday-school teacher. Fond of Christian company. Firm and lasting in friendship. Health and strength failing. The end approaching. Passing away. Appropriate remarks by his Pastor. Hope and joy in reference to the departed. Tributes to his memory.

CHAPTER XIV.

DR. CHARLES SWING.

Habits of reading and study. Studying medicine under the tuition of Dr. Ewing, of Greenwich. Entered the University of Pennsylvania. Graduated. The first year's practice at Greenwich, Hopewell and Stoe Creek. Three good doctors. Removal to Salem. Partnership with the late Dr. Benjamin Archer. Marriage. Removal to Pennsville, where he became successful and popular, and remained for several years, until the death of his wife. Removal to Sharptown. Elected to the New Jersey Legislature. Second marriage. Names of father Swing's children. Approaching seventy years. Return of his son, John, from the gold mines of Colorado and Pike's Peak. Crossing a provision train. Accident on a ferry-boat. Drowned in Snake River. Marriage of Rev. Firman Robbins to Miss Hannah A. Swing. Recollections of Mr. Robbins while in the ministry. Names of the circuits traveled during a period of twenty-eight years.

CHAPTER XV.

LEONARD SWING.

CHAPTER XVI.

EBENEZER HARRIS.

CHAPTER XVII.

CAPTAIN JOHN M. SWING.

CHAPTER XVIII.

CHAPTER XIX.

HISTORIC MEMORIES.

CHAPTER XX.

OUR RELATIVES IN THE WEST.

CHAPTER XXI.

NOTES OF TRAVEL.

CHAPTER XXII.

OUR FAMILY IN THE WEST—CONTINUED.

Leaving New Jersey in 1804. Settlement in Clermont county. Building the first stone dwelling house in 1808. The first set-·tlers made great havoc with the timber. Raising corn, wheat, hogs and cattle. When our people first settled here Southern Ohio was one of the grandest forests in the world, and abounded with deer and wild game. The streams of water were full of fish, but my grandfather never ceased to long for fresh mackerel, haddock, sea bass, Jersey shad, and the fish that were caught from the ocean. Cincinnati was only a village, twenty-seven miles from our settlement, and the public roads were little more than cow paths. A large poplar tree. When I was a boy, I happened to be at my grandfather's house. Letters received from New Jersey. Failure of the Farmers' and Mechanics' Bank. Devoted to the church. Recollections of my grandmother. Miss Nancy Crane. Emigration to Ohio a success, alike to himself and family. They become respected and honored citizens. His mind and memory well preserved to the close of life. Another branch of our family. Visit of Captain John M. and Nathaniel G. Swing to Ohio. I love our family name in the United States.

CHAPTER XXIII.

Notes of the campaign at Yorktown, Va., and Newbern, N. C. Correspondence with Capt. G. P. Riley, captain 6th Regt. United States colored troops.

CHAPTER XXIV.

Notes of the Gettysburg campaign by Geo. W. Swing, captain 12th Regt. N. J. Vols.

CHAPTER XXV.

SHADRACH D. SWING.

Another branch of our family settlement in Illinois.   Products of the land described.   Raising of cattle, sheep and hogs.

———

CHAPTER XXVI.

MERRITT J. SWING,

Of Ohio.   Western correspondence continued.

———

CHAPTER XXVII.

ZACHARIAH RILEY,

A soldier of 1812, fallen.

———

CHAPTER XXVIII.

SAMUEL SWING.

———

CHAPTER XXIX.

Biographical sketch of Frederick Carman, soldier of the war of 1812, stationed at Billingsport, on the Delaware river.

CHAPTER XXX.

MICHAEL POTTER.

Incidents of the life of one of Salem county's centenarians. Born July 18, 1784. Celebrating his 99th, 100th and 101st birthdays. Extracts from the speeches of Messrs. Coombs, Swing, Connelly, Woolford and Edwards at the 101st anniversary. Memorial notice, James Coombs.

CHAPTER XXXI.

Reminiscences of life of A. R. Swing, of Washington City, D. C.

CHAPTER XXXII.

GEORGE M. SWING.

In their day and time the people of Fairfield were possessors of farms, orchards and gardens which Adam, in his innocence, might have coveted ; fine horses, carriages, and stock of expensive breeds. Looking back over the space of fifty years to the humble period when employed as teacher of public schools. From boyhood he was earnest, active and industrious, and in manhood fully sustained a noble reputation. Engaged in the lumber trade. Purchasing timber land. Supplying the ship-yards at Mauricetown, Millville and Bridgeton ; he is also engaged in mercantile pursuits. The oyster boats receive their supply of provisions mainly from the store of Swing & Tomlinson. Personally he was a high type of the "American gentleman," cordial in his manners, warm-hearted in his methods, and fluent in address. While giving direction to matters of business, there was little that escaped his notice. "Don't go to men of leisure when you want anything done ;

2

go to busy men." In the meridian of life death takes out of the list of living men one of the most noted citizens in his native place. Extract from the *Dollar Weekly News*. Obituary notice by Rev. J. Atwood.

———

CHAPTER XXXIII.

CHARLES P. SWING, ETTA T. AND ELIZABETH G. SWING.

———

CHAPTER XXXIV.

PHILIP B. SWING,

Of Batavia, Ohio.

———

CHAPTER XXXV.

Autobiographical sketch of the author, Gilbert S. Swing.

———

CHAPTER XXXVI.

Recollections of a Salem county school teacher. The end.

PREFACE.

The following biographical sketches and scraps of history have assumed their present form from the study and examination of ancient dates and records.

Conversation with the oldest and most reliable inhabitants of the counties of Salem and Cumberland has brought to light many important facts hitherto unknown. ·

This is a biography of men whose early history is little known to the present generation, and as an attempt to recover the personal and intellectual attainments of eminent families from oblivion this work is very valuable. Our people have the right to be informed of the principal events in the lives of those whom they delight to honor, but this cannot be unless these events are recorded and put in shape, and no apology is necessary for adding one more to the numerous biographies which already fill a large space in our literature.

The author has bestowed upon these pages both labor and research, supplemented by the utmost fidelity in the arrangement and presentation of dates and calculation. All the information within reach has been used to make the statements trustworthy and reliable, as no diary had been kept, and no friendly hand had hitherto attempted to rescue the memory and deeds of our ancestors from oblivion.

The incidents herein related were founded upon fact, and written in testimony of a close and unbroken friendship with aged members of the family who are passing away. It has been said, " The way to guess the future is to know the past," hence this work contains important information for the young nowhere else to be found.

We would hereby acknowledge our indebtedness to the *Pioneer*, *Chronicle*, Bridgeton *Evening News*, *National Standard* of Salem, N. J., and the Cincinnati *Gazette* for brief family *extracts*, and also to the many friends who have so kindly responded to " letters of inquiry," and those whose personal recollections give additional interest to this work. It is sincerely desired that these sketches may be found instructive and entertaining, and read with pleasure and profit, not only by the present generation, but become more and more appreciated as the years roll on.

With this end, a brief review, and hastily written, is all that can be attempted within the limits of this book, although much of interest might be related of other families ; and if I have not referred to each by name, it is not because they have not deserved such mention. Much of what the writer saw, heard, and experienced himself is related in these pages, and the memory of the past is with us to-day. If the scientist, or learned critic, should be disappointed in not finding here profound historical expressions, he will please bear in mind that the majority of readers do not feel interested in hieroglyphics. Hence we have used the most plain and truthful language, and when in want of information in this direction it will be well for the reader " to look within."

THE AUTHOR.

G. S. SWING.

EVENTS IN THE LIFE AND HISTORY

OF THE

SWING FAMILY.

CHAPTER I.

HISTORY is a narrative of past events; it is intended to bring truth into the world; and it is truth and knowledge that make man intelligent and free. It is usually the recital of national incidents, leaving out the individual lives of all except the most prominent persons; and yet there are events transpiring in family circles which, to those interested, surpass in importance many historic narratives. Memory fails and is lost in the decline and ending of life, but a written document, or a book, reveals the past to present generations.

The biographical history of a family contains a source of information that improves the understanding, strengthens the memory, and is usually attractive both to the young and the old. It might be styled the philosophy of teaching by example; or moral philosophy exemplified by the lives and actions of men. It adds to our own experience an immense treasure of the experience of those who lived before us, and thereby enables us to enter upon the duties of life with the wisdom and example of our ancesters. It is a matter of regret that we have the means of obtaining so little knowledge of the early history of our family. Had our people kept a faithful journal during the long and eventful period of time covering an epoch in our "national history" the most stirring and eventful, it might prove more interesting reading than the "Problems of Euclid," or "Greeley's Recollections of a Busy Life."

Whoever has had occasion to trace his lineage back to the first settlers of the country has learned the very loose way in which family records are usually kept, and been surprised to find how little intelligent men know about their ancesters. It is not unusual to find family records, but they are in an imperfect state, on stray pieces of paper, liable to be lost, or in small blank books mixed up with family expenses, the births in one place and the marriages in another. It is quite common to find people who cannot tell who their grandparents were, or if they know these, they are ignorant of their grand uncles and aunts. Many who are intelligent thus far, perhaps by reason of a personal acquaintance with these relatives, can trace their kindred no farther back. Not one in a hundred preserves even the names of his ancestors beyond the third generation. As a people we have little pride of ancestry, and are quite too busy with the present to think or care much for the past. And yet the past has had much to do with our present; and we who are now upon the stage will have quite as much to do in moulding the characters and shaping the destiny of those who are to come after us. It is a duty that we owe to our children, and children's children, to put them in possession of the names and dates in the family history with which we are familiar, and which will soon be forgotten if they are not recorded.

Town, church and cemetery records are important in their places, but they ordinarily contain only fragments of a family history. It is always interesting to know where our ancestors lived and what their occupations were. It is desirable that a man should preserve in permanent form not only his own family record, but that of his father and those of his paternal ancestors as far back as he can trace them.

" But what is the use of the record?" some will ask, who have a sharp eye to the dollars and cents. It may be of no pecuniary value whatever. It will add nothing to the fertility of your fields and make no better sales for your crops. Pedigree may count for much less pecuniarily in a man than in a horse. And yet it may be worth a man's while, as a matter of intelligence, to know something of his origin, something of the homes, occupations and characters of his ancestors. The knowledge certainly would do him no harm, and it might throw some light upon the tastes and peculiarities that he sees cropping out in his children, and help him to better methods of training.

It cannot be expected that in a brief sketch of this nature we should attempt to give anything like a connected account of each family, the intention of the writer being only to record some of their most prominent characteristics, and thereby perpetuate a brief memorial of their life. The truth is, the majority of them are of that class which it is rather the province of the biographer than the critic to describe.

Many of the events herein written transpired a number of years ago, and were composed by a writer who lived long after the transactions of which they treat. They were compiled from scattered records, fragments and traditions. Letters of inquiry have been written, and conversation with aged men has brought to light a vast amount of interesting facts previously unknown.

When our forefathers emigrated to America, during the great exodus of independent patriots, probably about the year 1750, two brothers left their home in the south of France, emigrated to the United States, and very early identified themselves with the doctrines and followers of the reformation. Both the French and German language were used and spoken by our ancestors and by many people at that time in this department of France. Among the collection of books we find "The History of France;" also an ancient volume entitled "Exercises to the Rules and Construction of French Speech," containing a vocabulary of passages extracted out of the best French authors, with reference to the grammar rules, written by "Monsieur Louis Chambaud," the book referred to being the fifteenth edition, revised and corrected with many improvements, published in Paris in the year MDCCXXXXVIII, price one crown, bound in leather; a book entitled " The Treasury of the French, English and German," containing a vocabulary; 2d, familiar forms of speech upon the most common and useful subjects, the best, if not the only, help extant for foreigners to attain this knowledge, the eighth edition, printed in London in MDCCXXXXIV (1744). Also an ancient manuscript written on parchment many years ago and marked " Historical," Alsace being spoken of as the birthplace and former home of our ancestors. Alsace-Loraine lies west of Baden, and south of Prussia and Belgium. This province borders the River Rhine; Strasburg, the capital, and located opposite to the German principalities. Hymn books and Bibles were brought with them from the mother country, and were printed in the French and German language. In the old family Bible, printed in London in the year 1712, in the Dutch language, we find the following record: " Samuel Swing, born September 15th, 1729, emigrated to the United States when in his twenty-third year. He was accompanied by one brother, named Jeremiah."

After passing safely through the storms of mid-ocean the vessel in which our heroes sailed arrived safely in the harbor of New York.

They had considerable means in their possession, it is said, and were fond of adventure, and had brave and daring dispositions; their active life in Germany, France, and other lands, and their journey across the sea, had taught them habits of economy and self-reliance.

Soon after their arrival in America, Samuel journeyed

on horseback through Pennsylvania, New Jersey, and portions of the state of New York, ultimately settling on Long Island, and nearly opposite the city of New York, where several years of life passed away.

He is said to have been a clement, kind-hearted man, with a benevolent face and mild and kindly expression, so like the early fathers of the Church that our hero attracted the sympathy of a lady of great personal beauty, of modest bearing and fine social qualities, whose cognomen is given as Sarah Diament, with whom he formed acquaintance. This acquaintance soon became intimacy, and finally ripened into mutual admiration and love. He was comparatively a young man when he arrived there. His suit prospered, and he was accepted. This young lady who had inspired his heart was the daughter of a wealthy resident of the southern part of Long Island, and there being no objection offered by the parents of Miss Sarah Diamant to this union of hearts and hands, the lovers had nothing else to do but to get married, which they did; and soon after this event they removed from Long Island to the southern part of New Jersey, purchased land, and settled in Salem county.

The keen eye of enterprise fell upon the spot, capital was invoked, its magic hand was laid upon the place, and, lo! all was changed.

It is related of himself and wife that they were a strictly religious people, their names being found recorded among the foremost members of the Presbyterian denomination at Pittsgrove, where they continued to

reside for nearly half a century, winning the confidence and esteem of the whole community. He was willing to live by the sweat of an honest brow, and content to transmit the same heritage to his sons, without hoping that they would aspire to the canvas bags of the money changer, the spindle of the manufacturer, or the pen of the reformer. By constitution the family is conservative; old wine he never drinks, but they do love old friends and old ways, and believe the generation before him knew something. He is a thoughtful builder, does everything for solid use and nothing for display. On Sabbath morning it was his custom and delight to call the family around him and assure himself that he was

> "traveling home to God
> In the way the fathers trod."

In the process of time an interesting family of children was born to them, and nothing broke the harmony and happiness of the forty-four years of their married life, till death called him away and separated them from each other, which event transpired in the year 1801.

THE GENEALOGICAL TREE

of the family embraces the following familiar names:

Jeremiah Swing, born in Pittsgrove township, Salem
    County, N. J. . . . . Dec. 31, 1760
Sarah Swing,   do.   do.   do. . . . . . . Oct. 27, 1762
Christiana Swing,   do.   do.   do. . . . . . . Oct. 25, 1764
Samuel Swing,   do.   do.   do. . . . . . . Nov. 4, 1767
Ruth Lawrence Swing, do.   do.   do. . . . . . . Oct. 4, 1769
Abraham Swing,   do.   do.   do. . . . . . . Oct. 27, 1771

The hardy pioneers who began to populate the semi-wilderness of central New Jersey in the first decade of the century had a fancy for digging out of ancient history names for their children and the towns and villages which they founded.

CHAPTER II.

THE original heads of the families bearing our name in the United States were two brothers, respectively named Samuel and Jeremiah Swing, genial and pleasant in manner and conversation, and to whom the present generation trace their lineage directly.

The descendants were located in New Jersey, Pennsylvania, Ohio, Indiana and Illinois, and are justly renowned as a liberty-loving, law-abiding people, of sober and industrious habits, and of thrifty and generous dispositions.

The families residing in Salem county were the descendants of the first named, while those who were born and settled in Fairfield township, Cumberland county, including Uncle George, who emigrated to Ohio in the year 1805, were the descendants of Jeremiah.

Among the list of relatives in the western states were the names of Geo. L. Swing, counsellor-at-law; Philip B. Swing, United States District Judge of the Southern District of Ohio; Rev. Prof. David Swing, of Chicago, and "other lights of the world," whose deeds will be remembered through all coming time, and whose abiding place may be mentioned hereafter.

The families residing in Salem county at the present writing are the immediate descendants of my grandfather, Abraham. Some of these became merchants, mechanics, teachers and professional men, while others were farmers, tillers of the soil, and still continue " to occupy the land" purchased by our ancestors. The purchase of a part of this property and record of deeds in the clerk's office are found, bearing the date of 1760, when the corner-stones were laid in what was then a wilderness of trees, and where our ancestor erected his dwelling-house " in the wilderness of the New World."

Various circumstances have concurred to promote the increase and progress of the family. Extensive tracts of fertile land, suitable for agricultural purposes, were then procured on moderate terms, and the means of subsistence were abundant and easily obtained.

The different varieties of timber then growing in this locality were known as white oak, black oak, hickory and poplar. These trees originally attained large size and admirable proportions, and in later years became very valuable for shipbuilding and also for the keels of vessels.

TREES WITH A HISTORY.

A gentleman informed us recently that about the year 1811 or '12 he was living on the road from Alloways-town to Woodstown, and that in his immediate neighborhood there was cut a white oak measuring five feet in diameter and fifty-two feet in length, requiring two wagons for its transportation with a team of sixteen horses and ten oxen. The stick was taken to Fogg's Landing, or Alloways creek, with the intention of floating it to the Navy Yard, Philadelphia, but the chain that connected it with the wood flat broke while on the way, and the great log sank to the bottom of the river, and there remains.

The above we have from most reliable authority, and can vouch for its truthfulness.

Tradition informs us that wild game was very abundant in this vicinity. The black bear and the grey wolf were often seen around the settlements at that early day.

For many years after, Indian arrow-points and tomahawks were found imbedded in the soil, and were frequently ploughed up on the farms of Abraham Swing, indicating plainly to us that the Indian once roamed here and his bark canoe floated upon the waters of New Jersey.

There is every evidence in the surrounding country, as well as from authentic tradition, that this entire section of the state was at an early period occupied by aborigines or so-called American Indians, who contentedly thrived and enjoyed the abundance of food furnished by the waters of the bay and its numerous tributaries, and there are yet tracts of land located in Cumberland county known at this day as " Indian fields."

One hundred and twenty-five years have already passed away since the first settlement of our ancestors in the southern part of the state. The woodman's axe and the advance of civilization and improvement have been steadily going on. Indians and wild beasts have long since disappeared from sight and almost from recollection, while long continued industry and perseverance have had their proper reward.

It may truthfully be said that the surrounding country was well adapted to attract the attention of the lovers of the beautiful in nature and of the anxious cultivator of the soil. The surface of the country is generally level and undulating, interspersed with living streams of water and sufficiently rolling to make it admirably adapted for agricultural purposes.

Salem county is a fair sample of West Jersey, both in the variety of its soil and in the advancement of its agricultural departments ; it was the favorite resort of the first Quaker emigrants, who constituted a large part of its early settlers, and who long maintained a commanding position in the religious and political affairs of this county. The members of this denomination at Salem and Woodstown are still numerous, owning a large amount of real estate, and have maintained their social and religious influence to the present day.

In our school geographies, the first information given the urchin of the last generation was that " New Jersey was settled by the Swedes and Finns." This was true to a limited extent. A few colonies of Swedes landed at different points along the low sandy coast, and to some of them great tracts of territory were given, upon which titles were based which later authorities respected, and the broad foundation was thus laid for hereditary family wealth and culture. But these instances were by no means numerous. The choicest lands along the Delaware were selected and cleared by that mild and patient race of plain men and kind women of whom George Fox was the type and bright efflorescence. In the wholesome and modest precepts of their religious thinkers the tilling of the soil was recommended as the safest, the noblest and most useful of all the employments; and when the Quaker first began to move about with his broad-brimmed hat in our native wilds; when he laid aside that plain drab coat for a wrestle with the primeval woods, he set the foundations broad and deep for some of the soundest agriculture and the ripest and truest civilization of our age. His plain speech and modest bearing proclaim his religion. He has no large words, no boasts, no ostentation, but informs us that from yonder field of six acres he took two hundred bushels of wheat. This corn-field yielded last year seventy-five bushels to the acre.

He has had no rain for six weeks, and will not make so much this year, but not less than sixty, he thinks.

He commenced poor thirty-five years ago as a tenant, when he thought his crop good if an acre yielded him twenty-five bushels of corn or twelve of wheat. He gave forty-five dollars when he bought several years ago, when Polk was President. Now he would look away from an offer of two hundred. He has no idea of going West. Omaha has no charms; he cares nothing for the price of land on the line of the Pacific Railroad, nor amid the hills of East Tennessee. And now the reader asks for a reason for all this. Why are these farmers so happy and content? Why does their land so steadily appreciate? We answer that such success is won only where favoring nature has been aided by skill and industry on the part of man. These Salem county farmers are proud of their business, and earnest to know the secrets and established rules of successful agriculture. They compare usages and grow wise by mutual instruction. By the application of marl and lime, land once comparatively worthless has been reclaimed and rendered very productive. In later years the state of New Jersey has often been called the "kitchen garden" of Philadelphia and New York.

At the present writing the county of Salem presents to the eye of the traveler a fine agricultural development. Gentlemen of wealth and taste have purchased land and settled here, finding it a desirable investment, while orchards and vineyards have been planted.

The days of the ox team, the scythe, the sickle, and the flail are rapidly departing ; steam power is taking the place of the horse and the mule, and the rumbling train of cars bearing on its fashionable multitude have crowded out the old stage coach of former days.

LARGE TREES.

A chestnut tree growing on a farm near Friesburg, owned by the late Leonard Swing, measured twenty-eight feet in circumference, standing alone near the centre of a field in which corn and other crops of grain had been cultivated for seventy-five years past, and where children for two and three generations have gathered hundreds of bushels of nuts. In 1875 this venerable tree, supposed to have been one hundred and fifty years old, was sawed down, making a vast amount of rails, fence posts and building material. On a farm near "Swing's corner," owned by the late Jonathan DuBois, Esq., may be seen a chestnut tree recently growing on the premises, which measured thirty-one feet in circumference at its largest part, and is fairly proportioned throughout.

It is somewhat remarkable that the two largest oak trees in New Jersey are growing on land owned by the society of Friends. One is in the grounds of the Friends' meeting-house at Crosswicks, Salem county, and measures twenty-two feet and seven inches in circumference. The other, of almost precisely the same size, is a magnificent white oak, standing in the Quaker burying ground in Salem, N. J. It is more than 200 years old, and is remarkable for its amplitude of shade. In one direction its branches have a spread of 112 feet.

THE FAMILY PROPERTY.

Many years ago substantial houses and farm buildings were erected upon the original purchase of land in Pittsgrove township; additional properties have been added thereto from time to time, and there are yet five highly cultivated farms still owned and occupied by the descendants of the family, while other properties in this locality, either by marriage, death or sale, have passed out of the family name. The only wonder to persons of the present age is, how Samuel found his way to the spot chosen for a dwelling place.   It cannot be gainsaid, however, that he selected a level tract of land in probably one of the most fertile sections of the state, and while he felled the neighboring forest his children grew up around him.

In later years the inhabitants of the village named the post office Shirley, and yet the finger boards at Deerfield street and other places in the county continue to inform the uninitiated traveler that the distance by the public highway is

FIVE MILES TO SWING'S CORNER.

This place is located near the central part of Salem county, and at the intersection of four public highways, the road leading north going direct to the city of Philadelphia, Pa., a distance of twenty-eight miles; south, to Deerfield and Bridgeton; west, to Allowaystown and Salem, the county seat, ambitious, thrifty and rich, and raised to importance by having both railroad and steamboat navigation.   Still further on in your line of travel and in an easterly direction lie the villages of Elmer, Malaga, May's Landing, Atlantic City and the seashore.

CHAPTER III.

MY GRANDFATHER.

ONE of the most central and prominent figures in our narrative who, at the age of sixty-six years, passed into the shadow land which lies beyond the tomb, was my grandfather, Abraham Swing. He was the son of Samuel, the hardy emigrant who had braved the storms and danger of mid ocean at a time when vessels were poorly constructed and navigation imperfectly understood. "Unfurled the banner of freedom on American soil, and ultimately planted the footprints of civilization in distant corners of the earth." He is remembered as being a freeholder and interested in real estate transactions, and in the improvement and prosperity of the surrounding country. He married early in life, raised a family of sons and daughters, and his hopes and affections were with the young and rising generation; a man of plain speech and solid piety, while his social standing and influence in his own community made him an exceedingly useful member of the Presbyterian church to which he belonged. He was a man of strong constitution, vigorous in mind, faithful in duties, sound in doctrine and was all through life the holder of responsible positions. At least he held a respectable place among his neighbors, and soon after the commencement of the war of 1812 was appointed an officer in command of a company of men to defend his country. From this circumstance it would seem that he was prominent among his fellow-citizens; for be it remembered that the officers of our government, and the commanders of the army and navy, stood high then, whatever political troubles have met it since.

In company with Brigadier-General Jeremiah DuBois, Major-General Bloomfield, Lieutenant Stewart, and other prominent Jerseymen engaged in active service themselves, he proceeded to the front, and shared with others the danger and excitement of military life.

For the first six months they were stationed at Billingsport, on the eastern shore of the Delaware river, with a large number of soldiers to intimidate and keep the British army from taking possession of Philadelphia.

After being stationed here for six months, and having some disastrous battles with the enemy, the British retreated down the river in boats, landing at the mouth of Salem creek, Cohansey river, and also at Cape May. Horses and cattle began to disappear, and great excitement prevailed throughout the State.

A portion of the army moved down by land to drive the British away, and encamped at the Pole Tavern, in Pittsgrove township, where the arsenal was then located for the southern part of the state.

Major-General Bloomfield, Lieutenant Stewart, and a portion of the army encamped on the farms of Abraham Swing. It is related that my grandfather selected this stopping place, and that his barns were filled with gun-powder and surrounded with muskets, ambulances and artillery wagons.

Mr. Leonard Swing, then a boy twelve years old, re-members opening the apple and the turnip caves while my grandfather treated the soldiers.

This war lasted nearly three years. The bill declaring war between Great Britain and the United States passed the House of Representatives June 18, 1812. The day after, it passed the Senate and was signed by the Presi-dent, James Madison.

" The first battle was fought in Canada, by General Hull, July 16, and the British commander, General Brock, was killed. History informs us that while negotiations were in progress for peace between the United States and England, a large armament, under the command of Sir Edward Packingham, was fitted out by Great Britain for an attack on New Orleans, with the intention of ending the war with some *eclat;* but the design met with a most signal and fatal defeat. The British, after enduring great fatigue and numerous difficulties, and sustaining some desperate encounters, assaulted the works thrown up for the defence of the city on the 8th day of January, 1815, when they were dreadfully cut to pieces and repulsed by the Americans, under General Jackson. The loss of the enemy in killed, wounded and captured amounted to about 2,600. Among the slain was the commander-in-chief, General Packingham, and many other principal officers. The loss of the Americans was only seven killed and six wounded. This was the last important operation of the war of 1812."

After peace was declared between Great Britain and the United States, my grandfather returned to Salem county, and once more engaged in agricultural pursuits. A few years later he was elected to represent the county of Salem in the Legislature of New Jersey. Taking his seat in that august body in 1821 he heartily espoused the cause of freedom and independence. Endowed with mental and physical life the imprint of his genius is found deeply engraved in the legislative enactments of the state, while his dignified bearing, calm courage and " national reputation " enabled him at once to become a prominent and useful member, and also enlarged his acquaintance with the leaders of his party.

From his first entrance into public life his voice was always used in behalf of the people, in the defence of their rights, and he had the courage to storm the intrenchments of vice and intemperance wherever found, his aim being to protect the rights of all, and thus secure to all mankind "peace and good will among men." But, although dead in the body, yet he lives again in the illuminated pages of history.

Abraham Swing was born October 26, 1771. Hannah Lummis, his wife, October 10, 1773. They were united in marriage on the 2d day of December, 1794, and the outgrowth of this union was seven children—four sons and three daughters :

Jonathan L. Swing,	born	. . . . Oct.	23, 1796
Nathaniel G. Swing,	"	. . . . March	30, 1798
Ruth Swing,	"	. . . . Jan.	3, 1800
Leonard Swing,	"	. . . . March	11, 1802
Hannah Lummis Swing,	"	. . . . May	6, 1804
Sarah Swing,	"	. . . . Nov.	27, 1806
Samuel Swing,	"	. . . . March	17, 1810

GRANDMOTHER.

From the earliest days of civilization women have figured prominently in history, and the records of female influence are peculiarly interesting to many readers. Nothing is more creditable to the American people than the daughters of our early settlers and chief magistrates, and the women most conspicuous in history and in song were those who were renowned for virtue as well as beauty.

My grandmother is remembered as being stately, dignified and attractive. She was also a Christian and patriot down to the close of life. She carefully superintended the household duties of her family, keeping the children in a healthy and flourishing condition. The higher domestic life of that long ago is revealed in all we know of its refinement and elegance; its dignified courtesy can be contemplated with respectful admiration, for it was in keeping with the sincerity and frankness of the "olden time." She was regarded as a very industrious and enterprising character, and never allowed herself or the family to lead an indolent life, and next to the blessings of heaven we are, perhaps, indebted to her for our industrious habits and subsequent prosperity and

4

success. Encouraged by her kind and motherly ways her children learned household duties, and the art of making butter and cheese. The sound of the spinning wheel, and the knitting of socks and stockings formed a very interesting and important part of the education of girls in the olden time. When the duties of the day were ended, with shutters closed, curtains drawn, and on either side of the large hearth was placed the favorite chairs, the head of the family reading aloud the weekly papers, after which the two sat talking of days gone by, of little episodes in the history of their lives, while my grandmother occasionally indulged in smoking her pipe. This incident, which is among the earliest recollections of the writer, reminds us of the

DREAM OF A QUAKER LADY.

There is a beautiful story told of a pious Quaker lady, who was much addicted to smoking tobacco. She had indulged herself in this habit until it had increased so much upon her, that she not only smoked her pipe a large portion of the day, but frequently sat up in bed for this purpose in the night. After one of these nocturnal entertainments she fell asleep, and dreamed that she died and approached heaven. Meeting an angel she asked him if her name was written in the book of life. He disappeared, but replied on returning, that he could not find it. "Oh!" said she, "do look again, it must be there." He examined again, but returned with a sorrowful face, saying it was not there. "Oh!" said she, "it must be there. I have an assurance that it is there. Do look once more!" The angel was moved to tears by her entreaties, and again left her to renew his search. After a long absence he came back, his face radiant with joy, and exclaimed, " We have found it! we have found it! but it was so clouded with tobacco smoke that we could hardly see it!" The good woman, upon waking, immediately threw her pipe away, and never indulged in smoking again.

In the process of time the family grew up to manly and womanly stature and years of accountability. They all married well, owned their own farms and homes and enjoyed life as well as ordinary people. They were also temperate and industrious. But in the years that have elapsed, with the exception of Nathaniel G., who is still living, all have passed away, have yielded to the immutable decree of time, and as we humbly trust, entered into the joys of a blessed immortality, leaving large families of children behind, and the record of useful lives. The descendants have inter-married with many of the leading families of the country, and are to be found widely disseminated throughout the state and beyond its limits. Among the number were the names of Du-Bois, Craig, Shough, Harris, Hires, Newkirk, Johnson, Burroughs, Lippincott, Woodruff, Whitaker, Willis, Fuller, Moreland, Downham, Tomlinson, and others.

STORMING A BATTERY.

CHAPTER IV.

HISTORY OF THE ARSENAL, POLE TAVERN; MILITARY OR-
GANIZATIONS IN SALEM COUNTY.

OF the military organization of Pittsgrove township,
previous to the Revolution, but little is known,
except the information gathered from those who
participated in the " training days " and in active service
in the war of 1812.

The year before the Revolution the whole county was
stirred up against the British and their unjust and illegal
taxation and other oppressions, and the tax on tea had
caused especial hard feeling.

When the people of Salem county heard the news of
the Boston Tea Party, as it was called, there was some
division of opinion, but nearly all of the young men and
most of the older ones were on the patriotic side.

History informs us that after the battle of Lexington,
on the 19th of April, 1775, the county was alive with
military preparation. Companies formed, officers were
chosen, and frequent drills took place. The practice of
bearing arms and meeting for exercise produced a spirit
of independence and self-reliance, while the holiday
served to bring many people together, and cultivate
kind and generous feelings. During the Revolutionary

war Salem county was noted as a place of resort for refugees, and also for foraging parties. When the British fleet sailed along the Delaware on the way to Philadelphia, they frequently landed and scoured the country for miles around, driving off cattle, horses, sheep, swine, and anything that could be used to advantage. Among the former residents of Pittsgrove township were those who had shared in the toil of the march, the peril of the fight, the dismay of the retreat; night after night had sat beside the same camp fire; had heard the roll of the reveille which called them to duty, or the beat of the tattoo which gave the signal for the retirement of the soldiers to the tents.

About one mile north of the Pole Tavern it is related that " the Whigs and Tories " had a fierce engagement, in which the former named were successful in the fight. After the retreat a British officer and his staff took possession of a large brick house owned by a wealthy farmer, and occupied it for a considerable time. Our troops, being notified, surrounded the house during the night, and the whole nest of Tories were captured. The house above alluded to is still standing, and to this day the village is known as " Whig Lane."

There is an old eight-day clock in possession of a Salem county farmer that is more than two hundred years old. During the Revolutionary war the house in which this clock was kept was burned to the ground, and the clock carried off and pawned in Philadelphia. The house was afterward rebuilt, the clock reclaimed, and to-day occupies its old place as of yore.

When peace was declared at the close of the war of 1812, the old hotel was the scene of a brilliant pageantry, being illuminated from top to bottom and thronged with merry lads and lasses, tripping " the light fantastic," and singing patriotic airs.

In front of the tavern referred to is a sign bearing the following inscription, " Pole Tavern." It derives its name from the fact that a Liberty Pole has long stood in the central part of the village, and traditionally claimed to mark the site of the first Liberty Pole erected in Salem county. It has had many successive landlords, and is perhaps one of the oldest hostelries in the country in point of continuous service.

Organized troops for the conflict were sworn into the service under the roof of this venerable structure by Brigadier-General DuBois. Salem county established a training ground at Pole Tavern, and desiring to own their own armory purchased ground and erected the arsenal building. General DuBois purchased from the Government three large brass cannon, and three smaller iron ones, 100 flint-lock muskets and rifles for the use of General DuBois' body guard. The imposing stone edifice and the beautiful grounds surrounding it bristled with ambulance and artillery wagons. Around this place cluster the memory of fair women and brave men, and many interesting incidents connected with our Revolutionary struggle in 1776.

In 1802, a post-office was established here, called Pittsgrove, named in honor of the township. The first mail carrier between this place and Philadelphia was

Beniah Parvin, making two trips a week on horseback.

At the commencement of the war of 1812, a military drill was established here, and soldiers trained for duty by Brigadier-General Jeremiah DuBois, Major Bloomfield and Lieutenant Abraham Swing. After peace was declared, the guns were returned to the arsenal and military training days appointed by the Governor to be observed at various places in the state. Majors Judah Foster and Nathaniel G. Swing were the officers in command. Training days became very popular with the young people; they were observed and continued at this place for many years.

During the war of 1812, and for several years afterward, every male citizen of New Jersey was compelled by law to train for military duty, or pay a fine. Many persons preferred to pay this fine rather than occupy the time in training, and in this way a large fund came into the possession of the brigade paymaster, Thomas Yarrow, of Salem county, who paid the bill for the 287 muskets from the " Fine Fund " of this county, and the guns have remained, as they belonged, the property of said county.

NAMES OF THE FIELD AND STAFF OFFICERS OF THE MILITARY COMPANY.

Heavy Artillery—Colonel, Abraham DuBois; Lieut.-Colonel, David Sithens.

Majors—Judah Foster, Nathaniel G. Swing.

Captains—Cornelius D. Hulick, John Burroughs.

Ensign or Acting Sergeant-Major—J. L. Swing.
Lieutenants—Leonard Swing, Henry J. Frieze.
Sergeant—John Carter.
Corporals— —— Newkirk, Nathan Lawrence.

An old resident says, " When I was a boy, and for a number of years succeeding my minority, the state law, made and provided, required all able-bodied white male citizens of the age of twenty-one and over to train or drill so many times a year, and training days then were *the* great event in our social happenings. I remember," he continued, " there was considerable rivalry between two infantry companies, organized respectively at Woodstown and Sharptown. Dr. Israel Clawson recruited the foot company at Woodstown, and Captain McCallister the company at Sharptown. Clawson was particularly desirous that his company should excel in uniform, equipments and numbers, and so banded together a hundred men and uniformed them at his own expense, only stipulating that the wearer of the goods should pay for them, if then able, or at any time becoming so. You may smile, if you will, but I tell you honestly that, although I have seen the brilliant, dashing soldier in every variety of outfit many times since, yet I never saw any in these latter days that, to my notion, were half so handsome as those which pleased my youthful fancy in the years 1816–18.

" Our uniform was dark blue pants, corded with red up and down the seams, and coat cut swallow-tail fashion, with the same red cord running diagonally across the breast and looping over great shining brass buttons washed in gold. The hats were of the second-story regulation pattern, surmounted by a beautiful plume of red and white, and we carried the best shot-gun or rifle we had at hand. Of the feminine hearts that fluttered and the feminine heads turned topsy-turvey at the sight of the brave 'sojer boys' and their rattling, martial music, but few now remain, though now and then I see their children of the third generation.

"Was I ever in a sham fight? Oh, yes, I took part in three in my time, although I have only a vague recollection of incidents that occurred at the time. The first sham battle we had came off at Pole Tavern, which was, as near as I recollect, about the year 1817. Captain Clawson divided his squad of a hundred or more men into two bands, the one to act as Indians in ambush and the other as infantry soldiers, and we were to fight it out very much as General Harrison had been doing but a short time previous in northwestern Michigan and the territories. Well, we had a high old time for quite awhile, the Indians shooting from behind trees and dodging our fire, we driving them at times, and at times being repulsed, until at length a luckless shot (wad) ripped open the coat of Commander Clawson, when hostilities at once ceased. It was announced in the programme that we were to defeat and drive the Indians, but we didn't. The next fight came off at Salem, or rather near Quinton, Captain Rowan, of Salem, who was also a doctor, commanding a company of light dragoons, which were to oppose the militia force of Captain Clawson. I remember, in this fight, that the cavalry was to charge on the infantry, and the instructions were for the horse to close well on to the infantry and then suddenly wheel about, fall back, and reform, etc., and that my brother rode a horse with a hard mouth which, when in coming up the line, instead of wheeling about, leaped entirely over the head of a terribly frightened soldier. Of course, my brother was taken prisoner. My last and third fight was at Bridgeton, which I believe was on the Dutch Neck road. This was in 1818, and the fight was between two opposing cavalry bodies. In this fight we were to break through each other's lines at open ranks, strike swords as we passed, and then form and re-attack, etc. This was highly exciting and grand fun, but at one charge two fellows collided, and they came together with so much force that their steeds almost stood erect."

This reminds us of a story they used to tell of the genial and humorous captain, Cornelius D. Hulick, of Pittsgrove. Old H. was a famous member of the ancient and honorable artillery corps. One day when marching through Fenwick street, Salem, in column of review before Major Foster, his steps became very irregular. "Uncle H.," said a friend, "have you been taking too much hard cider?" "Not a bit of it," said Hulick; "there is a band both before and behind our company, and I am marching to two tunes."

The first band of music organized in Salem county was long known as the Pittsgrove Clarinet Band. At the military parades and political occasions their services were in great demand, not only in their own, but also in the adjoining counties, instrumental music being well received and highly appreciated by the citizens of Salem county. The following named persons composed the original organization:

<table>
<tr><td>Leonard Swing,</td><td>Lewis DuBois,</td></tr>
<tr><td>Samuel DuBois,</td><td>Daniel Nash DuBois,</td></tr>
<tr><td>Cornelius Burroughs,</td><td>Thomas DuBois,</td></tr>
<tr><td>Andrew Hann,</td><td>John Harding,</td></tr>
<tr><td>Ephraim DuBois,</td><td>* Edmund DuBois,</td></tr>
<tr><td>Matthew N. Foster,</td><td>Samuel Swing.</td></tr>
<tr><td>* Nathaniel G. Swing,</td><td></td></tr>
</table>

At the commencement of the year 1888, but two members of this band (indicated by *), who participated in these social and political gatherings, and were foremost in bearing on the standard of musical conquest in Salem county, were still living. When old members died or moved away others were initiated into their places, and the band continued in existence for many years. In fact, some of the instruments are still in occasional use.

During the summer of 1889 the Robeson Post, a military organization of veteran soldiers in the late war, desired to hold a Fourth of July celebration in Bridgeton, and through the influence of ex-Senator I. T. Nichols obtained an order from the quartermaster at Trenton for the removal of the cannon into Cumberland county. After the removal of the guns from the arsenal at Pole Tavern the question of ownership was warmly debated in the county newspapers, as to whether these muskets and cannon belonged to the citizens of Salem county or to the state of New Jersey. An investigation of the history of the arsenal at Pole Tavern revealed the fact that six members of the old battalion are still living—Ananias G. Richer, of Whig Lane, aged 82; David Shimp, Friesburg, 87; Jonathan S. Wood, Fairton, 88; Nathaniel G. Swing, of Shirley, 91; Major C. F. H. Gray and Col. I. W. Dickinson.

Mr. Swing related to the writer that when the rifles for Gen. DuBois' body guard arrived he assisted in cleaning the guns, and they were used here for military and training purposes from 1812 to 1830, when the training was discontinued, and the guns have remained until recently the property of Salem county. Mr. Swing trained in the militia ten years. He was then commissioned as adjutant and afterward promoted to major of the First Battalion, First Brigade, which commission he held from the year 1828 to 1861, when he was appointed brigade paymaster.

[Extract from the Elmer Times of June 8, 1889.]

A *Times* representative has thoroughly investigated the placing of the arsenal at Pole Tavern and published the following

HISTORY OF THE CANNON.

The cannon taken to Bridgeton last week has a remarkable history, and is a valuable piece of artillery. It is an Italian cannon, and bears the date of 1763, also an inscription in Italian.   When Napoleon crossed the Alps in 1800 he left most of his cannon behind him, owing to the great difficulty of transporting them up rugged sides and through the ice and snow of those famous mountains.   When about to embark in the perilous undertaking one of his marshals is said to have remarked to him: "Sire, what shall we do for cannon when we get on the other side?"   To which Bonaparte replied: "We will take them from the Italians."   And he did take them.   Among them was the gun to which reference is made.

It was with Napoleon in many of his great battles; afterward being transferred to the custody of the French army during the seven years' campaign in Spain.   Here it fell into the hands of the British by capture, and finally was taken, with many of Wellington's veterans, to America to participate in the war of 1812.   It was captured by the American army at the battle of Plattsburg, New York, and became the property of the nation.

BRING BACK THE CANNON—INDIGNATION MEETING NO. 2.

Last Saturday night the second indignation meeting was held at Pole Tavern.   J. N. Gray presided.   It was reported that Col. Dickinson and Director Griscom, of the Board of Freeholders, had been to Trenton, searched the records and found that Salem county purchased the four cannon of the state for $624, and 287 muskets at a cost of $900.   Gen. Perrine was sick and the committee was unable to see him.   They were informed that by making affidavits to the records the cannon would be returned to Salem county. Joseph Richman reported a conversation with Hon. Nathaniel Swing, of Shirley, and gleaned in addition to the facts published in the *Times* two weeks ago, the information that he at one time cleaned and burnished all these guns (muskets) to the number of 287 at a cost of forty cents apiece, and was paid with county funds. The state would not pay for the work.

Mr. Swing was a musician in the brigade, and remembers when Ballinger's mill pond was used for target practice when they first commenced, and had a sheet at the head of the pond for a target. Major Judah Foster fired the first shot, which went about thirty feet above the mark, cutting the tops off the trees that high from the ground; afterwards lowering the elevation of the guns, the balls were buried in the hill at the head of the pond, and were dug out and used again. The first ball the major shot was found years afterwards on the Lawrence property, having been ploughed up a long distance from where they were shooting. Mr. Richman also reported having seen the Rogers Bros., wheelwrights and blacksmiths, who were located at Daretown, who were ordered to repair them *by the county*, at a cost of $60, and were paid by the county.

The following were appointed a committee to secure the cannon and return it to the arsenal: Joseph Henry, James T. Mayhew, Isaac T. Prickett, Joseph Richman, Jr., and Joshua Fox.

On motion it was ordered that a committee be appointed to get the wheels of the dismounted cannon, said to be in possession of private parties. The following were appointed: Henry Coombs, Frank D. Evans and Gottlieb Kress.

MORE ABOUT THE CANNON.

To the Editor of the Times :

My DEAR SIR:—As a former citizen of Pittsgrove township, I was greatly interested in reading the advice recently published in the Elmer *Times*, entitled "A Bold Deed. Salem county cannon and muskets taken from the arsenal at Pole Tavern and removed into Cumberland."

This incident should not be permitted to pass unnoticed by the people of Salem county, who collected money and purchased from the government an armory of guns three-quarters of a century ago.

At the commencement of the war of 1812 a military training ground was established here and soldiers trained for duty by Brigadier-General DuBois, Major Bloomfield and Lieutenant Abraham Swing, the officers herein named were subsequently stationed at Billingsport on the Delaware river, with regiments of soldiers to intimidate and prevent the British army from taking possession of Philadelphia. After peace was declared the guns were returned to the arsenal at Pole Tavern, and military training days appointed by the governor of the state.

Training days became very popular with the young

people, and were observed at Pole Tavern for many years.

From 1813 to 1823 Salem county paid over $3000 for guns and cannon.

When a boy the writer of this article remembers being sent to Salem, the county seat, to buy "flints" and assist Major N. G. Swing in cleaning the guns for military parades, and Fourth of July occasions.

Later in life we remember the spring and summer of 1861–62, when all the patriotic young men in this part of Salem county were invited to meet at the military parade ground at Pole Tavern once a week for training and drill exercises, companies being formed and drilled here by Majors Judah Foster, N. G. Swing, Captains Crooks and John W. Janvier. All the muskets in the arsenal were in constant demand, while many trained with rifles and double-barreled shot guns.

On Saturday afternoons Captains Crooks and John W. Janvier and Lieutenant Joshua Lippincott occasionally drilled their companies on a vacant lot opposite the old Presbyterian church, Daretown. Wishing to test the rifles, they procured five hundred cartridges and placed the targets at a distance of one hundred and fifty yards, intending to shoot down the valley into the hill beyond. At first the range of the rifles was too high, and most of the bullets flew over the hill and across the Janvier farms, where three colored men were at work in the cornfield. Presently the firing in the valley commenced, and presuming that the war really had begun in Salem county, the colored men quit work, and taking

5

their horses galloped up to the farm house at full speed.
"And what is the matter now?" inquired Mrs. Janvier.
"Lord a massa, Missus, nobody can work in dat corn-
field while de war is going on. De bullets am flying
ober our heads eb'ry minute."

Major Foster was a man of splendid appearance in
the saddle; he owned and rode for many years a very
stylish looking white horse. He was also a fife and
drum major. Names of the members of his band were
G. S. Swing, C. Whitaker, William M. Swing, Charles
Richman, Aaron Shoulders, Robert S. Harris.

Many of the young men of Pittsgrove township, who
were trained here, joined the 12th New Jersey regiment,
and passed through a three years' campaign; others preferred the Pennsylvania or New Jersey cavalry. In 1861
these muskets were inspected and sent to Trenton;
the locks were exchanged from flint to percussion, and
afterwards used by our volunteers in the battles of the
Wilderness, and also at Harper's Ferry and Gettysburg,
places famed in the history of the war, and in the soli-
tudes of which lie sleeping thousands of brave men.

At the end of three years, and the close of the war,
the Jersey troops were mustered out of service at Trenton, and our soldiers came home with guns. The impression of the writer is that the muskets used in the
late war never were returned to the county of Salem,
where they belong.

I believe in individual as well as state rights, and
hereby propose that an order be issued and signed by
the six living members of the old battalion, Nathaniel

G. Swing, Ananias G. Richer, David Shimp, Jonathan S. Wood, Col. J. W. Dickinson and Hon. Charles F. H. Gray, who holds the commission of major, chosen at the re-organization of the brigade in 1861, requesting Quartermaster-General Perrine, at Trenton, to return the said muskets and cannon to the arsenal at Pole Tavern.

GILBERT S. SWING.

[Extract from Salem Standard.]

"The heavy clouds which have hung over Salem county ever since the departure of 'that cannon' are dissolving and the people are smiling once more. The cause is the following letter which Col. J. W. Dickinson has received from Quartermaster-General Perrine, after the affidavits setting forth that the four cannon were purchased with Salem county funds were forwarded:

"'Your letter, together with the records and minutes of the Brigade Board of Salem county, is received. As soon as I am able to take the matter up I will do so. No disposition will be made of the property until I have thoroughly examined into the subject, and of which you will be duly advised.'

"The citizens of Salem think that this settles the case, and are so jubilant that it is proposed that the patriotic Pittsgrovers, when the cannon arrives, celebrate their victory in several rousing salutes."

CHAPTER V.

SAMUEL AND JEREMIAH.

SAMUEL SWING and his brother (as before stated) soon after the landing of the vessel at New York, procured employment on Long Island, where they continued to reside for a short period of time, and where the marriage of the first-named person was duly celebrated.

During the fall of the following year, and after the crops of vegetables had been gathered and marketed in the city near by, they removed from this place to the southern part of New Jersey, purchased a tract of land and settled in Salem county.

His brother Jeremiah accompanied him to Pittsgrove, where he remained about four years, assisting in the clearing of land, construction of houses and purchase of stock, gaining much valuable information in regard to the agricultural interest of this country, the rapid growth of cities and towns, and the demand then springing up in Baltimore and Philadelphia for ship timber, lumber and building material. After reconnoitering the country round about, he chose for his future home and abiding place the State of Pennsylvania. On the borders of the Susquehanna river, among the large and stately hemlock, the ash, the elm and the white pine, he saw an extensive field of labor, if not a fortune or a gold mine, in the distance.

Here, in 1764, accompanied by three hired men, he made a clearing near the banks of the river, built his cabin and engaged in the lumber trade, floating rafts of logs down the river to Baltimore. Immense tracts of timber were then standing along the headwaters of the Susquehanna. In the valleys bordering the stream, many of those trees were two hundred feet high and straight as a gun-barrel, as yet undisturbed by the approach of civilization or the sound of the woodman's axe.

In this wild and romantic locality the marriage of Jeremiah Swing was subsequently celebrated, and here they commenced " housekeeping " together. They were blessed with abundant health and strength, and the providence of God seems to have smiled upon their labors, crowning their life with success, and following the family and their descendants in a remarkable manner.

At that time York was the oldest town, except Shippensburg, west of the Susquehanna river, in Pennsylvania. During the French and Indian war two forts were erected there, Fort Morris in 1755 and Fort Franklin in 1756, the ruins of one of which, until within a few years, were still to be seen. These fortifications were erected as a protection to the village and to make arrangements for receiving supplies for General Braddock's army. The dwelling-houses were built of stone and wood, and were the birthplace and early home of many distinguished men.

Around the family board of Jeremiah Swing were gathered, beside himself and wife, two sons and one daughter. The eldest, named George, was born at York, Pa., in the year 1766, Michael in 1768, and Mary in 1772.

The family remained in this locality until the children had become of age. They were successful in business, quiet and reserved in manner.

Of the daughter but little is known, except that she grew up to womanly stature and married a gentleman by the name of Gibson, who was engaged in the lumber trade on the Susquehanna river. For several years after their marriage they continued to live in the vicinity of York, and eventually became influential and wealthy citizens of the Cumberland Valley. Among their descendants were born those who subsequently became noted leaders in the military and political history of Pennsylvania.

CHAPTER VI.

TWO SONS OF JEREMIAH.

MANY years ago two young men came over on horseback from York, Pa., to visit relatives in Jersey, having a desire to become better acquainted with the families living in this state. After spending a few weeks in Salem county they returned home, but soon after these young men decided to leave the state of their nativity and join the "Jersey settlement."

From the bold and fearless spirit of their father, who was a strong, athletic man, and whose life had been full of adventure, enterprise and stirring events, these sons had inherited the same spirit of industry and perseverance, and their early years were not spent in idleness.

From the sale of valuable tracts of timber land in Pennsylvania they were enabled to come to New Jersey with considerable means, having in their possession a good constitution, good character, good name and some capital in cash on hand. To a friend in Salem county one of them wrote:

"Brother George and myself propose selling out our property here and coming to New Jersey, as most all of

our kindred reside there, and we admire both place and
people, although the present outlook for ourselves is
peculiarly bright and encouraging, and everything points
to a successful termination of the past year's work."

During the following year, 1789, the two brothers
removed to New Jersey, and soon after this event Michael
Swing was united in marriage with Miss Sarah Murphy,
daughter of Rev. John Murphy, of Salem county.

It may be interesting to our readers to state that Mr.
Murphy belonged to one of the first Methodist families
in this section of the state, and was licensed to preach the
Gospel soon after the close of the Revolutionary war.
Upon his own farm in Pittsgrove township he built a
church, which was long known as " Murphy's Meeting
House."

Extending his labors into the adjoining counties, he
often held religious service at " Greenwich Chapel," in
Gloucester county, where a society had been previously
formed.

Methodism was introduced into the town of Salem
about 1774. It is related that Rev. Daniel Ruff was the
first minister in that place, his first sermon being preached
in the Court House. In commencing the service he gave
out the hymn beginning:

> "Fountain of life, to all below
> Let thy salvation roll."

In 1784 the first Methodist church was built and dedicated, and in 1788 the name of the circuit was changed

from " West Jersey " to Salem Circuit, James O. Cromwell, presiding elder; Nathaniel Mills and Joseph Cromwell appointed to the circuit. The immortal Benjamin Abbott, who joined this society when a young man and afterwards became a useful and zealous minister of the Gospel, and preached many years in this state, and by whose instrumentality thousands of people were converted and brought into the church, died on Salem circuit, and his remains rest in peace near the site of the present South Street M. E. church.

Michael Swing was the pioneer of the Methodist church in Fairfield, to which place he came about the year 1790. He was a very zealous Christian, and began to hold meetings at private houses. Being a man of property and influence he soon organized a society in this neighborhood. His early Christian life must have given promise of usefulness to the church, for during the following year, 1791, he was licensed to preach the Gospel by Rev. John Merrick, presiding elder of the district (which then embraced Salem, Cumberland, and part of Gloucester counties). The same year a class was formed at New Englandtown cross-roads, and the home of Michael Swing was the resting place of the weary itinerant of those days.

The society increased in numbers ; and chiefly at his own expense he built a church on his farm, which was long known as " Swing's Meeting House."

Mr. Murphy, who had been a local preacher for several years, accompanied his daughter and her husband to

New Englandtown, and aided in establishing the church at Fairfield.

Happy allusion has since been made to the organization, growth and grandeur of this society. When churches wisely plan and earnestly toil, and nobly give according to their ability, the pastors and their families are sustained and made happy in their work. Methodism was identified in its rise here with its rise and origin as a denomination in other places.

Michael Swing purchased a farm of Rev. Daniel Elmer, pastor of the Presbyterian church at Fairfield, the property being located on the south side of the Cohansey river, the finest and best navigable stream in the southern part of the state, and with facilities for building their own wharfage at which vessels of four hundred tons burthen could land. The soil was rich and productive, and on the river shore was an excellent shad and herring fishery. At almost any time during the year fish and oysters could be obtained for the taking of them out of the water.

The first settlers in this part of New Jersey are said to have been a mixed population of half-civilized American Indians, who were loth to leave so good and desirable a country, Dutch and Swedes, and emigrants from New England. Lieutenant Stratton, an Englishman, who resided for some years in Cumberland county, on his return to his native land, published an account of his adventures in America, and what he saw in the province of West Jersey.

EXTRACT

" Describing the Delaware bay, Cohansey river and its tributaries, where the otter, beaver and muskrat abound, and where the inhabitants used to kill vast numbers of wild ducks and geese, many of the latter being captured for their feathers only, the down being in demand for filling beds, and in some instances quilted in the lining of overcoats for a protection against the severe cold in winter."

The names of Michael Swing's children by his first wife were as follows :

Dr. Charles Swing, born 1790
Captain John M. Swing, born 1792
Elizabeth Swing, born 1794
Polly Swing, born 1796
Anna Swing, born 1798
Priscilla Swing, born 1800
George M. Swing, born 1803
Simon Sparks Swing, born 1805
Sarah S. Swing, born 1808
Michael Coates Swing, born 1811

This comprises the first crop.

THE HOME OF MICHAEL SWING.

Standing well back from the road, and nearly in the centre of a large tract of level land, enclosed by a high fence of cedar rails, is a large and stately farm house two and a half stories high, broad veranda in front, and porches running around the side of the building. As I entered the broad, green gate and passed up the newly repaired gravel walk leading between two lines of shrubbery and trees to the steps of the porch, where stood large iron urns holding beautiful evergreens on each hand, I cast my eye over the enclosure, and it presented an air of quiet, comfort and peace. A short distance to the west are three large barns and other out-buildings used for the storage of hay and grain, and the accommodation of horses and cattle. Long rows of Flemish Beauty, Dutchess, and Bartlett pears greet the eye, while on either side orchards of peaches and apples hang loaded with fruit. A few yards north of the house a beautiful spring of water is found gushing up from the rocks below, always lively, cool and refreshing. The sides of this spring are walled up in imitation of a well, and enclosed by a frame building, the bottom paved with brick and stone, and used as a summer house and cool retreat.

Following the stream a short distance through the woods, the road leads down to the beach. A great expanse of water stretches off toward the west, farther than the eye can reach, and the gentle surf from the sea, the rising and falling tide, washes the white pebbles upon the shore. Now and then a cheering sail boat relieves the monotony of land and water, and occasionally the shrill whistle of a passing steamer or a tug breaks upon the stillness of the morning air. In the background lies a vast expanse of rich marsh land, capable, as society advanced, of being converted into meadows, with pasture green, and herds of sheep and cattle grazing quietly thereon.

The scene before and around the residence of Michael Swing is in many respects charming. Here beautiful children enjoyed the early years of their lives, and sang out the long summer months, and prosperity and wealth laid its golden hand upon every thing calculated to make life a success and existence a joy. Rustic youth related their stories of love and devotion, and father and mother, full of pride in what they saw and enjoyed, made merry with family and friends.

CHAPTER VII.

MICHAEL SWING.

THE first son born in the family, and named Charles, is remembered to have been a very bright, intelligent lad, and in his youthful days gave tokens of native cheerfulness, energy and ability.

He soon evinced that thirst for knowledge and love of independence which lie at the foundation of all successful characters; for this attainment he attended school, and studied closely during the fall and winter months, and worked on his father's farm throughout those of summer.

In the course of time he became a student of medicine under the tuition of Dr. Ewing, of Greenwich, rapidly winning the honors and reward of his chosen profession. He was graduated at the Medical University of Pennsylvania, and subsequently became one of the most eminent physicians in the county of Salem.

In 1815, when in his twenty-fifth year, he decided to gratify the long-cherished desire of visiting his "Uncle George," in Ohio; and with the exception of the first fifty miles, he traveled all the way on foot.

No railroads were then built in the United States, the crossing on the river and bay were the Indian canoe and

FISHING BOAT—MICHAEL SWING'S FISHERY.

the old-fashioned boats propelled by horses. The postage on letters was twenty-five (25) cents each. In 1790 there were only twenty-five (25) post-offices in this country, and up to the year 1837 the rates of postage were twenty-five cents for each letter sent over four hundred miles.

Many persons still live who remember the time when letter-writing was comparatively a rare accomplishment. As it cost from ten to twenty-five cents to pay the postage on a missive, naturally persons wrote letters only when there was something important to say. Much use was made of friends to carry communications from place to place, although the government tried to protect itself from this practice by imposing a heavy fine upon those who were caught dodging the post-office. Of course, the speed with which letters were delivered was very slow before the introduction of steam. Mounted postmen, armed with a horn, carried the mails into remote districts once or twice a week.

But with the growth of the country and the more rapid methods of communication, this slow system has given way. In 1792 the postal law fixed the following rate : Six cents for the first thirty miles, and a proportional increase for each additional ten miles. So it cost fifteen cents to send a letter from Pittsgrove to New York, and twenty-five cents to Cincinnati. In 1799 the rate was changed, standing at eight cents for the minimum distance, forty miles, and twenty-five cents for the maximum, 500 miles, or over. In 1816 the standard of 1792 was re-adopted, and held until 1845, when a further change, in the direction of cheapness and uniformity, was taken by classifying all letters as " single " or " double." Single letters paid five cents for each half ounce carried 3co miles or under, double letters paid ten cents for all over that distance. In 1851 a further reform made three cents the rate for all distances under 3,000 miles, and all letters to be prepaid by stamps.

One hundred years ago not a pound of coal, not a cubic foot of illuminating gas, had been burned in this country. No iron stoves were used, and no contrivances for economizing heat were employed until Dr. Franklin invented the iron-framed fireplace, which still bears his name. All the cooking and warming in town and country were done by the aid of fire kindled in the brick oven on the hearth. Pine knots or tallow candles furnished the light for the long winter nights, and sanded floors supplied the place of rugs and carpets. The water used for household purposes was drawn from deep wells by the creaking sweep. No form of pump was used, so far as we can learn, until after the commencement of the present century. There were no friction matches in those early days by the aid of which fire could be easily kindled ; and if the fire " went out " on the hearth over night, and the tinder was so damp that the sparks would not catch, the alternative was presented of wandering through snow a mile or so to borrow a brand of a neighbor. Only one room in any house was warm, unless some of the family were ill ; in all the rest the temperature was at zero many nights in the winter. The men and women of a hundred years ago undressed and went to their beds in a temperature colder than our modern barns and woodsheds, and they never complained.

After nearly three weeks' travel, the doctor arrived in Cincinnati, and on the following day at the home of Uncle George, in Clermont county.

The frost of winter had recently come out of the ground, leaving it soft and spongy. Ox-teams were met on the road hopelessly mired in the mud, unable to draw the wagon or get out themselves without assistance. Few bridges were then built in Ohio, the streams of water were difficult to cross, and Charles felt disgusted with the country.

" We found Uncle George located between Poplar and Sugar Tree creeks, his land extending from one creek to the other, a few miles back from the Ohio river, and about twenty-eight miles above the city of Cincinnati. He had purchased a large tract of land, and built thereon a stone dwelling house, in which he then lived. His family consisted of himself and wife, four sons and one daughter."

After a visit of a few weeks' duration, and becoming acquainted with the people in the neighborhood, the doctor was induced to teach school in the " Swing settlement," in which capacity he served with great acceptability for one year.

The school-house stood upon the property of Uncle George, located along the high banks of Sugar Tree creek. The house was built of logs, with one middle aisle, two doors and four windows.

School teaching in Ohio is pretty much the same

as in other portions of the country, and "boys will be boys" the world over. The compensation for teaching was not as much for the same amount of work as then paid in New Jersey, and after the term expired the doctor purchased a horse and saddle and started for home. He took the old stage road up the north side of the Ohio river to "Fort Pitt," at that time a military station established by the government to protect emigrants and settlers from attack by Indians on the frontier. In later years this place was called Pittsburg, and since has become a city of considerable importance.

The doctor arrived safely, and rode the horse all the way through to Fairfield. Letters were written from Ohio to his father, and the time appointed for his return to New Jersey. George M. Swing, then a lad thirteen years of age, and his father, promised to meet the doctor on his return at Little York, Pa., as they wished to look again upon the "home of their childhood," and to visit a married sister living there.

"We rode in a two-wheeled carriage called a gig, with large side-lights and leather top. This was greatly admired by ladies and looked upon as a very stylish conveyance at that day. Few covered carriages were then in use, traveling by men was almost exclusively on horseback, the women riding in side-saddles and sometimes behind their male friends.

"The first night on the road we stayed at Abraham Swing's, Pittsgrove, and on the following morning arose early to pursue our journey, and drove to 'Cooper's Ferry,' at Camden, crossing the Delaware river in boats propelled by horses. Night coming on we stopped at a hotel near the Schuylkill river, in West Philadelphia. The next day we drove on to Lancaster, a distance of forty-six miles, feeding the horses and taking supper at the latter place. The charges for dinner were eighteen cents, supper twelve and a half cents; feeding horses, one shilling each. After resting one hour we drove sixteen miles further on, arriving at York, Pa., some time in the night.

"Our first visit was at the residence of Mr. Gibson, a large, portly gentleman, who was extensively engaged in the lumber trade, and some years before had been united in marriage to Mary Swing, the only sister of my father.

"'Any increase in the population or improvements since I left York twenty-eight years ago?' asked my father. 'Oh, yes,' replied Mary, 'although the country looks wild, and the settlements are few and far between, our own little village has more than doubled itself in population. You remember,' she continued, 'the large tract of timber land that father cleared below the village? The soil was sold and is now occupied by an industrious colony of farmers called the "Pennsylvania Dutch."'

"'Are the winters very cold?' 'The winter of 1799 was long and severe. About the first of January snow fell three feet deep, and covered the ground until spring. The Susquehanna river was frozen two feet thick, and continued fast three months. The weather was intensely cold. Bears and wolves, prompted by hunger, came out from their hiding places in search of calves and sheep, or anything they could eat.   Many cattle and deer were found frozen to death.   Bread and provisions were so scarce and high many persons in the state subsisted chiefly on wild game.'

" 'We like the climate and soil of South Jersey best,' said my father; 'the country is very level, with few hills or valleys; not so much large timber or wild game, but plenty of fish and oysters.   At almost any time of the year they can be caught on the Cohansey river adjoining my own farm.'

" 'What kinds of fish inhabit these waters?'   ' Rock, shad, bluefish, mackerel, and most of the varieties found in the ocean.   Immense numbers of them swim up the bay and river in search of food and fresh water.'

" 'How are they caught?' inquired sister.   ' In seines and nets.   Fortunes are made in the fish business. Those not sold when fresh were put in barrels, salted, and sold in cities for table use.'

" 'What induced brother George to leave New Jersey and emigrate to the west?'   ' This removal surprised his friends, as he was pleasantly located and owned his own farm in Salem county.   He is credited with being very ambitious and enterprising, and one of the most daring and adventurous members of our family.'

" ' Dr. Charles, your eldest son, gives a good account of him.'

" ' Has Charles arrived?' asked my father.   ' Yes, sir,' replied my sister.   ' The doctor arrived on horseback from the west three days ago ; has already made his visit at York, and the morning before your arrival started on for home.'

"'Is that so? How is it we did not meet him on the road?' 'He took the nearest route for Jersey,' replied Mary; 'passing through Lancaster and Chester counties, Pennsylvania, and Newcastle county, Delaware, to Port Penn,' [where a ferry was then established and much in use, boats crossing the Delaware from Port Penn to Elsinborough Point, New Jersey.]

" We missed the doctor on the road and did not see him again until our return to Fairfield on the following week."

The year subsequently became memorable to us not only on account of our visit at York, and the return of Dr. Charles from the west, but from the fact that the summer of 1816 was one of the coldest on record, very little corn or vegetables of any kind being raised that year in Salem county.

THE "YEAR WITHOUT A SUMMER."

We continue to receive occasional inquiries concerning the "year in which there was no summer." Some persons appear to have a wrong idea as to the time. It was the year 1816. It has been called the "year without a summer," for there was sharp frost in every month. There are old farmers still living in Connecticut who remember it well. It was known as the "year without a summer." The farmers used to refer to it as "eighteen hundred and starve to death." January was mild, as was also February, with the exception of a few days. The greater part of March was cold and boisterous. April opened warm, but grew colder as it advanced, ending with snow and ice and winter cold. In May ice formed half an inch thick; buds and flowers were frozen and corn killed. Frost, ice and snow were common in June. Almost every green thing was killed, and the fruit was nearly all destroyed. Snow fell to the depth of three inches in New York and Massachusetts, and ten inches in Maine. This weather is very perplexing to the honest agriculturist, who does not know whether to put in his potatoes or go sleighing. July was accompanied with frost and ice. On the 5th ice was formed of the thickness of window glass in New York, New England and Pennsylvania, and corn was nearly all destroyed in certain sections. In August ice formed half an inch thick. A cold northwest wind prevailed all summer. Corn was so frozen that a great deal was cut down and dried for fodder. Very little ripened in New England, even here in Connecticut, and scarcely any even in the Middle States. Farmers were obliged to pay four or five dollars a bushel for corn of 1815 for seed for the next spring's planting. The first two weeks of September were mild, the rest of the month was cold, with frost, and ice formed a quarter of an inch thick. October was more than usually cold, with frost and ice. November was cold and blustering, with snow enough for good sleighing. December was quite mild and comfortable.— *Extract from the Hartford Times.*

Did you ever ride in a stage coach? If you have lived in South Jersey it is presumed you have. The "stage" is one of the favorite conveyances of Jersey, and although it is not a peculiarity to this state, the Jersey stage is in some respects peculiar. Years ago, before the advent of the railroad, the "stage" was wont to drive out of the hotel yard ere yet the morning was gray, and gathering in its load of passengers by four o'clock in the morning, start off with a flourish of whip for Philadelphia, Cape May or Salem. Previous to 1850 it was no pleasant matter to attempt a journey to Philadelphia, or, as some would have to do, to Cape May, in the winter time. The would-be visitors to Philadelphia would make all their preparations and conclude all their business the night before starting, and in the morning at four o'clock they must be ensconced in the stage ready for the long and tedious ride. The journey was not often made, yet there were passengers to go every day. The Philadelphia mail, Mark Lloyd, stage-man, left Bridgeton on horseback on Saturday morning, January 14th, 1831, but the carrier was nearly all day before he reached Deerfield, only seven miles, and came near perishing at that. The drift of the snow was so great as to render the main roads in many places almost impassable. He succeeded in reaching Philadelphia on Monday evening, but with great difficulty. The snow was said to have been on the level about two feet deep. The late William Parvin, of this city, drove the down stage to Bridgeton, and the late Henry Graham, father of John R. Graham, our townsman, had the Greenwich stage. They were finally set across the Delaware in a row boat to Camden on Sunday just before sundown. Mr. Parvin had three passengers on board his sleigh on Monday morning for Bridgeton—Nancy Seeley, Jacob Woodruff and the late Peter Cambloss, of Newport. They had a very rough passage down, floundering in snow drifts every little while, but reached Deerfield that night, and came on to Bridgeton Tuesday morning. Mr. Graham had two passengers to Greenwich—Nancy Griffith and a sea captain, whose vessel, loaded with corn, was frozen up at the mouth of the Cohansey. His way was several times blocked by snow banks, but by the aid of neighboring farmers, who dug him out, he got as far as Woodstown some time after dark. The Jersey stage is not a soft-cushioned, swinging, easy pleasure wagon to ride in, by no means. It is a heavy, rattling concern, mostly of a peculiar build—a sort of a cross between a farmer's market wagon and a wood carter's wagon, and is constructed more upon principles of durability and rugged service than mere show. It can, on a pinch, transport a dainty city lady on a visit to a country cousin, or a barrel of pork to an inland storekeeper; and all of them have passengers to carry and errands to perform.

CHAPTER VIII.

THE first M. E. Church society in Bridgeton was organized in 1804, and owes its origin in a large measure to the labors and influence of Rev. John Murphy and his son-in-law, Michael Swing, two zealous men who had been instrumental in forming societies elsewhere and in building another church previous to this time.

A plain frame house of worship was erected here in 1807, 30 by 36 feet, the deed for the lot of ground and cemetery on Commerce street bearing date of that year. The oldest tombstone noticed in this yard, also bearing the date of 1807, was erected to the memory of James Smith.

The congregations at this time were small; did not exceed twenty-five or thirty members. As years rolled on, the membership having largely increased, this society was admitted within the bounds of Salem circuit. With the exception of Bishop Asbury, who had previously traveled through New Jersey, John Murphy and Michael Swing were among the first ministers who preached here.

An old member of the Methodist Episcopal church hands us the following reminiscence of the aforesaid denomination, which, half a century ago, was very weak in this community, but is now powerful and vigorous,

and growing yet more so year by year. It will doubtless be very interesting to many of our readers :

"About fifty-six years ago I was sexton of the old
Commerce street church. Salem and Cumberland were
in one circuit. There were two preachers on the circuit
together, who received about $250 each as their salary.
The presiding elder at that time traveled the whole state,
and received for his pay what was taken at each quarterly
meeting by collection. I was then at the church in
Bridgeton, which was lighted with candles hung up
around the wall in tin candlesticks. I went around in
time of service and snuffed the candles, and I opened the
church, swept it, and made the fires, burning wood only,
stone-coal not being used here for fuel, nor to any extent
anywhere, nor for years subsequently. I received for
my services eight dollars a year and candle stumps, after
the candles were too short to burn in the tin sticks.
The members paid to make up the preacher's salary,
some 12½ cents, some 25, and some 50 cents every
quarter. One year four persons volunteered to act in
the capacity of sexton gratis, three months each, and at
the end of the year the stumps were sold at auction."

In later years the membership of this society increased
to 650. The first house of worship was removed to
make room for the present neat and imposing structure
erected on its site in 1833. During the pastorate of
Rev. Isaiah D. King, in 1871, the church was again
rebuilt and enlarged, and it has ever been regarded as
the "Mother Church" of Methodism in this city.

The remaining years of Mr. Murphy's ministry were

spent in Cumberland county, where he died in the year 1813. His remains were buried in the Commerce street church cemetery by the side of his daughter, who had preceded him a few months before. In this quiet spot " he rests from his labors, and his works do follow him."

Rev. William Walton, an esteemed acquaintance and former school companion of the writer, during his successful pastorate of three years' duration at the Commerce street M. E. church, raised subscriptions among the Methodists of the city and county, for the purpose of erecting a monument to John Murphy, the founder of Methodism in Cumberland county. Mr. Murphy's remains lie in the Commerce street cemetery, and they have had no stone to mark the place, but a monument has now been erected such as is a credit to the church and an honor to the memory of the man who did so much for Methodism in South Jersey.

For many years Michael Swing was an influential member of the Cumberland County Bible Society. He was an excellent preacher, a very useful man, and much esteemed, not only by his own society, but by people of other denominations. In public speaking he prepared sufficiently to give command of the subject and of the congregation, and yet left himself free for those thoughts which often occur under the excitement of the hour. In all his religious utterances there was a freshness which showed it to be a heart exercise. Under the influence of the movements which he originated, and through his instrumentality, many persons were converted and added to the church.   Others were led to greater devotion, and to a higher and more perfect Christian life.

His first wife, Sarah, died in the month of February, 1813, after a brief illness, and was buried by the side of her father, Rev. John Murphy, in Commerce street churchyard, Bridgeton.

Standing by the side of her grave we read the following inscription :

" IN MEMORY OF OUR MOTHER,

SARAH,

WIFE OF REV. MICHAEL SWING,

DIED FEB. 16, 1813, AGED 48 YEARS.

' Children, meet me in Heaven.' "

For more than twenty-four years she went forth, cheering the heart of her husband in every good work.   She cheerfully submitted to the toil and privation of the early settlers of our country, and in the various changes which took place made many acquaintances and friends. As a wife and mother she was devoted and faithful, and though called away from a large family of children who were dependent upon a mother's care (the youngest, Michael Coates, being only two years old), yet her decision of character made impressions upon that family which cannot fail to benefit them through all the years to come, saying unto them, " This is the way, walk ye in it."   Thus the beauty of her life was seen, and its influence felt by many."

CHAPTER IX.

MICHAEL SWING, CONTINUED.

SINCE the days of Adam and Eve, when they were created and placed in the Garden of Eden, there has been found no spot of earth so nearly resembling that garden of beauty and blessedness as a happy home. He who made man and knew his nature, declared from the beginning of the world that it was "not good for man to be alone." The Bible picture of a truly blessed man is not a lonely bachelor in his garret nor a solitary monk in his cell, but a father in the midst of a happy home, enjoying the fruit of his labor and the affection of domestic life.

Near the farm of Michael Swing there lived a highly respectable and interesting family by the name of Newkirk, their broad fields adjoining. In this family were a number of daughters, and Mr. Swing, being one of the nearest neighbors, and a widower, was frequently invited to call, and it is presumed that this acquaintance was both pleasant and profitable, and many happy seasons here enjoyed. In the process of time Michael Swing found it not good to be alone, and in 1814 took unto himself another wife in the person of Miss Susannah Newkirk. He believed in the scriptural injunction, "Be ye fruitful and multiply and replenish the earth." By this marriage five children were born to them, namely: Joseph, Margaret, Pengam, Rebecca and Benjamin Franklin.

B. F. Swing, the last person named in the family, became a very large and portly gentleman, and for several years was engaged in business at Fairfield, Harmony and Roadstown, in Cumberland county. In the earlier years of his life he began work as a farmer on his father's estate, and for some time was a successful tiller of the soil. Subsequently, finding this a slow and unsatisfactory way to ascend the ladder of fame or amass a fortune for himself and his increasing family, he entered into cattle droving, buying and selling stock. He was acknowledged to be a good judge of horses and cattle, a good business man, and when in the meridian of life one of the largest representatives of our family in New Jersey.

Daniel R. Powell, a lad eleven years of age, applied at the farm of Mr. Swing for employment. He was informed that the owner of this property had a modest supply of boys in his own family, but if the lad really wanted work and wished to become industrious and useful he could find something for him to d. .

"Here, in 1824, I was apprenticed to learn the farming business, occasionally mending nets, fishing and catching oysters. I remember the winter of 1829. That year Michael Swing was elected member of the New Jersey Legislature, and spent the winter in Trenton. Two days were occupied with a good team of horses in reaching the capital of the state. It being a long and tedious ride in the stage coach, or private conveyance, he returned home only twice during that session.

" I remember a clear, beautiful night in the month of February. The girls were at home, the house illuminated, and company in the parlor. In the kitchen a large fire was blazing on the hearth, and the small boys were sent out to have a good time. Joseph, Benjamin and myself were ranged around the fire in a circle, smoking pipes. In the midst of our amusement and hilarity the door suddenly opened, and in came Mr. Swing from Trenton. He advanced rapidly toward us, and said:

" ' Boys, boys, this will never do! I had much rather find you studying books than smoking pipes.' Then he bumped our heads together.

"In the parlor he found Mr. Tyndall, Ephraim Whitaker, and another young man named Wescott. Priscilla immediately arose and said: ' Father, you have greatly surprised us; we were not expecting you home to-night; we have been very lonesome until Mr. Whitaker and Mr. Tyndall came over. Give me your hat and cloak, and sit down by our fire.'

" Handing his hat to this lovely daughter, he said : ' Ah, girls, I see how it is. When the old cat is away the mice will play.'

" Then he entertained the company by relating some funny stories. He said that when he was first elected an assemblyman, and the time came for him to go to the capitol at Trenton, he feared that he would be paled by the flashing of bright intellects all around him. He took his seat on the first day and resolved to remain quiet;

but in ten minutes he was perfectly at ease. This was what wrought the change in his mind: ' Mr. Speaker,' said one of the assemblymen from Bergen county, ' there are no ink in the inkstands.' Up rose another member, since famous in the history of the state, and known to most Jerseymen : ' Mr. Speaker,' said he, ' there are ink on my stand, but it is frozen in the bottles, and, as regards this new style of writing pen, I would prefer a *goose*-quill.' A broad smile illuminated the countenance of some of the members, and that was all Swing needed to put him at ease in the legislature."

The family long enjoyed a wide reputation for the beauty and grace of its women. This distinction was acquired, not so much from the number of its beautiful women, as for their industrious habits, sprightly manners, cheerful and entertaining conversation, and fitted as they were by nature and education to adorn mansions.

"It was my pleasure and good fortune," said Mr. Powell, "to remain with this family until twenty-one years of age, and after that time was hired to continue at good wages."

He remembers many happy days enjoyed here, and also in the Sunday-school at " Swing's Meeting House," where he subsequently united with the church, became a pious and useful man, attained a good old age, and at the present writing (1889) is a resident of Cumberland county and also a local exhorter in the church of his choice.

In relating his experience recently, Mr. Powell stated that he had been a member of the M. E. church for fifty-six years, and was still greatly attached to this society and all its institutions. Notwithstanding the fact that, fifty years ago, when a young man, he found no marriageable young ladies in this denomination at Fairfield who seemed to care much for him, although he had looked diligently among them for a companion to share with him the joy and happiness of this present life. In this emergency he was induced by a friend to attend the Presbyterian church, and subsequently courted and married a pious young lady belonging to that denomination.

"To this day," he said, "we will bless God for the Methodists, bless God for the Presbyterians; for we know from experience that the two, when united in marriage, will work harmoniously together, and hence no man can shake our faith and admiration for the Presbyterians."

The associates of Mr. Swing, while in the ministry, were Revs. Holmes Parvin, Walter Burroughs, Jonathan Brooks and Bartholomew Weed. While young in years Mr. Parvin died, apparently in the prime of life and in the midst of his usefulness, and was buried in the cemetery at "Swing's Meeting House."

The author recently visited the ancient and now crowded burial place of the family in "Rural Cemetery," a sloping tract that lies upon the south bank of the Cohansey river, in Fairfield township, one mile below Fairton. This cemetery has been used to an equal extent by the citizens of this community, and beneath the shade of venerable trees the remains of many distinguished men are interred. The plainest kind of tablets mark the resting places of Rev. Mr. Parvin and his wife, and probably some twenty-five or thirty deceased members of the Swing family, while a more elaborate one bears the inscription :

IN MEMORY OF
REV. MICHAEL SWING,
DIED JAN. 17, 1834,
In the full assurance of eternal life,
Aged 65 years, 10 months, 9 days.

He joined the M. E. Church in 1790, and soon after was licensed to preach. He labored extensively and usefully as a local preacher and filled acceptably the office of Class Leader, Deacon, Elder and Steward.

" Servant of God, well done,
Rest from thy loved employ.
The battle's fought, the victory won ;
Enter thy Master's joy."

With his armor bright, and amid his most active usefulness, he has fallen, just as he had attained the meridian of greatness and his concentrated activity was reaping a golden harvest. His ardent enthusiasm had brought him to eminence, when he was suddenly withdrawn from life's work. That manly form has vanished from earthly view ; that sympathetic voice charms no more the delighted ear nor inspires others to the attainment of a nobler and better life.

It is grateful to express the tribute of affection to the memory of one so much esteemed. To those who knew him well he was valued as a friend, dear to his brethren as a co-laborer, and, to his associates, revered as a faithful assistant.

The funeral services of the deceased took place at "Swing's Meeting House" on the 20th day of January, 1834, at half-past 10 A. M. Upon the platform were seated Revs. Walter Burroughs, Jonathan Brooks and Bartholomew Weed. After the reading of Scripture and the singing of the hymn commencing:

> " The hills of Zion yield
>   A thousand sacred sweets
> Before we reach the heavenly fields
>   Or walk the golden streets.

> " Then let your songs abound
>   And every tear be dry,
> We're marching through Emanuel's ground
>   To fairer worlds on high,"

Rev. Bartholomew Weed delivered an appropriate eulogy, taking as a motto the words, " He that reapeth receiveth wages, and gathereth fruit unto life eternal ; that both he that soweth and he that reapeth may rejoice together. And herein is that saying true, One soweth and another reapeth. I sent you to reap that wherein ye bestowed no labor ; other men labored, and ye are entered into their labors." " Jesus introduced the work of saving the world with the simple description, ' The sower went forth to sow,' not with pomp nor display, nor with the exhibition of a showy apparatus, but quietly, often in solitude, unnoticed by men. It often happens that not until the sower enters into his rest, and his completed work passes in review, is it all thoroughly understood. The great men of the world are the seed-sowers. Moses, Elijah, Plato, Aristotle, Paul, Peter, John will be remembered when the great warriors will be forgotten. It is cheering to know from the lips of Jesus himself that the sowers have a common bond of brotherhood, and that they shall rejoice together; ' he that soweth, and he that reapeth, shall alike rejoice.' Our dear brother who has left us, and whose memory we shall continue to cherish, was himself a beautiful illustration of this. His whole life is an illustration of his willingness to accept his reward in heaven. His associates have the honor in being pioneers in church organization. I now refer," said the speaker, " to the organization of this society, the building of the Fairfield M. E. church, and also the organization of the Methodist society at Bridgeton, of which your speaker is now pastor. When two intimate friends called to converse with our departed brother for the last time, they were greeted with the assurance that ' I feel better ; am resting calmly and peacefully,' and, before leaving, requested them to sing one of his favorite hymns :

> " ' There is a land of pure delight,
> Where saints immortal reign.
> Infinite day excludes the night,
> And pleasures banish pain.'

" Not long after he seemed as one enjoying a beautiful vision, and exclaimed : ' Death is the happiest hour of the Christian's life ; the time of my departure is near at hand.

Rivers of life divine I see, and trees of Paradise.' Thus passed our departed brother into the port of peace."

INSCRIPTIONS ON OLD GRAVES.

The following appear on the covers of two adjoining vaults in the old graveyard at Swing's Corner:

" Beneath this stone lies the remains of

REV. WILLIAM RAMSAY,

For fifteen years a faithful pastor of the Presbyterian church of this place, whose superior genius and native eloquence shone so conspicuously in the pulpit as to command the attention and gain the esteem of his hearers. In every station of life he discharged his duty faithfully. He lived greatly respected, and died universally lamented, Nov. 5, 1771, in the 39th year of his age."

" Here was deposited the body of

SARAH SMITH,

Successively the wife of the Rev. William Ramsay, of this place, and the Rev. Dr. Robert Smith, of Pequa. She was highly distinguished for the exercise of the estimable and amiable qualities in the various relations of a wife, mother, friend and Christian. Having survived her last worthy husband a few years in great weakness of body, she fell asleep in Jesus, Aug. 9, 1801. Aged 65 years."

"IN MEMORY OF

SUSANNAH,

Second Wife of Rev. Michael Swing,
For 34 Years his Widow.

She departed, in hope of eternal life, the first day of May, 1867,
aged 81 years, 6 months, 13 days.   For 63 years a member of the
M. E. church, and faithful in her religious life.

" Gently, she is sleeping,
She has breathed her last ;
Gently, while we are weeping
She to heaven has passed."

At the commencement of the present year (1889) it
may be written of this large and interesting family group
that only one of them is now living, to wit, Mrs. Rebecca
N. Smith, who in advanced years resides with her son,
Mr. Eleazer Smith, a well-to-do farmer of Mannington
township, Salem county, N. J.

CHAPTER X.

MEMORIAL NOTICE OF SARAH S. ATWOOD.

[Reported originally for the "News" by the Author, G. S. Swing.]

IN recording the death of Sarah S., wife of Rev. Joseph Atwood, after a brief sickness of about one week, it may be interesting to many readers to state that Mrs. Atwood's maiden name was Swing, she being the fifth daughter of Rev. Michael Swing, of Fairfield township. Her father and her grandfather, Rev. John Murphy, being the original founders of the first Methodist society in Bridgeton in the year 1804. With the exception of Bishop Asbury, who had previously traveled through New Jersey, Revs. Murphy and Swing were among the first ministers of this denomination who preached here. The youthful days of the deceased were happily spent on her father's farm along the banks of the Cohansey river, in Cumberland county, and after she had attained the age of womanhood, was united in marriage to Captain Moses Husted, by whom she had one daughter who grew to womanhood. She was soon called, in the providence of God, to part with both husband and daughter, and was left a widow in destitute circumstances. After the death of Captain Husted, which event occurred in

1852, she took up her residence in this city and remained here until the time of her second marriage to Hon. Cornelius M. Newkirk, a prominent and honored citizen of Upper Pittsgrove, Salem county. To the last named place they afterward removed and subsequently enjoyed many pleasant years of life together. After the death of her second husband, Mrs. Newkirk returned to her former home on Jefferson street, but not long destined to remain a lonely widow. Her earnest character and Christian demeanor attracted the attention of Rev. Joseph Atwood, and she was united in marriage with him.

Mr. Atwood was admitted into the New Jersey Conference in 1837, and has been a very successful minister, traveling large circuits and filling many important stations in the conference for a period of forty years. Until recently both have enjoyed excellent health. The deceased was an untiring Christian, courteous in manner, kind to the poor, and a model of hospitality and politeness, warmly attached to the church and its interests, and so remained for all the days of her pilgrimage. She was born March 28, 1808, and was a consistent member of the Methodist Episcopal church for fifty-three years. She passed away in great peace January 18, 1884, in the seventy-sixth year of her age. Her funeral services were held in Commerce Street Methodist Episcopal church on Tuesday morning, January 22d, at 10.30 o'clock, and were very impressive. They were opened with prayer by Rev. E. C. Hancock, of the Central church. Scripture lesson was then read by the Rev. W. S. Zane, of the Trinity church, from the 23d

Psalm, also part of the 21st chapter of Revelation. The sermon was preached by Rev. Jesse Stiles, II Cor., 4:18: "While we look not at the things which are seen, but at the things which are not seen; for the things which are seen are temporal; but the things which are not seen are eternal."

In the course of the speaker's remarks, he said : "The soul of the departed will cease to speak and exist among us, but her influence will not cease to live and be felt in this community."

She had read the Bible through many times, and committed passages of Scripture to memory, often repeating the 23d Psalm, " Yea, though I walk through the valley of the shadow of death I will fear no evil, for thou art with me, thy rod and thy staff they comfort me." To her husband she said, a short time previous to her death, "I feel my dying day is coming ; shall soon walk the golden streets."

> " Yonder's my house, my portion fair,
> My treasure and my heart are are there."

On another occasion she sung with a clear voice:

"There are lights along the shore that never grow dim," &c.,

then asking the question, " Don't that sound nice?" "Yes," replied her husband, "I believe it ; I believe it."

A large circle of friends from the surrounding country paid their last sad tribute of respect to the departed one. Deceased was buried in a black cloth coffin with

silver handles.   Forty-five couples followed the remains
to the grave.   Commerce Street church was full, and
among them we noticed a number of the Newkirk family,
relatives of the deceased's second husband, from Pittsgrove.   There were also persons from New York, Jersey
City, Woodstown, Salem, Millville and Philadelphia.

Mr. Atwood, her surviving husband, was born near
Tuckerton, Burlington county, N. J., April 22, 1804.
He grew up on a farm, was converted at the age of
eighteen, and while very young was licensed to preach by
Rev. Bartholomew Weed.   He is a ready and fluent
speaker, with full, strong voice and bright, keen eye.
As pastor on many charges he was active, earnest and
devoted.   He has a portly, well-built form of full six
feet in height, a large, noble head covered with the finest
growth of hair, now almost white, and his brown, benevolent face gives him the appearance of the "typical
grandfather of the olden time," in personification of all
that is good, kind and manly.   His long service in the
New Jersey Conference gives him a large acquaintance
and happy experience, while his countenance is comparatively free from the wrinkles and ravages of time,
although drawing near to the eighty-second year of
his age.

FOUR TIMES WEDDED.

[Extract from the " Daily News," March 28, 1885.]

Rev. Joseph Atwood, the well-known Methodist clergyman of our city, has recently been thinking that it was

about time he was taking another partner for life, to share his joys and his sorrows, through sickness and through health, for better or for worse. Accordingly, on Tuesday last, he took unto himself a better half for the fourth time, in the person of Mrs. Margaret Humphrey, manager of the Humphrey House, Broadway, Ocean Grove. The ceremony was performed at the Humphrey House by Rev. Dr. Stokes, manager of the Ocean Grove Camp Meeting Association. As a result of this union Bridgeton is to lose the Rev. Mr. Atwood, as he is now packing away his furniture and making preparations, and will take up his residence at the Humphrey House on Tuesday next.

Rev. Mr. Atwood has been a resident of this city for eight years, and though having retired from the active ministry has done a good work in our midst. During that time he has visited, he informs us, all of the 500 families in the Second ward, 800 in the First ward and 200 in the Third ward, not having had time to complete the latter ward, and has distributed tracts and prayed with all who would allow him. He has also, during that time, placed eighty-eight couples in the same happy state into which he has just entered, for the fourth time, himself. He has been a frequent visitor of our Sunday-schools, and few of the scholars of our city have not heard one or more of his addresses at the close of the regular Sunday-school services.

He will be known to readers outside of Bridgeton by the carpet-giving episode in Camden a few years ago, when a carpet manufacturer offered a roll of carpet to

any couple that had lived together a certain length of
time happily and without a cross word. The offer was
accepted by Rev. Mr. Atwood and his third wife, who
was then living, and they were paraded around Camden,
led by a brass band, as a result.

The marriage of Rev. Joseph Atwood and Mrs. Margaret Humphrey, the proprietress of a large and flourishing boarding-house at Ocean Grove, has created considerable interest. The groom is eighty-two years old, and
the bride but ten years his junior.

After the decease of his fourth wife, which occurred at
Ocean Grove, he again returned to Bridgeton and engaged in local mission work. He was of an active,
stirring make, and at times supplied the pulpits of the different churches in town, and of the neighboring towns,
and his sermons were always characterized by great
plainness of speech and unction of manner. He frequently related and dwelt upon the happiness of his own
Christian experience, the advantage of being always ready
to die, and without long sickness or lingering decay pass
suddenly from earth and awake amid the glories of immortality.

In the autumn of '86 he sold his residence on Jefferson street, Bridgeton, removed to Camden, and being
one of the oldest members of the New Jersey Conference,
was preparing to preach his semi-centennial sermon at
the next conference in March, 1887, when suddenly he
was stricken with apoplexy, fell from his chair and expired.

CHAPTER XI.

NATHANIEL G. SWING.

IN writing brief articles of prominent men, few are more worthy of notice, or more favorably known throughout the community, than the subject of this memoir, who was born at Pittsgrove, Salem county, N. J., March 30, 1798.

Every town and community have their "oldest inhabitant" and representative men, and in a certain sense Mr. S. may be regarded as one of these. His boyhood was not more remarkable than that of any other child in the same circumstances, although his early surroundings were attractive and pleasant. Nathaniel was next to the oldest of the children in his father's family, and his youthful hands were an indispensable help in the clearing of the land; and while he cultivated his own mind and the soil of his father's farm, the lad wrought for himself a training and discipline in the fields and at the fireside such as make honest-hearted heroes.

His first recollection of attending school was in a log school house near "Newkirk's Mill," known in later years as "Kean's," and now as "Ballinger's Mill."

In this rude and ancient amphitheatre of learning the seats extended around the outer wall, and long, low

NATHANIEL G. SWING.

benches without backs.   But we were a progressive and
enterprising people, and improved the house by turning
the long desks around against the wall, putting the long
seats in front, and sat with our backs toward the teacher.
Our school books were limited in variety, and the
pens were contributed by the "immortal goose," and
during the writing hour the request, " Please mend my
pen," was heard from all parts of the house.   The names
of the teachers in those days were Lewis Hall, David
Austin and Mark Peck.

In very early boyhood Nathaniel was regarded as
particularly bright and promising in intellect, and at an
early age sent to a higher and better school, Union Seminary, the *alma mater* of many accomplished scholars
and learned men, where, under the tuition of Professor
John Rose, he received sound physical as well as mental
training.

From his first entrance into this school the teacher
showed an ardent interest in its welfare, and was proud
of the material of which it was composed—sons of
farmers chiefly—a manly body of youth, which for
strength, activity and health, I think, was not surpassed
by any in the state.

Nathaniel gave himself diligently to his studies, won
the respect and affection of his comrades, and graduated
with honor to himself and the teachers in charge.   To
this day the names of his school companions are fresh
in his memory, and the lessons learned in 1811 were
never forgotten.

In 1812 the war broke out between England and the

United States. Ships of war and English vessels were numerous in Delaware bay, and also at the mouth of Salem and Alloway creeks; horses and cattle began to disappear, and great excitement prevailed throughout Salem county. His father talked the subject over with his family and friends, and decided to leave mother and the boys to manage the farm, while he went to war.

Although a lad of only fifteen years of age, Nathaniel took charge of the farm, and by attentive cultivation and continued industry good crops of corn and wheat were gathered during that year.

Years rolled on; the war with Great Britain at length was ended; our state was blessed with wise and competent rulers, and the country was at peace with all the world and the rest of mankind; and when all things became quiet and serene Mr. Swing proceeded to open a school for the instruction of children and youth, his first appointment being at Newkirk's Mill in 1819–20. This school house stood upon a very high piece of land, and was surrounded by large and stately trees. It overlooked the mill and the pond, and also a beautiful stream of running water.

One of the students of the class of 1819, Mr. Samuel D. Craig, who is still living in the same neighborhood, recently called at the residence of the writer, and, in relating his experience, said that his recollections of this school were both pleasant and agreeable. In fact, the subsequent life of both teacher and scholar had been smooth and tranquil as the running stream by which they sported in childhood.

John Carter, Esq., for many years a prominent merchant, justice of the peace and ex-member of the Legislature from Cumberland county, was also a pupil in the school at " Kean's Mill," and adds his testimony to the subsequent value and usefulness of the instruction received here in 1820.

Some years later Mr. Swing resigned his position as teacher, and proceeded to build a new house, a large barn and other outbuildings. These were pleasantly located at the intersection of four public roads crossing each other, and as the family owned the land on either side of the way, the place was subsequently named in honor of himself, " Swing's Corner."

His marriage to Miss Ann Parris was duly celebrated in 1822, and soon after this event they took possession of their new home and commenced their life work. He had the advantage of sociability, and saw on the horizon of his future the perpetual star of hope. In 1825, on the west side of the road and nearly opposite his residence, extended a beautiful tract of large timber, which subsequently withstood the storm and tempest of a hundred years; and in those days the woods abounded with squirrel, partridge and turtle doves, and when perched upon the topmost branches usually were safe from the attack of the boy with the ordinary shot gun. Upon the edge of this grove extensive machine works were erected for the turning and carving of wood and ornamental designs; carriage hubs, spokes, chair bottoms, and settee rounds, formed a part of the stock manufactured at this place, and which when finished found a ready sale in the markets of Philadelphia and New York. Like most of the industries of the olden time the belts and machinery at this establishment were propelled by horse power, and the hum of the revolving wheels of industry were heard for many years as if propelled by divine inspiration.

Prosperity in business brings gladness to all parties who have capital invested, and the familiarity and skill of the proprietor in the manufacture of the articles named, the most useful and ornamental in their day and time, were of a fashionable and satisfactory order. In connection with this he also owned a store for the sale of goods and general merchandise; and while superintending these industries the early years of life passed rapidly and pleasantly away.

At the commencement of the present year, 1889, Mr. and Mrs. N. G. Swing were both living, having enjoyed a good old age, their intellectual powers and memory but little impaired, and physical vigor good for persons so far advanced in life; and they may fairly be regarded as the eldest and most prominent representatives of our family now living.

For the past half century they have lived upon the farm at "Swing's Corner," and during that time were actively engaged in agricultural and mercantile pursuits. Throughout life he was vigorous, active and careful of his health, with an unfailing flow of good spirits and kindly feelings, of which his countenance gives abundant indication ; he also understands the sentiments of life as well as its logic, and to this day is not a bad dinner companion.

In early years he had struggled and toiled against the disadvantages of pioneer life; he had seen the forest disappear from the area of our country, and lived to see the day when friends and neighbors were surrounded by all the comforts and conveniences of civilized society.

I do not remember a man who is more familiar with the religious and political history of the last half century than he, nor one whose conversation is more to be enjoyed than his. He has been a great reader, a man of books and newspapers, and is well posted in all the current events and literature of the times. Before the township was divided he was collector of taxes for the years 1845–46 ; town superintendent for three years, from 1849 to 1852, with authority to examine and license teachers of public schools. Re-elected to the same office from 1863 to 1866. In these important offices he gained the prestige which in the course of time brought to him other leading distinctions of his life—that of representing the county of Salem in the legislature of New Jersey.

With a high degree of literary culture he has the sturdy integrity and substantial common sense which so eminently characterize the members of the Swing family.

He was also interested in military affairs, and connected with the arsenal at Pittsgrove (Pole Tavern), a teacher of the military drill, and also held the commission of major from the year 1828 up to the breaking out of the late war in 1861, when he resigned the last-named office and commission.

Like William Penn, Benjamin Franklin, and other distinguished Americans, he loved peace rather than war. His was a nature made for friendships, and his life fully exemplified the Shakespearian idea of man : tender, humorous, large-hearted, modest and obliging. We may think of him as one whose name was on the roll of merit when the late General U. S. Grant was a barefooted boy and Cornelius Vanderbilt was lying in his cradle, unconscious of his future greatness.

> He hears men say he's growing old ;
>   It seems but yesterday
> That he was young, and strong, and bold—
>   'Tis all a mystery !
>
> To him the clear, melodious song
>   Of birds rings forth as sweet
> As when a boy he ran along
>   With little, swift, bare feet
>
> The cow path in the " pasture lot,"
>   Or waded in the brooks,
> And in his happiness forgot
>   His errands and his books.
>
> Great changes he has lived to see ;
>   " The trusted and the true "
> Have gone to vast eternity,
>   The land " beyond the blue."

To say he was a moral man, a good counsellor and friend, is not enough : he is a religious man, having been an exemplary member of the Presbyterian denomination during the greater portion of his life, and held in honorable esteem by the church, contributing to the support and advancement of the Gospel, both at home and abroad. He is now among the oldest of the church in years and in membership, and his memory will brighten with the years of Christian progress. It may also be said that few more remarkable examples of religious life illuminate our church history.

Recently an intimate friend remarked: "I have been with him in seasons of toil, in transactions of business, and in tours of recreation, when all thoughts of education, agriculture, mercantile or military life might be thrown aside. Yet the purity of thought and expression, the affinity with all that is generous in human nature, and his unfailing command of harmonious language will continue to attract our reverence and admiration.

In later years he is apparently giving little attention to politics, although greatly interested in our state and national prosperity, a keen observer of passing events, and is keeping an eye upon the condition of the party in all parts of the state, being at the present time the oldest living ex-member of the New Jersey legislature from Salem county. He attended the last election, Nov. 6, 1888, and was offered the choice of either of the two candidates named, Wm. Henry Harrison or Grover Cleveland, this being his sixteenth presidential vote, having voted at all the presidential elections since the days of John Quincy Adams in 1825.

Two children grace the household, a son and daughter, Frank Marrion and Sallie P. Swing. The first named has been actively engaged in both agricultural and mercantile pursuits in his native state, and also in Pennsylvania, where he now resides, while the daughter, for several years past, was teacher in the female department of the public school at Millville, afterward at Bridgeton and other institutions of learning in the same state.

Tough of fiber and stout of heart, Mr. Swing has survived nearly all the companions of his youth and those who settled around him in early times. Notwithstanding his advanced age, his general health and memory is good. He is able to talk by the hour of events in the early part of the present century, and is regarded by young people as a walking encyclopædia of religious and political history.

When his ninetieth birthday arrived (on the 30th of March last) the event was commemorated by the planting of corn and vegetables in the field; then, mounted on a favorite saddle horse, he called upon friends and relatives three miles distant.

He owns a pleasant home in Salem county, and since his retirement has lived a quiet and uneventful life among the people.

May no dark clouds arise to mar the beauty of his declining years.

CHAPTER XII.

HISTORICAL REVIEW OF THE PRESBYTERIAN CHURCH, PITTS-
GROVE, SALEM COUNTY, N. J.—SKETCH OF ITS PASTORS
AND PEOPLE.

THE history of the Presbyterian church, Pittsgrove, opens in the latter part of the year 1738, when Rev. Daniel Buckingham, a traveling missionary, first visited this part of New Jersey. He was a man of great energy, fertile in resources, modest in manner and thoroughly consecrated to his work. It was his constant care not only that his people should be more pious, but gaining in knowledge, and willing to join their struggles in building a house of worship; sing and pray, and with Bibles and hymn books invade the wilderness. His native genius and transparent soul gained multitudes of admirers; and by providential opportunity and religious zeal succeeded in banding twenty converts together for mutual advancement in scholarship and piety. The people who settled here were industrious, and improved their condition by building houses, clearing up farms and erecting mills. They also knew their religious wants, and to this community the present generation accord the honor of building the first Presbyterian church in Salem county.

REV. GEORGE W. JANVIER.

It is not the intention of a missionary to settle himself over his congregation. He usually is sent out as an ambassador to open new fields of labor, gain converts, form societies, and impress upon his hearers the importance of keeping the Ten Commandments.

Three years later the church was organized by the Presbytery of Philadelphia—April 30, 1741. Rev. David Evans was installed the first regular pastor. My grandfather, Abraham Swing, who resided near by, relates that the original building was constructed of cedar logs and called "The New Missionary Meeting House." At once the place became the centre of attraction to large numbers of people and a sacred spot to the households of the forty-nine members who signed the church covenant. Two large stoves with their ruby light gave out a cheerful glow, and the plain wooden benches presented a neat appearance, and were suggestive of the primitive character of its worshippers. Louis DuBois sold to the trustees two acres of land for building purposes, and a few years later fifty acres adjoining the same.

In 1744 the trustees decided to make an additional purchase of fifty acres of land of Abraham Newkirk, to be used for a farm or parsonage, upon which suitable buildings were erected for the pastor and his family. A few years later the congregation came into possession of a large tract of valuable timber land to be used for church purposes.

Rev. David Evans continued pastor over this congregation for a period of ten years. He was a man of piety, learning, ability, and manifold experience. In his inter-

course with the people he was prompt, unwearied, reso-
lute, and full of kindness, of courtesy and courage.
Ten years later he was suddenly transferred by death
from earthly toil, and entered into heaven and history on
the 4th day of February, 1751. The future will take
care of his fame; and of him it may be said, "The
righteous shall be in everlasting remembrance."

The second pastor of the church was Rev. Nehemiah
Greenman, ordained and installed December 5, 1753.
Among other accomplishments he was a good singer
and musician, and often styled by country people a
native born orator. Crowds of people attended his
church, when it soon became necessary to build a larger
house of worship. During the month of October, 1765,
the congregation met and decided to build, giving subscriptions and appointing managers. The building committee was Jacob DuBois, Thomas Sparks and Matthew
Newkirk. The log structure was taken down and removed, and a new brick church erected in its place.
Over the south entrance a marble capstone bears the
following inscription:

N. G. V. D. M.
1767.

While living here Mr. Greenman purchased a tract of
land, enclosed it with a cedar rail fence, planted trees and
erected a dwelling-house thereon for himself and family.
His good knowledge of men, amiable temper and religious
zeal endeared him greatly to this people; and for

twenty-six years he continued as pastor over this congregation. Coming when in his thirty-first year, in his fifty-ninth year was called home to sing the songs of redeeming grace, and join the church triumphant in heaven. The elders of the church at this date were the six following: Matthew DuBois, Gideon Conkling, Jacob DuBois, Jr., James McClung, David DuBois and Joseph VanMeter. The church was next served by three young men, Revs. Schenck, Glassbrook and Isaac Foster; the last named died on this charge in June, 1794, in the thirty-ninth year of his age. After him came Rev. Mr. Laycock, who supplied the church for a brief period of time. Next in order was Rev. Buckley Carll. When quite a young man, and for several years after, Mr. Carll was employed in teaching a village school in the higher branches of learning. During this time he occasionally preached in his own school house and in churches as occasion permitted. The Presbytery of Philadelphia recognized his ability and eminent fitness for the gospel ministry, and in the year 1801 ordained and installed him pastor of the Presbyterian church at Pittsgrove. From that time until the year 1804 he continued to minister to this congregation. Next he received a call to one of the largest and most important congregations in the state, and was transferred to Rahway, N. J., where he was pastor of the First Presbyterian church of that place for twenty-three years. In 1828 his health failed, when he took a superannuated relation with the church, and removed to Deerfield township, where he owned a farm. His religious zeal, perseverance and industry were unflagging, and while living here he often occupied the pulpit at Deerfield Street. He frequently preached in the old stone church, Fairfield, and also assisted Mr. Janvier in pulpit work at Pittsgrove. He seldom wearied in Christian conversation or ministerial work, and did not preach because it was his duty, but because he loved to do so. He is remembered as being very intelligent, one who had read and studied many years; a firm believer in the doctrines taught, and the leading motive of his life was to win souls, honor God and the church.

He died on the 22d day of May, 1849, in the eightieth year of his age. Among his last requests to surviving friends was that his remains be buried among the other deceased ministers at Pittsgrove.

The next minister who lived long enough to make any permanent mark upon the history of the church is Rev. John Clark, who was stationed here in 1806, and for several years later. About seventy years have passed since the formation of this society. The population has greatly increased. Farms, orchards and dwellings have multiplied, and the "noon-time of life" has become brighter than the morning.

In 1811 a young student in the ministry, Rev. Geo. W. Janvier, came to preach on trial, as was the custom in those days. He was exceedingly admired by the people, and ordained pastor May 12, 1812. Besides the morning service in the church at 10 A. M., he preached every Sunday afternoon at either the Washington, Jefferson, or Whig Lane school houses.

In the early history of the church the congregation was scattered through the whole of Pittsgrove township and a part of Pilesgrove and Upper Alloway's creek, where as yet there was no church of this denomination, Salem and Pittsgrove being the only two churches organized in the county.

Mr. Janvier was united in marriage with Miss Margaret Friese, whose parents resided about four miles distant and formed a part of his own congregation.

At first the salary of the pastor was $300, with free use of the parsonage. Soon after his marriage this amount was increased to $500 per annum, including the rent or use of the large parsonage farm.

A clergyman of our denomination would not often invite into his pulpit a minister of any other denomination, neither would he recommend Sunday visiting among his parishioners, nor the wearing of side whiskers or a mustache, all these things being considered worldly and sacrilegious acts. In those days the congregation stood up during prayers and sat down when engaged in singing.

The old brick church in which our pastor preached so many years is yet standing, although exceedingly antiquated, having the old-style roof and the keystone arrangements peculiar to structures of that date. Inside it is even more ancient in appearance, with very high pulpit, and galleries almost as capacious as the first floor itself. It contained very high seats, two aisles, two side and one end galleries, and was capable of seating 800 people.

9

Formerly it was surrounded by a grove of large forest trees, with a running stream of water near by.

Back of the church are the old-time carriage sheds, where the young men of former generations tied their "trotters" while the sermon was going on.

After the benediction, in the hallway and galleries, young men and maidens exchanged. glances with each other, and there were courtship and flirtation in the air.

In those days the writer occupied a seat among members of the choir, and during a period of almost half a century the leaders were the four following named: Thomas DuBois, Jonathan L. Swing, John W. Janvier and Henry Harding. About twenty-five persons, male and female, belonged to this choir, and their musical attainments were greatly appreciated by both pastor and people.

Years ago Fourth of July celebrations were held in the grove near by, and every summer the old church is still used for a brief time for holding a "picnic," or strawberry festival, for the benefit of Sunday schools. In front of this church a venerable oak yet remains standing, apparently as sound as it was fifty years ago, when, as a lad, we stood beneath its shade, admired its grand proportions, its strength and beauty. Looking upon it recently recalled to memory the following lines:

> " Woodman, spare that tree ;
> Touch not a single bough ;
> In youth it sheltered me,
> And I'll protect it now."

Then I thought of these words, contained in the good book, and of which men are so forgetful and indifferent: "They that be wise shall shine as the brightness of the firmament, and they that turn many to righteousness as the stars forever and ever."

Sir Matthew Hale, chief justice of England, is said to be the author of a little stanza the wisdom of which has been demonstrated in a busy life:

> " A Sabbath well spent
>   Brings a week of content,
> With rest for the toils of the morrow.
>   But a Sabbath profaned,
>   Whatever be gained,
> Is sure to be followed by sorrow."

> " I feel the happier all the week
>   If my foot has pressed the sacred aisle ;
>   The pillow seems softer to my cheek,
>   I sink to slumber with a smile;
>   With sinful passions cease to fight,
>   And sweetly dream on Sunday night."

To illustrate the faith of " old-time Christians " and the faithfulness of God to answer prayer, the following truthful incident is herein related:

In the latter part of the summer of 1849 a great drought prevailed throughout the lower part of New Jersey. People became alarmed at the condition of their corn-fields and other growing crops, and requested the pastor to pray for rain. As dry weather had long contined, the pastor consented to this proposal, and on the following Sabbath commenced reading a Bible description of the flood, taking for his text, " Noah and all his household entered into the ark."

Among the announcements were the following: "On Monday and Tuesday next a public meeting will be held in this church, at 3 o'clock P. M., to pray for rain."

The farmers could not plough in the fields, so they attended the rain services; and on Tuesday afternoon the congregation had largely increased in number. People were talking together in the grove, and outside the church, when Mr. Janvier approached a group of elders and, with his eagle eyes scanning the clear, bright horizon, said (so the story goes): " Brethren, is there any use praying for rain to-day? Not a cloud can be seen."

Entering the church the deacons gathered around the altar, and the services begun. As the meeting progressed in interest, Deacon Gilbert H. Craig arose and said he believed the coming of rain was only delayed by the lacking of our own faith in God. He believed in God. Ever since the days when the shepherds watched their flocks by night on the plains of Judea, God had watched over his people. And to-day he believed in the same overruling providence.

> " God moves in a mysterious way
>   His wonders to perform ;
>   He plants his footstep on the sea,
>   And rides upon the storm."

Elders Moses Richman, Foster, Swing and Harris followed with touching language, bearing testimony to the remarkable providence of God since the birthday of creation. The audience became electrified, when, as in the days of Pentecost, a mighty power came down.

> " Heaven came down our souls to greet,
> And glory crowned the mercy seat."

When the services ended dark clouds approached from the west, rain came on; in the evening the wind changed to east and met another shower, and it continued raining all night and a part of the next day. The dry ponds were filled, and before morning mills and bridges floated away.

At that time a millwright by the name of Hulick was employed in repairing a mill near by, and experienced some difficulty in saving the property from destruction. The next morning, and while the rain was still falling, he called at the parsonage on horseback, and said: "See here, parson, have thee been holding 'rain meetings' for three days? I have come to tell thee that Foster's and Kean's mills were both undermined by water last night and came near floating away. I have already more work than I can do this summer, and when the mills are gone we'll have neither flour nor bread to eat. Now, parson, I want thee to stop these 'rain meetings' at once."

Turning his horse in the direction of the mill pond the millwright galloped away, leaving the astonished parson alone, meditating, perhaps, upon the power and greatness of the Ruler of the universe.

Kind words will never die. Though they do not cost much, yet they will help one's good nature and good

will, and produce their own image on the souls of men.
Kind words will produce a cheerful temper, make youth
and beauty attractive, and cheer us on through life's pilgrimage.

When Mr. Janvier first came to preach to this people
he was in the twenty-eighth year of his age, and the
membership of the church at that time was ninety-eight.
He continued pastor until his resignation in October,
1857, a period of almost forty-six years. The records
will show additions of between four and five hundred
members. And, it may be said, that songs of praise to
God arose from the assembly, and the "wilderness and
the solitary place was glad."

All through this extended period we find him going
in and out before the people, blessing their homes, cheering their hearts and improving their lives, baptizing
children, marrying the young people and burying the
dead.

The meetings in the old church were always well
attended, its spacious galleries being filled with young
people, and many found the light and the peace of God
that passeth all understanding.

Samuel Swing and Sarah, his wife, whose names are
mentioned elsewhere, were prominent members of this
society.

In the cemetery we read these inscriptions on tablets
of marble:

Samuel Swing, born Sept. 15, 1729. Died March 13,
1801, aged 72 years, 6 months. As a man of piety he
was much revered, as an elder he was truly useful. La-

mented by all who knew his worth, he died as he lived, in the full confidence of a glorious immortality.

Sarah, his wife, survived her husband seven years, and died June 7, 1808, aged 78 years, 2 months, 24 days.

Jeremiah Swing, one of the early settlers of Salem county, died at York, Pa., June 24, 1794, and sleeps among his kindred at Pittsgrove, where so many ancient and modern tombstones are strangely mingled together.

Mrs. Ruth S. Lawrence died at Pittsgrove, Sept. 8, 1793.

My grandfather, Abraham Swing, departed this life Oct. 10, 1832. In domestic life he loved the Gospel; he was a Christian at home, commanding his children and his household to keep the way of the Lord.

Hannah, his wife, survived him seventeen years, and died February 24, 1849, in the seventy-seventh year of her age. The funeral sermon was preached by Rev. George W. Janvier; text, Genesis 23:2: "And Sarah died in Kirjath-arba; the same is Hebron in the land of Canaan; and Abraham came to mourn for Sarah, and to weep for her."

Fronting the church is a stone bearing the following: "Albert Coombs, Vol. of 12th N. J. Reg., died April 26, 1863, at Stanton hospital, Washington, D. C., aged 25 years;" and at the north side of the church another as follows: "Asa R. Burt enlisted Aug. 14, 1862, in Co. H, 12th Reg. N. J. Vols. Wounded in the battle of Chancellorsville, Va., May 3d, 1863, fell into the hands of the enemy and was buried on the field of battle."

Abraham Swing Harris enlisted at Pittsgrove, Salem

county, August 14, 1862, in Company K, 12th Reg. N.
J. Volunteers; wounded at the second battle of the Wilderness; captured by the enemy, and subsequently died
at Andersonville, Va.   These are those of whom our
poet sings:

> " How sleep the brave, who sink to rest
> With all their country's wishes blest,
> When Spring, with dewy fingers cold
> Returns to deck their hallowed mould?
> She there shall dress a sweeter sod
> Than Fancy's feet have ever trod;
> By fairy hands their knell is rung,
> By forms unseen their dirge is sung;
> There Honor comes, a pilgrim gray,
> To bless the turf that wraps their clay;
> And Freedom shall awhile repair
> To dwell a weeping hermit there."

A little further on we find the following inscription
written over the grave of Alfred Swing, member of Company C, Sixth Pennsylvania Cavalry, died at Harper's
Ferry, July 10, 1865:

> " He died afar from his sunny home,
>   Beneath a southern sky;
> And they bore him o'er hill and dale,
>   In his native land to lie.

> " And wrapt him in his soldier garb,
>   And placed him 'neath the sod,
> Where oft in childhood's halcyon days
>   His feet had lightly trod.

> " And yet he died, fair freedom's son,
>   In the holy cause of truth,
>   And slumbers with the great and brave ;
>   Alas! the noble youth."

Near the junction of four roads stands the church, the school house and the cemetery, where generations of people sleep in the silence of death, while other generations of the descendants are hard at work in the fields close by.   Among the monuments we notice the names of Bewster, Burt, Foster, Alderman, Craig, Coombs, Janvier, Elwell, Harding, Krom, Wood, Newkirk, Richman, Lawrence, Johnson, Swing, Mayhew, VanMeter, Brooks, Carll, Cole, Stratton and DuBois, and these are the names one hears everywhere in this "garden country" to-day.   Thus be it remembered that Salem county has given to the country, the world and humanity some of the proudest names in history.   She holds in her bosom to-day the ashes of some of the noblest and greatest men that have illustrated the glories of this community.

BEYOND THE RIVER.

[Selected Poetry.   Author unknown.]

> Time is a river deep and wide ;
>   And while along its banks we stray,
> We see our loved ones o'er its tide
>   Sail from our sight away, away.
> Where are they sped—they who return
>   No more to glad our longing eyes?
> They've passed from life's contracted bourne
>   To land unseen, unknown, that lies
>   Beyond the river.

'Tis hid from view, but we may guess
  How beautiful that realm must be;
For gleamings of its loveliness,
  In visions granted oft we see.
The very clouds that o'er it throw
  Their veil unraised for mortal sight,
With gold and purple tintings glow,
  Reflected from the glorious light
                Beyond the river.

And gentle airs, so sweet, so calm,
  Steal sometimes from that viewless sphere;
The mourner feels their breath of balm,
  And soothed sorrow dries the tear;
And sometimes listening ear may gain
  Entrancing sound that hither floats,
The echo of a distant strain
  Of harps' and voices' blended notes
                Beyond the river.

There are our loved ones in their rest;
  They've crossed Time's river—now no more
They heed the bubbles on its breast,
  Nor feel the storms that sweep its shore.
But there pure love can live, can last;
  They look for us their home to share
When we in turn away have passed,
  What joyful greetings wait us there,
                Beyond the river.

FIFTY YEARS OF CHURCH HISTORY—1839 TO 1889.

On the 5th of November, 1839, the Presbytery of West Jersey was organized with ten ministers, viz: Revs. Ethan Osborn, Buckley Carll, George W. Janvier, Samuel Lawrence, Moses Williamson, Alexander Heber-

ton, Benjamin Tyler, S. Beach Jones, Samuel D. Blythe
and Cortlandt Van Rensselaer; thirteen churches, viz:
Fairfield, Pittsgrove, Greenwich, Cold Spring, Salem,
Deerfield, Bridgeton, Woodbury, Blackwoodtown, Burlington, Millville, Cedarville, and Mount Holly, and with
a territory equal to one-third of the state.

In 1839 Atlantic county was without a Presbyterian
church, now it has eight; Camden county then had
one, now it has nine; Gloucester at that time had one,
now ten; Salem county then one, now four; Cape May
then one, now four; Cumberland, the stronghold of
Presbyterianism in '39, had eight churches, now ten of
this denomination.

THREE REMARKABLE MEN.

It will be remembered that Revs. George W. Janvier,
Ethan Osborn and Buckley Carll were three remarkable
men and eminent ministers of the gospel. They were
fine classical scholars; had warm and generous hearts,
and delighted to read and converse upon the theme of
Christian holiness. During their long and useful lives
they obtained a character and influence in the Presbyterian church and throughout the state which few can expect to attain. One of them passed away from earth
at the age of ninety-nine years, nine months and eleven
days. Mr. Janvier continued to preach to this congregation almost forty-six years, when failing health admon-
ished him to retire by resignation in October, 1857.

Rev. Edward P. Shields, a student from the seminary at Princeton, was next ordained and installed pastor June 2, 1858, and continued in this relation almost thirteen years; eighty-six persons were added to the church on profession and forty by certificate, making 126 in all.

In the spring of 1863 a proposition was made by the elders for the building of a new church, and through the efforts of the pastor and people $5,800 were subscribed for a beginning. The building committee chosen was Charles Wood, John R. Alderman, James Coombs, Enoch Mayhew, Benjamin F. Burt, George Coombs and John W. Janvier. The building committee met at the parsonage July 4, 1863, and signed articles of agreement with Joseph Allen, a builder and contractor of Salem, New Jersey. The question of location was decided August 6, '63; vote 16 north, 23 south, side of the public road; corner stone laid in the presence of a large assembly; addresses delivered by Rev. S. J. Baird, C. R. Gregory and Daniel Stratton. Messrs. Janvier and Shields deposited the box of documents, and set the corner stone in its place.

The church was not completed in one year from date; the war of the rebellion was then going on, and some patriotic members of the church enlisted for three years, or during the war. Carpenters, masons, bricklayers and hod-carriers became demoralized and refused to work. Various obstacles presented themselves, in the way of lumber, building material and skilled workmen, until it became impossible to carry out the original contract as to date of completion. Three years expired before the steeple was finished, the bell set in its place and pealing forth its cheerful sound, inviting the congregation to attend divine service in the new church building erected at a cost of twenty-five thousand dollars ($25,000).

It was dedicated Aug. 11, 1867; sermon by Rev. Charles W. Shields, of Princeton, assisted by Rev. C. E. Ford, of Williamstown, and others.

Rev. Mr. Shields continued pastor until Dec. 25, 1870, on which day he preached his farewell sermon and resigned his pastoral connection with Pittsgrove church, a cordial invitation to another church having been extended to him, and he soon after removed to Cape May. Pittsgrove was his first charge. He served his people well as a faithful minister of the Gospel, and was greatly beloved by his congregation.

Rev. Wm. A. Ferguson, of Ohio, next received a unanimous call to the pastorate Nov. 27, 1871. When preaching his centennial sermon, July 9, 1876, to this congregation, he said:

"During the five years of my ministry with you, 106 persons have been received on examination, and 21 by letter—127 in all. When I first came here the membership was 212; now it is 300. The amount given the benevolent boards of our church during my pastorate is $1825.00. Exclusive of this amount for the boards, there have been raised, including salary, incidental expenses and church debt, $13,194.76."

The elders who have served the church during the first sixty years of its history are as follows:

Isaac Harris . . . . who died in 1808
Abraham DuBois . . . .   "   1811
Samuel Swing . . . .   "   1801
John Stratton . . . .   "   1814
Hosea DuBois . . . .   "   1822
Benjamin VanMeter . . . .   "   1826
Eleazer Mayhew . . . .   "   1828
Jeremiah DuBois . . . .   "   1844

The following named persons were elected elders during the ministry of Janvier and the other later pastors:

Abraham Swing . . . . elected Feb. 25, 1814
John Mayhew . . . .   "   "   "
Jeremiah Foster . . . .   "   "   "
Jonathan L. Swing . . . .   "   Dec. 7, 1826
Erasmus VanMeter . . . .   "   "   "
Moses Richman . . . .   "   April 22, 1833
Leonard Swing . . . .   "   "   "
Gilbert H. Craig . . . .   "   "   "
Ebenezer Harris . . . .   "   June 6, 1844
Richard Burt . . . .   "   "   "
Thomas Harding . . . .   "   May 4, 1857
Samuel D. Krom . . . .   "   "   "
Garret DuBois . . . .   "   "   "
Enoch Mayhew . . . .   "   "   "
Joseph L. Richman . . . .   "   Aug. 30, 1868
Benj. F. Burt . . . .   "   "   "
Adam S. Groff.
Richard B. Ware.

Continuing, Mr. Ferguson said:

"Among the elders of our church, Benj. F. Burt, Jonathan L. Swing, Garret DuBois, Leonard Swing and Richard Burt have died during the present pastorate.

They were all good and useful men, and we can say, as
we think of their virtues, what you can say of them and
the other elders known to you, who are longer absent
from the body :

> " 'With us their names shall live
>   Through long succeeding years,
>   Embalmed with all our hearts can give,
>   Our praises and our tears.'

" These have been pleasant years in the Gospel ministry, not only because of God's blessing upon our union
in the ingathering of many souls, but because of the
uninterrupted kindness which I have received at your
hands. Many of the young have united with the church,
and a considerable number of the older. It is a pleasant
reflection to me that the first aged person with whom I
met on the cars, on my first visit to this place, was one
who has since joined the church under my own ministry."

Mr. Ferguson was pastor for ten years, from 1871 to
1881, and then accepted a call to another church in
Ohio.

Rev. John D. Randolph was the next pastor. His
sermons were thoroughly scriptural and classical, and
during the years of his ministry at Pittsgrove made impressions upon the minds and hearts of his hearers.

The date of the building of the new missionary church,
Rev. Daniel Buckingham, pastor, was 1738; the brick
church, Rev. Nehemiah Greenman, pastor, 1767.

A large modern church, with steeple and bell, was
built during the pastorate of Edward P. Shields, in

1867. Size, 51 by 92 feet; with projecting tower, and spire 125 feet high. Cost of building, $21,150; furniture, $700; steeple bell and fixtures, $4,196; total, $26,046.

Many eventful scenes have transpired during the one hundred and fifty years of the church's history. These walls have resounded with the voice of prayer and praise, and many souls converted to God. Some have gone out from these congregations into the ministry, making honorable records. Among the number you remember the name of Rev. Levi Janvier, a son of your former pastor, who for twenty years was a missionary in a foreign land.

Following are the names of the pastors of the church from the year 1738 to 1889:

First Missionary, Rev. Daniel Buckingham; pastors, Revs. David Evans,* Nehemiah Greenman,* Isaac Foster,* John Laycock, Buckley Carll,* John Clark, Geo. W. Janvier,* Edward P. Shields, William A. Ferguson, John D. Randolph, John Ewing, D. D., the last named being the present beloved pastor; in all, one missionary and twelve stationed pastors during a period of one hundred and forty-eight years.

The remains of five of the above named ministers (*) were buried in the old yard, passing away in advanced years. Doubtless they have met together in heaven to recount the mercies of God to their souls, and in the councils of eternity compare the results of their services to mankind and the church on the earth.

CHAPTER XIII.

MEMORIAL NOTICE.

ANOTHER of the prominent and influential men of Pittsgrove township, whose birthplace and home were here, was Jonathan L. Swing. In speaking of his early life, he said when he was a boy there were few schools in his neighborhood, and our school houses were of the most primitive and rudimentary character. He attended them only about four months during the fall and winter seasons. Here he became active in athletic sports, and with exercise his figure gained in fullness and in strength. One of the leading qualities of his mind was a remarkable memory, and in this he excelled other members of his class. Blessed with an excellent constitution, a joyous and obliging disposition, his mind was improved by extensive reading, and subsequently by long acquaintance and extensive intercourse with the most noted and intelligent people of the land, he became familiar with the early events of the country in which he was born, and appreciated all that was noble and excellent in mankind. "Our amusements," he said, "partook largely in the study of music and in practicing the military drill at the arsenal

10

JONATHAN L. SWING.

near by, for be it remembered that during the war with Great Britain, in 1812, the spirit of '76 filled the minds and hearts of young America."

Mr. S. has always retained a warm affection for his youthful companions, and recalls with pleasure the memory of the pioneers of Salem county, and their zealous celebrations of Washington's birthday and the Fourth of July.

" When I was of age," he said of himself, " I had almost completed my apprenticeship and learned a trade." At an early age he was impressed with the beauty and value of religion, and desired to make it the subject of his choice. Without any remarkable experience he united with the Presbyterian church, and some years later was elected one of its ruling elders. With the welfare and prosperity of the church he was largely identified, working in harmony with pastor and people. He took a great interest in theological matters ; was active in church work ; but his religion took the form of quiet doing rather than noisy profession. In the Sunday school he was a diligent and successful laborer ; he particularly enjoyed teaching the young, and was instrumental in gathering many children into the fold, being either teacher, chorister or superintendent of the Washington and Jefferson districts for a period of thirty-five years.

This noble system of instruction reached all classes of society and involved a quadruple blessing—a blessing upon the parent, the teacher, the pupil and the community, and through all these upon the vast interests of society itself.   It may be said that he greatly enjoyed congregational singing, instrumental music and sacred song. His love for the church and Sunday school increased with the years, her worship and her songs being a source of great delight.

While employed in teaching music in the village of Deerfield he met Miss Rebecca McQueen, who, at that time, was gifted with a remarkably cheerful spirit, and full of zeal and honest joy.   A romantic attachment followed which, while life lasted, never lost the beauty of its attraction.   They were united in marriage on the 15th day of July, 1818, and she not only cheered his life, but proved herself a most efficient helpmeet during the fifty-six years she was permitted to be his companion.

Jonathan L. Swing was born at Pittsgrove, Salem county, N. J., October 27, 1796, and the farm adjoining the one on which he lived was his birthplace.   By trade and occupation he was a farmer and mechanic, a builder of wagons, carriages and agricultural implements, making a specialty in the construction of the revolving hay rake, ploughs, cultivators and farming machinery. In business he was industrious, regular and reliable; humorous in conversation and firm and lasting in friendship.   He was a man of the people; enjoyed being among people, and could talk intelligently upon agricultural, political and religious subjects.   Of modest nature, he was seldom cast down by reverses, nor elated by great prosperity.   The writer, who knew him intimately in a social and business relation, and admired him for his honest and obliging disposition, can only speak the sentiments of the community in which he lived, by saying in brief that his character was strong, like the iron, the oak and the young hickory of his wagons; it was for use and reliability, though smooth and beautiful in finish.

The greater portion of the life of Mr. Swing was devoted to the pursuit of his trade and the cultivation of his farm adjoining the ancestral acres so long owned and occupied by his father. Another feature, and perhaps the most beautiful of his virtues, was his magnanimity; his clemency was as great as his courage. He trusted and reposed the utmost confidence in friends and associates, and, like all great men, had an honest faith in the teachings of his youth.

Of his family of children it may be said that they were educated and refined, reared in the most pretentious society, and suitors were not few. At the time of his death Mr. Swing left a widow, two sons, John M. and George W., and four daughters, to wit: Mrs. Ruth Woodruff, Mrs. Mary Asher DuBois, Mrs. Harriet Woodruff and Miss Eliza L., all of whom were still living and pleasantly located in the counties of Salem and Cumberland, the married ones presiding at the heads of interesting families, and in many instances over elegant homes, the pride and ornament of our best society.

Advanced years and a busy life began to show their heavy traces upon the previously sturdy frame, and compelled Mr. S. to desist from active work, and amid the scenes of his childhood and the associations of early life awaited the summons which should gather him to

the " home of the just made perfect," and he doubtless
felt with the poet, Montgomery, that

> " There's nothing terrible in death,
>   'Tis but to cast our robes away,
> And sleep at night without a breath
>   To break repose till dawn of day."

Through every period of his public and private career
we observe the religious tone of mind and the natural
color given by kind action and pious thought, and when
in advanced years sickness laid him low and he stood in
the presence of death, mark that courageous spirit which
calmly said " Thy will be done." Sustained by this
heavenly power, slowly and unmurmuringly he passed
along the weary road of almost eighty years, and at last
solved the mystery of death. At the funeral the following lines were sung by the choir:

> " How blessed the righteous when he dies ;
>   When sinks a weary soul to rest ;
> How mildly beam the closing eyes,
>   How gently heaves the expiring breast.
>
> " A holy quiet reigns around ;
>   A calm which life nor death destroys ;
> And naught disturbs that peace profound
>   Which his unfettered soul enjoys.
>
> " Life's labor's done; as sinks the clay,
>   Light from its load the spirit flies ;
> While heaven and earth combine to say,
>   How blest the righteous when he dies."

Rev. William A. Ferguson, the pastor, then referred to the character and finished life of the deceased; he said: "His social character, combined with his religious life, was such as to endear him to the people, and cause him to hold a prominent place in the confidence of his fellowmen. His life, which neared the extreme limits of the Psalmist, was one unbroken process of labor, and his continued activity added lustre to them all. You can remember him as one of the elders of our church who has, for more than half a century, gone in and out among this people; devoted in his work, and living so as to claim the promise, 'Lo, I am with you alway.' Near this quiet country village his life began, and when it had worn out the body and taken its flight to unknown realms the casket it had inhabited was given back to earth to sleep among its kindred. And while we recognize the fact that the church still needs the services of her ablest and best men, we also read,

> " ' God moves in a mysterious way
> His wonders to perform.'

And what now seems an affliction and a mystery may be revealed in the life to come. Let us believe that good deeds and kind thoughts have endless fruit, and that a noble, self-denying life beautifies the moral life of man, and assures a future grander than the past.

> " ' Oh, may we tread the sacred road
> That holy saints and martyrs trod;
> Wage to the end the glorious strife,
> And win, like them, a crown of life.' "

CHAPTER XIV.

DR. CHARLES SWING.

CHARLES SWING, eldest son of Michael Swing and Sarah Murphy, his wife, was born in Fairfield township, Cumberland county, March 4, 1790. His father was a prominent citizen of Fairfield, for many years a local preacher in the M. E. church, and, indeed, was regarded as one of the founders of Methodism in the southern part of the state. This son was blessed with the example and instruction of godly parents. Early in life he manifested a love for literature, and after finishing the course of study in the village school he employed his leisure moments in reading such scientific works as he was then able to procure. He not only employed his time in this way, but was known often to take his books with him into the field, and when following the plough would hold the reins in one hand and his book in the other. His father used to say that Charles' habit of reading and study made the horses lazy, they would not work. This incident reminds us of Burns, Coleridge, and many others, who composed some of the finest poems while at work in the field. While engaged in agricultural pursuits he began the study of medicine, under the tuition of Dr. William Ewing, of Greenwich;

in 1812, walking once a week from his home, a distance of twelve miles, in order to recite his appointed task and receive assistance in the further prosecution of his studies. As the winter season approached and walking became tedious and disagreeable on account of mud and slush in the roads, he then went down the river in a boat, frequently rowing for hours against a strong current of wind and tide. Night coming on before reaching his destination, and weary with the day's doings, he was often compelled to turn his boat in the direction of the shore, making fast to a neighboring tree, and, climbing up the bank of the river, pursue the balance of the way on foot. To test and prove his courage at every step Providence seems to have erected a barrier across his path; but, like a gallant soldier, he dashed up and over every hostile parapet, planted on it the standard of his invincible purpose, and left it to melt away behind him, while he assailed with a soul of victory each succeeding obstacle.

Disciplined in such a school, his body toughened, his mind invigorated and his spirit strengthened, his youth ripened into an honorable manhood, to become the envy of the luxurious and the inspiration of the poor.

He was an attentive student, and when graduated from the University of Pennsylvania was thoroughly furnished and prepared for the responsible work of a physician.

The first year after his graduation was spent in practicing medicine in connection with his preceptor at Greenwich, their field of labor extending over a large extent of country, including the townships of Hopewell and Stow creek, where his practice became large, and embraced a large circuit, especially so from the fact that much of it had to be performed on horseback.

THREE GOOD DOCTORS.

The best of all the pill-box crew,
  Since ever time began,
Are the doctors who have most to do
  With the health of a hearty man.

And so I count them up again, and praise them as I can;
There's Dr. Diet, and Dr. Quiet, and Dr. Merryman.

There's Dr. Diet, he tries my tongue.
  "I know you well," says he:
"Your stomach is poor and your liver is sprung,
  We must make your food agree."

And Dr. Quiet, he feels my wrist,
  And he gravely shakes his head.
"Now, now, dear sir, I must insist
  That you go at ten to bed."

But Dr. Merryman for me
  Of all the pill-box crew!
For he smiles and says, as he fobs his fee,
  "Laugh on, whatever you do!"

So now I eat what I ought to eat,
  And at ten I go to bed,
And I laugh in the face of cold or heat;
  For thus have the doctors said!

And so I count them up again, and praise them as I can;
There's Dr. Diet, and Dr. Quiet, and Dr. Merryman.

Upon the following year he transferred his residence to Salem, entered into partnership with the late Dr. Benjamin Archer, and soon after married a Miss Mary Lambson, of Penn's Neck. Dissolving his partnership with Dr. Archer, he commenced practice the third year in the village of Pennsville. He was very successful and popular in the latter place; by his prescription and advice many persons were restored to health. He remained here for some years, until the death of his wife. Later he married Mrs. Hannah Ware and removed his residence to Sharptown. Here, and on a farm which he purchased in this vicinity, he remained until his death.

The doctor had a family of nine children; three by his first marriage, Matthias L., Sallie C. and Mary F.; last marriage, Charles P., Hannah A., Harriet, Margaretta A., Abigail S. and John Swing, most of whom are still living. Two of the daughters were married to ministers of the New Jersey Conference.

The doctor, in stature, was above the medium, large and portly. He was always lively and exuberant in spirits, and very popular as a physician. He acquired and retained an excellent practice, and had the reputation of being an excellent prescriber in difficult cases. He was frequently called in cases of consultation, and was very courteous and gentlemanly in his bearing toward his professional brethren. The study of medicine was his delight. Being accessible to Philadelphia, he made it a point very frequently to attend the lectures of his *alma mater*.

The writer remembers Dr. Swing, some twelve years

ago, in the amphitheatre of the university, intensely listening to every word as it fell from the lips of the professor of anatomy and surgery. He thus kept fully abreast with the improvements in medicine, and was justly regarded as one of the ablest and best informed practitioners in the southern portion of the state.

Upon one occasion a distinguished citizen of Salem county, Mr. Job Ridgeway, approached Dr. Swing in a jovial sort of way, and said: "Doctor, did you ever shorten the lives of your patients or kill any one during your practice in medicine?"

The doctor remained thoughtful a moment, then said: "I never trifle with drugs nor with the health of my fellow men. My life has been devoted to the pursuit and study of my profession, and the recovery and life of my patients are precious in my sight. Had we known more thirty years ago, I think that I might have prolonged the lives of some of our fellow citizens."

The profession of medicine presented to his mind a great attraction. The relief of suffering humanity from disease and pain seemed to him a truly noble work, and throughout a long life of study and practice he had prepared himself for this work.

Dr. Charles Swing was elected a member of the New Jersey Legislature from Salem county, in 1823. In the legislature, as elsewhere, he was true to the interests of the working people, always sustaining their rights and advocating their cause.

The public school system of New Jersey owes much to the early and persistent efforts of the doctor, who was for many years its advocate and pioneer. In the board of education he was an active member, and lived to see the success and good result of the establishment of a State Normal School for the better education of teachers, and free public schools for children throughout the state.

Approaching seventy he contracted a severe cold, causing an attack of asthma, and the afternoon previous to his death, paralysis setting in, terminated his useful life, January 3, 1860.*

Of Father Swing's children it will be remembered that Matthias L. engaged in business in Philadelphia.

Sallie C. married Mr. Sparks and removed to Texas.

Mary T. Swing was united in marriage with a Methodist clergyman, Rev. David Duffell, so well and favorably known to many members of the New Jersey Conference, and with him shared the labors and joys of an itinerant life for nearly forty years. When a young man Mr. Duffell was connected with Third Street church, Camden; was class leader, exhorter and local preacher; was admitted into the New Jersey Conference in 1839, and subsequently spent many years in effective work. He was a man of more than ordinary eloquence, and his ministry was attended with unusual success. His talents

---

*Note.—The thanks of the author are hereby expressed to Rev. Firman Robbins, a son-in-law of the deceased, for his interesting letter and conversation regarding this branch of our family, and from whose recollection and statement the following facts were written: Said Mr. R., "My father was conscious of his approaching end, and desired to depart and be at rest; said angels were in the room—were all around him, and he was going to meet the loved ones who had gone before."

as a public speaker commanded admiration wherever he went, and the dignity and real nobility of his character were very impressive. He was born in Camden, N. J., September, 1801, and died in Clayton, Gloucester county, July 11, 1884.

Harriet was united in marriage with Mr. Brown, of Burlington, and Abigail S. to Mr. Janvier, of Delaware.

John, the younger, aged 26 years, was drowned in Snake river, Montana territory, while fording it, on his return to the gold mines of Colorado and Pike's Peak. The ferry boats were propelled by a windlass and a strong cable rope extended from shore to shore. Few of the old residents of Salem county have forgotten the Gold Bluff excitement of 1850–54, when, by all accounts, old ocean himself turned miner and washed up cartloads of gold on the beach above Trinidad; nor have they forgotten the excitement a few years later caused by the discovery of both silver and gold at Pike's Peak. It was represented by the newspaper correspondents that any enterprising man could take his hat and a wheelbarrow and in a few days gather up enough to last him for life. The newspapers were full of intelligence from the mines, and every arrival from the mountains confirmed the glad tidings. Any man who wanted a fortune needed only to go over there and pick it up, and no one staking out claims could go amiss. Among those who crossed the plains en route for the mines was John Swing and a few other heroic young men from Salem county. After working the mines for a considerable length of time John realized the great need of improved machinery for separating particles of gold from the earth, and also noticed the exhorbitant price of provisions at the mines. He returned to the border states, purchased improved machinery, and fitting out a cattle and provision train, again started on his return across the plains.

LATER INTELLIGENCE.

We learn with regret that John Swing, son of the late Dr. Charles Swing, formerly of Salem county, was drowned at Central Ferry, on Snake river, Montana territory, on the 31st of last May. Mr. Swing was a young man of great enterprise and perseverance. He was proceeding westward with a train of eight provision wagons which he had succeeded in getting safely across, and had turned back to assist a neighbor in crossing with another train, when the cable rope used in ferrying broke suddenly. The stream was very rapid, and the river shore high and rocky below the ferry; to avoid being carried away with the boat he jumped overboard, intending to swim ashore, but sank from exhaustion and disappeared before reaching it.

STILL LATER INTELLIGENCE.

About twenty-four years since Mr. John Swing, a trader residing at Virginia City, Montana, was drowned in Snake river while crossing on a ferry, his last words as he went down being "help, help." Mr. Swing was a son of the late Dr. Swing, of Sharptown, and had $4000 in gold dust and two navy revolvers about his person at the time. Further than that the family and relatives hereabout know but little. Yesterday the Hon. H. H. Mood, horse dealer from Montana, now in this city, in conversation with the writer, spoke of an old friend of his, Mr. John Swing, who, he said, was drowned in Snake river, Montana, his home.

CONVERSATION WITH MR. ROBBINS.

"In the early years of my life, and while yet a student for the ministry, it was my pleasure," said Mr. Robbins, "to form the acquaintance of the doctor and his family; was united in marriage with Miss Hannah A. Swing, January 12, 1850. We have two sons, William W. and Charles F. Robbins; the former is engaged in mercantile business in the city of Bridgeton, N. J.; the latter died at Dickinson College, Carlisle, Pa., February 11, 1876. I was admitted into the New Jersey M. E. Conference in the spring of 1853; have been in the ministry twenty-eight years; passed through and enjoyed many blessed revivals of religion during that time, and admitted hundreds of people to the communion and fellowship of our church; was appointed to the following places: Cape May City, 1854–55; Port Elizabeth circuit, 1856–57; Glassboro, 1858–59; Cedarville and Fairton, 1860; Clayton, 1861–62; Allentown, 1863–64; Jacobstown, 1865.

"In 1866, by request, I received a superannuated relation, which continued until 1869, when, by request, my relation was changed to effective, and was appointed to the following charges: Paulsboro, 1869-70; Alloways-town, 1871; Sharptown, 1872-73; Sayreville, 1874; Windsor and Sharon, 1875-76; Port Elizabeth and Dividing Creek, 1879-80; Berlin, 1881-82."

At the annual conference of the M. E. church held at Millville, April 8, 1883, Mr. Robbins was received and classed among the supernumerary preachers. Since that time he has taken up his residence in Bridgeton, where he has built for himself and family a pleasant home, and retired from the active duties of ministerial life.

Mrs. Hannah Swing, widow of the late Dr. Charles Swing, recently celebrated her ninety-first birthday, February 28, 1889. She was born in Salem, N. J., February 28, 1798, and is still living.

CHAPTER XV.

THE subject of this memoir was an earnest, devoted man; he labored to excel, and was emphatically a man of work. Of a family of seven children he was the third, and a native of Pittsgrove township, Salem county, where he was born March 11, 1802. He commenced life as an agriculturist, and his youth and early manhood were spent upon the homestead farms. Favored by nature with a strong constitution, attractive face and figure, and when a young man conducted himself in a discreet, quiet and temperate manner, preventing any uneasiness on his account to his nearest friends. The peculiarities of great men may be pointed out for the admiration of others; their good qualities may teach youth to persevere, and that determination and work will elevate a man whatever be his position in life. A man's birthplace, his early life, his ambition to succeed, his struggles with wealth or poverty, and his final triumph may be recorded. By occupation a farmer, he believed labor, either of muscle or mind, to be the true source of wealth; and the man who makes two ears of corn, or two blades of grass grow, where but one grew before, is a benefactor to mankind. He considered the progress of agriculture to be a joint work of theory and practice, and in many departments great advances were made in his day; especially is this true in all that relates to farming implements, in machinery and the improvement of domestic animals. It may be said that he delighted in the works of agriculture, in the improvement of the soil and the successful growth of vegetation, so that "seed time and harvest might not fail upon the face of the earth."

Among literary men and the newspaper fraternity he was not altogether unknown. Upon his centre table was usually found the latest and most reliable information of the times, to wit: the "American Agriculturist," Philadelphia "North American," the "Presbyterian," "State Temperance Gazette," and "National Standard" (Salem, N. J.) To some of the above named journals he had been a continuous subscriber for a period of thirty years.

In the midst of a singularly busy life he found time for scholarly pursuits; has been upon school committees in his day, and moderator at town meetings over and over again; yet his eye still retains the same keen, bright flash in it from the depths of seventy-five years. His long and varied intercourse with the people and intimate knowledge of men have been supplemented by a more than usual acquaintance with books, and the result is a peculiar and ready fund of information which makes him a most instructive companion and gives a peculiar interest to whatever comes from his recollection and authority.

For many years he held important local offices in the township and county, such as chosen freeholder, judge of election, delegate to state and county conventions, and his judicious counsel and generous assistance have been of important service to the party in numerous campaigns.

His life began away back when the nation was yet in its infancy, and he was regarded as a sort of living record of the past. His memory of facts and dates was wonderful, and his own life was crowded full of interesting episodes. He could begin with General Washington and give you the name of every president of the United States down to the present time, with the date of their election; and the same may be said of his recollection of distinguished senators, legislators, governors and members of congress, who have within the past half century figured prominently before the country, and whose abilities and achievements were worthy of remembrance in the archives of political history.

The first temperance societies in Salem county, of which we have any account, were organized in a school house near Newkirk's Mill, by Thomas DuBois, Nathan Lawrence and Leonard Swing. A few years later societies were formed at the Washington school house, and also at the " Broad Neck " M. E. church and Allowaystown. In each of these places monthly meetings were held, the appointed time usually being the first evening of the full moon. In 1845 and '50, and for several years after, two reformed men and eminent speakers, from Baltimore, Daniel MacGinley and John Hawkins, visited Pittsgrove and addressed these societies. The speakers usually were invited guests at my father's house, and night after night the writer, when a small boy, drove the family carriage containing these worthies to meet their appointments.

Among the most prominent and zealous citizens then active in the temperance reform are remembered the names of Gilbert H. Craig, Isaiah Conover, William B. Heighton, Jonathan Hogate, William B. Rodgers and Nathan Lawrence. To live in such an age and be the participator of these historic unfoldings with men who lived so long and worthily is certainly an exalted privilege. Men who had been intemperate for years burst the bonds that had so long enslaved them, and became temperance reformers, many of whom kept the pledge to their dying day. Others still live, a blessing to their families and an honor to the community. Near the close of a meeting held in one of the rural districts an invitation was given to persons in the congregation to come forward and sign the temperance pledge; while this was progressing a Dutchman by the name of Coblentz arose in the assembly and said: "Mr. President, may it please your honor, I can tell you how it was mit me. I puts mine hand on mine head and there vash one pain; den I puts mine hand on mine body, and there vash another pain; den I puts mine hand in mine pocket and there vash notting; so I throw away mine pipe and whiskey, and jined mit de temperance. Now there is no more pain in mine head; the pain in mine body is all gone away; I puts mine hand in mine pocket and dere vash twenty dollars; so I shall stay mit der temperance peoples." Applause.

During the presidential campaign of 1860 and '64 New Jersey was the theatre of some of the hottest battles of the campaign. Its ablest men were enlisted in the contest, and prominent speakers of other states were sent here and took part in the agitation. The First Congressional district then comprised the counties of Camden, Gloucester, Salem, Cumberland, Atlantic and Cape May, with its division lines and districts extending from the river to the sea, to be supplied with speakers. During the latter part of the month of October, 1864, about twenty patriotic farmers of upper Pittsgrove township decided to hold a political mass meeting in the woods belonging to Garret DuBois, Esq., near Newkirk's station. The programme advertised was as follows: Military parade at 9 A.M.; music by the Pittsgrove Fife and Drum Corps; public speaking at 10 A.M. and 2 P.M.; music by the Woodstown and Daretown Brass Bands, and a free dinner for all; the meeting to be addressed by Hon. Alexander G. Cattell, of Camden, ex-member of congress.

The day dawned bright and beautiful. Although the October morning was frosty and cold, by 10 o'clock a vast concourse of people had assembled in the grove, when an escort of mounted cavalry and four horse coaches was sent to the railroad station to escort the speaker to the stand.

On the arrival of the train from Camden, Mr. Cattell stepped out on the platform, and stated that at the mass meeting at Woodbury on the previous day he had taken a severe cold, and did not think it advisable for him to speak in the open air, and asked to be excused, etc. A moment later the cars started on for Salem, where Mr. C. had another appointment the same evening.

When the procession returned to the grove without a speaker there was some anxiety manifested upon the countenances of its managers. In this dilemma "a council of war" was held among the boss politicians. Hon. Charles F. H. Gray called the meeting to order, when Mr. Leonard Swing, who appeared to be the star speaker of the party, addressed the citizens, dilating with enthusiasm upon the importance of the coming election. Then warming up with the subject, he pronounced a beautiful eulogy upon the life and public services of President Lincoln, and spoke enthusiastically about the energy, ability and integrity of Marcus L. Ward, our candidate for governor, William Moore of Atlantic county, for congress, and other local candidates on the county ticket; said they were plain, honest, straight-forward men, and worthy the confidence and support of our citizens.

While the people applauded, he related the amusing story of " Old Grimes and the Methodist preacher," how a heroic woman in Ohio " killed the bear," and made an excellent, if not eloquent, address.

Rev. A. B. Still, pastor of the Pittsgrove Baptist church, followed with matchless eloquence, and after a lofty panegyric inquired : " When will New Jersey redeem herself and reach the apex of her glory ? " " When Marcus L. Ward is elected governor and Wm. Moore for Congress," replied a voice in the crowd. The answer coming unexpectedly as it did created both laughter and applause, ladies waved their handkerchiefs and the bands played " Hail, Columbia ! " At the conclusion of the speaking and music, dinner, prepared by the ladies, was announced, to which the company did ample justice. In the afternoon, Hon. John W. Hazelton, who participated actively in politics, and was subsequently elected to Congress for two terms from the First Congressional district of New Jersey, occupied the stand, and was an excellent speech maker. The Pittsgrove glee club sang patriotic songs on the platform, and when the mass meeting adjourned it was pronounced a great success.

In marriage Mr. Swing was united to Miss Elizabeth Shough, of Upper Alloway's Creek, May 11, 1825. This couple subsequently enjoyed a married life of fifty-one years' duration. While the family were growing up the children were either sent to school or employed upon the farm, and the long winter evenings usually were spent in the study of arithmetic, drawing, penmanship, music and history. The governor himself was a good singer and musician, and the homestead was well supplied with musical instruments of various kinds.

THE FAMILY.

The family is like a book—
  The children are the leaves,
The parents are the cover, that
  Protection, beauty gives.

At first, the pages of the book
  Are blank and purely fair,
But time soon writeth memories,
  And painteth pictures there.

Love is the little golden clasp
  That bindeth up the trust ;
Oh, break it not, lest all the leaves
  Shall scatter and be lost.

One of the maxims of Dr. Johnson, and long observed in the family, was :

" Early to bed, and early to rise,
  Makes a man healthy, wealthy and wise."

The representatives were five in number—Abraham R., Gilbert S., Charles J., William M. and Christiana—all of whom, with the exception of the first-named, are still living.

In company with a large concourse of relatives and friends Mr. Swing celebrated his golden wedding, May 11, 1875. The meeting of relatives and friends, long and widely separated, the presentation of useful presents, sociability, and a sumptuous dinner, contributed much to the enjoyment of the occasion.

Rev. William A. Ferguson, the pastor of Pittsgrove

Presbyterian church, being present, addressed himself to the company, and recalled many pleasant incidents appropriate to the time and place. He referred to the tranquil life of the venerable couple and the good example set by them as citizens and members of the church, and the satisfaction all felt in this fiftieth return of their marriage day.

Two and a half years later, after a brief illness, the subject of these remarks, and "one of the beacon lights in history," passed away from the boundary of this life to the beginning and enjoyment of another. Though not in robust health for some years, he still kept about his occupation and attended to many duties on the farm until the last few months of his life. By fidelity and uprightness he inspired among the people respect, confidence and regard. Never did he shun, but always rather chose, the harder field of labor, and the monuments of success are precious and enduring.

[*Extract from the National Standard, Salem, N. J.*]

By the death of Leonard Swing, of Upper Pittsgrove, which event is recorded elsewhere in the *Standard* to-day, another good man and useful citizen has been removed from the stage of action. The deceased has resided for upward of a half century in the neighborhood in which his death occurred, and has always been held in high esteem by his friends and neighbors and the people at large throughout the township. During his long and active life he has often represented his township in the Board of Chosen Freeholders, and in other positions of trust and responsibility. He was an earnest Whig and an active political worker during the days of that party, and has since been an equally earnest Republican. He took a lively interest in education and in all matters pertaining to the public good. He was also a consistent Christian and an influential member of the Presbyterian denomination of Upper Pittsgrove.

The memory of the deceased will be long and favorably cherished by relatives and friends, and by the community in which he lived. He was a man of sterling character, a good counsellor, a kind father, neighbor and friend. Mr. Swing joined the Pittsgrove Presbyterian Church in 1825, and during a period of fifty-two years continued an active member. He was ruling elder of the same church forty-four years.

TRUE WEALTH.

Men of wealth from heaven are sent,
Sent to earth with good intent ;
Rich they are in gold that's pure,
Gold whose glitter will endure.

Gems are theirs, most costly gems,
Fit for regal diadems ;
Ephod stones of rarest hue,
Ever changing, ever new.

Pearls they wear—a glittering host—
Brighter than Columbia's boast ;
Diamond circlets, lo ! I see,
Full of burning brilliancy.

Men of wealth, indeed, are such,
Nor can aught their treasures touch,
For within they're hidden deep,
And their brilliancy they keep.

Men of wisdom—well they've lined
All the chambers of the mind;
Pearls and diamonds, rich and rare,
In profusion cluster there.

This is *wealth*—such wealth be mine,
Round the neck of Truth to twine;
Diamonds for the soul give me,
Full of burning brilliancy.

[*Extract from the Pioneer, Bridgeton, N. J.*]

In another column we notice the death of an old and esteemed resident of Salem county, Mr. Leonard Swing. Before his health failed he was one of its leading citizens, and filled many offices of trust and responsibility. For fifty years he has been identified with the business interest of Salem county, and filled with honor the duties of a long and useful life. A speaker in public, and in the years gone by a worker in the Sunday school, the church and the temperance reform. He was kind, generous, and ready to entertain at his home public speakers and ministers of the Gospel. He joined the Republican party at its organization, remaining a member to his death, not wishing office himself, but working for the success of others. The names of Sinnickson, Swing, Hazelton and Cattell will long be remembered as good soldiers in the Republican party of Salem county. We remember him years ago, and his services for the election of Dr. Clawson, of Woodstown, to Congress; also for Cattell and Star, of Camden. He did good work for the election of John T. Nixon, of Cumberland, who was elected to the Thirty-sixth Congress in 1858 and re-elected to the Thirty-seventh Congress in 1860; Wm. Moore, of Atlantic; Hazelton, of Gloucester, and Sinnickson, of Salem. He was a man universally respected throughout the county in which he lived—one whose faith had been tried and tested and whose influence for truth and justice should not be forgotten.

OBITUARY NOTICE OF ELIZABETH SWING.

The bright days of summer are gone; the breeze whispers softly no longer amid the hills; the flowers sleep, and little feet that never wearied with their tramps over field and dell, or by the sunny sea, may to-night be dancing with delight as the song of the angels has swelled with more distinctness above the discord of earth; and hearts may ache over vacant places, and

> " Sigh for the touch of a vanished hand,
> And the sound of a voice that is still."

It may not be an unwelcome thought that the bells of heaven ring in concert with the bells of earth to-day. Time spares nothing, animate or inanimate; it lays the destroying hand upon every household, and death is ever present in our land. The aged, the young, the beautiful and fair are constantly the subjects of his search. On Sunday morning, August 27th, gently passed away from this world of affliction and care, Elizabeth, wife of Leonard Swing. She was born in Upper Alloway's Creek township, Salem county, New Jersey, March 2, 1801, and died at her home at Pittsgrove, August 27, 1876. A few prominent traits in her character deserve mention. She became religious in early youth and united with the Presbyterian church, herself and her sister Margaret being the first in her father's family to embrace religion. Her circle of acquaintances and sphere of usefulness was widely extended, and the maternal solicitude for the welfare and prosperity of the family eminently fitted her to be the guide and educator of her children, directing their studies and entering into all their pursuits and joys with dignity that commanded respect. Blessed with good health, cheerful and kind in her social nature and wonderfully gifted in song. She was the possessor of a large family Bible, the former property of her father, published in London in the year 1750, which is said to be fully equal in typography and plates to issues of the present day.

The star of Bethlehem, which pointed out the way of the Saviour's birthplace, was the star which lighted her pathway to the " house not built with hands, eternal in the heavens." Her last sickness, though severe, was of short duration, when suddenly on the morning of August 27th the weary wheels of life stood still.

The funeral sermon was preached by the pastor, Rev. William A. Ferguson. Text, " Let me die ·the death of the righteous, and let my last end be like his." The services were very impressive and commenced with the

reading of Scripture, and prayer, and the singing of one
of her favorite hymns :

> "What a friend we have in Jesus,
>   All our sins and griefs to bear,
> What a privilege to carry
>   Everything to God in prayer.
> Oh ! what peace we often forfeit,
>   Oh ! what needless pain we bear,
> All because we do not carry
>   Everything to God in prayer."

For some time past her mind seemed to have contemplated this event, and many cheering expressions
made in regard to it.

This much we have thought proper and fitting to con-
tribute to the memory of one who has gone in and out
before us for nearly half a century, and whose bright
and shining light has left its reflection behind it.

> Our lives are albums written through
> With good or ill, with false or true ;
> And as the blessed angels turn
>   The pages of our years,
> God grant they read the good with smiles,
>   And blot the bad with tears.

CHAPTER XVI.

EBENEZER HARRIS.

IT may be of interest to the reading community to know that among the worthy and industrious mechanics of half a century ago few are more worthy of notice than the person herein named, Mr. Ebenezer Harris, who passed from life on Sunday evening, February 11, 1883. He was a native of Fairfield township, where he was born in the year 1801, and when a boy was apprenticed to learn the blacksmith trade at Cedarville. After completing his apprenticeship at that place, and having a desire to visit other states and see something of the world, he travelled on foot and by stage to Herkimer county, New York. The next three years of life were spent in working at his trade, and valuable information was gained in regard to the welding of iron and the tempering of steel.

While living at Albany, in the same state, the principal work consisted in ironing sleighs, shoeing horses, oxen and mules. During the holidays he visited Saratoga, Buffalo, Niagara Falls, and many other places of attraction in the northern states. To use his own expression, he sowed his wild oats in his youthful days, and returned to Fairfield a wiser and better man.

12

Having a desire to commence business for himself he removed to Salem county in search of employment, leased a strip of land, built a shop and commenced working therein. For many years he was the only blacksmith in this vicinity, and continued in active business here for a long period of time.

When first establishing himself in this locality in 1825, he found the greatest attraction of the place to be the society and companionship of Miss Sarah, third daughter of Abraham Swing. After a pleasant and agreeable courtship they were united in marriage by Rev. George W. Janvier on March 14, 1827, and soon after this event they took up their residence on a farm inherited by his wife, and located opposite Swing's Corner (now Shirley), where they continued to reside, surrounded by all the attractions of home, and the endearments of family and friends. In connection with his trade he was also interested in farming and agricultural pursuits. The representatives of the family group were four in number, Abraham S., Martha, Hannah and John, all of whom are still living, with the exception of the first-named, who deeply sympathized with the Republican party in its efforts to preserve the union, enlisted and became an active supporter of the government at the outbreak of the rebellion; was wounded at the battle of the Wilderness, captured by the enemy, and subsequently died in the prison pen at Andersonville.

Mr. and Mrs. Harris both united themselves with the Presbyterian church at Pittsgrove in 1827, and became good and useful members of that denomination, but she failed, however, to enjoy either robust health or great length of days. On the morning of October 8, 1846, after a brief illness, Mrs. Harris passed quietly and peacefully away from this world of affliction and care, and the funeral oration was pronounced by the same clergyman who had performed the marriage ceremony twenty years before. The management of household duties was then entrusted to and performed by his daughter, Miss Hannah L. Mr. Harris remained a widower for two years, when he found it not good to be alone, formed acquaintance and entered into the marriage relation with Mrs. Elizabeth Camm, May 16, 1848. He was elected ruling elder of Pittsgrove Presbyterian church in 1833, and at the time of his decease was one of the oldest official members of that denomination. His pastors ever found in him a wise counsellor and ready and efficient helper, acceptable and useful at home or abroad. He was characterized by intellectual ability of a high order, by moral uprightness, and courage which resisted temptation and braved opposition, and by a religious faith and loyalty that made his life admirable and his death the "death of the righteous." As a business man he was cautious, laborious and successful; not a politician, but an intensely loyal citizen, antagonizing rebellion, slavery and the rum traffic. He was of modest nature, one whose daily life spoke louder than his tongue. "In quietness and in confidence" was his "strength." His vigor and robustness were seen in the tenacity with which he clung to life, his great vitality causing him to rally time and time again, when death seemed to have fallen upon him.

The veil of unconsciousness covered the last moments, and in the thick gloom which humanity so dreads the life of this good man closed like flowers at set of sun, to bloom again in the gardens of the better land. His funeral was well attended, and his remains interred in the family plot in the old cemetery at Pittsgrove, by the side of his first and second wives, both having preceded him to the spirit land.

CHAPTER XVII.

CAPTAIN JOHN M. SWING.

CAPTAIN JOHN M. SWING, the second son of Michael Swing, was born in Fairfield township, Cumberland county, in the year 1792. He was one of a large family of children, and spent his childhood days on the banks of Cohansey river, where he learned to swim, and there, near the present location of "Tyndall's Landing," saved the lives of a young man and two children from drowning. Born with a love for the water, he prevailed upon his father to build a vessel and let him go to sea; and at an early age he donned the blue frock and trousers, and learned to land, reef and steer a boat, and was well trained in all that is required to make a thorough seaman.

The science of navigation he soon learned, and became familiar with the river and bay, explored Maurice river cove and many of the sounds and inlets along the Atlantic coast. In 1818, and for several years after, himself and father were engaged in building boats on the river shore not far from his father's house. Boats and sailing vessels were then in great demand for fishing purposes and for the navigation of these waters. In the markets of New York and Philadelphia a great demand for fish and oysters was springing up. Not many boats were then employed in this business on the Delaware, and Captain John soon realized more money in what he called "oyster farming," than in farming upon the land.

Delaware Bay and its tributaries afford a vast outlet of many miles in extent for the natural growth of the oyster, as well as all needful facilities for its rapid propagation and culture. Located in a suitable degree of latitude, its bottoms of sand and white pebbles, with abundant sea moss as a protection and home and breeding place, its waters suited in degrees of saltness, mingles with Alloway's, Salem and Stow creeks, the Cohansey river and various other streams bringing down a continuous supply of food to refresh and fatten the oyster.

For many years Captain John Swing was the owner of a vessel called the "Oyster Boy," a fast sailing craft engaged in the oyster trade between Maurice river cove and Philadelphia. He was a large and powerful man, about 280 pounds in weight, and acknowledged to be the "oyster king" on Delaware Bay. He became famous among the craft by saving the lives of shipwrecked companions. Upon one occasion, when off the coast of Cape May, a sudden squall of wind struck the vessel. Orders to reef the sail were given. In attempting to accomplish the command, a sailor fell overboard from one of the lower yard-arms into the sea; the vessel was going at a great rate of speed and a gale of wind blowing. Notwithstanding this disadvantage the captain jumped on the rail, leaped into the foaming billows and rescued the drowning man.

Daniel R. Powell, a young man living with the Swing family, relates the following incident: " During the winter of 1828 oysters were very scarce and high in price in the cities of New York and Philadelphia. The schooner 'Swan' and the 'Oyster Boy' were loaded for the latter city. In making the voyage up the Delaware we encountered a heavy storm, which continued for two days and nights, bringing in a high tide. Large blocks of ice became detached from the shore and came floating down toward the sea. In view of this unexpected and alarming state of the river, our captain ordered the vessels into the dock at New Castle. While nearing the shore and endeavoring to make the harbor, the fury of the storm increased, both vessels were jammed in the ice, keeled over, partially filled with water and sunk, the captain and crew making their escape to the land. At daylight the mast of the 'Oyster Boy' only was visible to indicate the place where she had disappeared. The 'Swan' sunk near the dock. After the abatement of the storm this vessel and cargo was raised, the water pumped out, and the boat towed to her destination. The cargo was sold to Baylis & Ware, commission merchants, of Philadelphia. Price received: Prime, $1.75; cullings, $1.00 per bushel. The sloop 'Oyster Boy' proved to be almost a total loss to him, the wreck being sold at public auction in Philadelphia for a few dollars. Captain John then purchased the Dolphin, a larger and better boat. After the wreck of the 'Oyster Boy' had laid under water for six months (all previous efforts to raise her being abortive) wreckers, with newly invented machinery were sent down, and were successful in raising and floating her to Philadelphia, where she was overhauled and repaired, and again, on the coast, did good service in the oyster trade for many years."

In later years many experiments have been tried and numerous inventions brought to light for the purpose of floating a sunken ship, one of the latest being a submarine diver, who goes down under the water, and makes an examination of the wreck. If the hull is sound and unbroken, the hatches are closed, the caps put on, and the deck made watertight. Then steam and air pumps are attached, the water being pumped out and air pumped in. If there be no bad leaks and the ship not sunk deep into the mud, she will be soon raised and appear floating on the surface of the water.

Could the sea give up its treasures, those who found them would have a very comfortable income. The New Jersey coast alone would offer some fine pickings, though not always in the precious metals. Recently a wrecking company started on a search at Elberon, near Long Branch, and a diver found the ship Europe, which was wrecked there thirty-five years ago. It was loaded with iron, steel and lead, and the question of values, even if raised, is a problematical one. Near this vessel is another one, the Chauncey Jerome, lost in 1854, and, curiously enough, also loaded with iron and steel. To get anything it will be necessary to blow the wrecks to pieces.

Delaware Bay and its tributaries have long been famous, not only for its propagation of fish and the productiveness of its oysters, but also for the immense flocks of wild fowl which congregate there in the fall and winter season. When cold weather sets in at the northern states the various species of duck begin to arrive, and congregate in the bays along the coast, where they find favorite feeding grounds. They are generally poor when they first come from the north, but soon improve and fatten rapidly.

The late Michael Coates Swing, sailing in company with a watchman employed by Captain John and other owners of private and planted oyster beds below Fortescue Island, and stationed here in a sloop to prevent trespass by sailors belonging to passing vessels, and dredging and loading of boats during the night, informed the author how thirteen wild geese were captured.

"Upon a dark and stormy night in December, 18—, our sloop lay at anchor near the mouth of Straight creek. The wind had been blowing very hard all day and night; toward morning it shifted north, and the gale increased in fury. The incoming high tide covered the marsh, and the waters of the bay were white with foam, and the rumbling of the sea, like 'the sound of many waters,' was heard in the distance.

" Our little bark tossed like a feather upon the angry waves so that I could not sleep; but towards morning, however, overcome by watching and fatigue, we fell into a restless slumber, and while dreaming the dreams of the just, the noise of the raging elements and the honk of wild geese filled the air.

" Viewing our situation at daylight, large flocks of

ducks and geese were seen on the marsh, others were passing over low down, almost within arm's reach from the mast of our sloop, and settling in a pond on the marsh near by. Ascending to the masthead our cook reported this pond as being full. Upon examining our stock of firearms we found one old musket and some gunpowder, but no shot could be found. 'We'll steal a march on those ducks,' was the command of the leaders, and accordingly the boy was sent to the cabin of a fisherman to borrow shot. Nearly an hour elapsed before his return, when he reported that there was no shot at the cabin, but he had borrowed three pieces of lead from the net of a fisherman. These were cut into slugs, and the musket loaded, the small boat lowered into the water and silently guided through a small inlet in the direction of the pond. Arriving there, and looking cautiously through the tall reeds, we saw that the pond was full, and apparently the geese were asleep. Springing to my feet I shouted at the top of my voice 'awake.' The birds were surprised ; they immediately arose in a body out of the water, and when a suitable distance off the musket was discharged in the air and thirteen large geese were captured."

A short distance below Swing's farm, and opposite Butter Cove Meadows, in the Cohansey river, a celebrated fishery is located. Great numbers of the finny tribe congregate here, coming up from the sea in search of food, and in the early spring to spawn and lay their eggs in streams of fresh water. Upon one occasion ten thousand rock fish were caught in a seine at one haul by Michael Coates, Benjamin Franklin and Simon Sparks Swing.

For many years Michael Swing had a large quantity of hay cut on the meadows adjoining the river and sent to Philadelphia by water.

Upon another occasion Captain John Swing came up the river in one of his vessels to load hay, and anchored at Tyndall's wharf. While standing on shore looking at two sailors in a boat shooting rail birds, two porpoises made their appearance on top of the water, and the men shot at them several times without effect, when Captain John offered his assistance. On going into the boat he found they could do nothing with the weapons at hand, and requested the sailors to set him ashore and he would run up to the meadow get a pitchfork and harpoon the fish. He did so ; got the fork, and just as he reached the river again the porpoises made another circuit right up around the vessel and side of the wharf. The captain made a thrust at one with his long-handled pitchfork, but missed his aim and fell into the water himself, exactly on top of the porpoise's back. Being as badly scared as was the fish, he grabbed hold of him, when the fish started across the stream as fast as he could swim, nor did he let go until they had reached the opposite side, when the porpoise gave a sudden whirl and threw his rider off. Next the boat came along and picked up the half-drowned man, when he exclaimed: "By the holy Moses! did you ever see the like of this? Let the d——d fish go; they are strong meat anyway."

The oystering season usually commenced about the first of September, when all the available boats were in demand. Upon another occasion while oystering in the Chesapeake Bay a great storm of rain and wind came on, and during the darkness of the night, and the heavy sea which followed, John's vessel collided with another boat. Next morning the commander of the injured craft, Capt. Clark, came on board of Swing's vessel at daylight and demanded $100 damages. Captain John refused to pay this amount; said the accident was unavoidable on his part, &c. After further conversation both captains became angry and finally challenged each other to fight a duel with rifles at long range. Captain Clark afterwards objected to this mode of warfare and proposed swords. Captain John objected to this also by claiming that he had not attended the military schools; was not proficient in sword exercise, but was willing to settle this dispute in any honorable way. He immediately ordered on deck one barrel of gunpowder, and knocking out the bung sprinkled a train of powder around the barrel and attached a long fuse to the other end, took his seat on the barrel, asking Captain Clark to sit down by his side, while the mate of the vessel touched off the further end. Just before the powder ignited Captain Clark sprang off the barrel, stamped out the burning fuse, exclaiming at the same time, "By Jupiter, Captain John, you are a brave man; I admire your courage and bravery. Let's shake hands, take a drink of wine and be friends forever."

Another industry worthy of notice and successfully carried on by our people at Fairfield was

SHAD FISHING.

The season of shad fishing fairly commences in Delaware bay during the month of March, and next to the salmon, probably, no fish in the American waters is more highly esteemed. At low water mark the nets are put down, and as the tide comes in the shad, in swimming up the river, run their heads through the meshes of the net and are caught by the gills, where they hang until the net is drawn up. The fishing grounds in the Delaware bay extend as far up as Trenton, and above Lambertville a distance of 100 miles; fish are also found in great quantities in all the bays and rivers bordering the Atlantic ocean. The usual size of the shad will average four pounds weight, but many are caught weighing seven pounds each. When the water is muddy more fish swim against the net and are caught, and on this account the fisheries are considered to be more profitable up the river than in the bay, where the water is very clear and deep. The first shad of the season command high prices; our hotel keepers sometimes paying as high as five dollars per pair for them, to serve up to the customers of the Astor House, St. James and Continental Hotels.

In marriage Captain John M. Swing was united with Miss Lydia Brooks, and when on shore resided in the township of Fairfield. They subsequently raised a large family of children, and in the process of time the daughters were chosen in marriage by some of the most influential citizens of Cumberland county. The eldest daughter, Miss Mary, was united in marriage with Mr. John Jones; Miss Lydia to James Elmer; Miss Jennie to David Roray; Miss Ann to Asa Smith; Abigail, the youngest, to Samuel Williams, and Sarah to John Willis, of the same place. Mrs. Lydia, the surviving widow of Capt. John M. Swing, until quite recently resided at the homestead in the classic village of Fairton, in reasonable enjoyment of health, and in the eighty-third year of her age. Later in her life she removed to Philadelphia, Pa. She has remained a widow for twenty-eight years.

The grim messenger death, however unwelcome, will come to each of us in time; to the captain he appeared when in his sixty-second year. After buffeting the storms of many voyages he sleeps by the side of kindred and associates in the cemetery near the old stone church at Fairfield. Let the hero lie peacefully where he falls; let us build his monument there, and cherish his memory to the end of time.

HUMAN LIFE.

After awhile—a busy brain
Will rest from all its care and pain.

After awhile—earth's rush will cease,
And a wearied heart find sweet release.

After awhile—a vanished face,
An empty seat, a vacant place.

After awhile—a man forgot,
A crumbled headstone, unknown spot.

CHAPTER XVIII.

SIMON SPARKS SWING.

ANOTHER of the strong men whose birthplace and childhood were here, but whom the waters of the bay and river attracted, was Simon Sparks Swing. Farming is not generally considered a very profitable business in this section of the country. Fancy stock, fish and oysters pay much better than ordinary farming, and it is stated that one acre of water will produce more food than five acres of land, and that, too, with less labor and expense. Many farmers have streams of water running through their land, which, when made into fish ponds, and stocked with trout, black bass, and other fish, yield a good return.

Nearly all the hardier young people of Down and Fairfield townships early in life engaged in fishing and oystering, and the people were always drifting away, even to the ends of the earth, seeking wealth. Some had been on long voyages to California, India and China, and after years of sojourn abroad, had returned without it. A seaport is an open door to foreign lands, and influences young people to venture out earlier in life than from inland villages. Among the many sea captains and navigators of Cumberland county, a few of them were successful and became owners of boats and vessels of their own.

Mr. Swing was twice married, and raised a family of sons and daughters. Among the representatives of this group the utmost love and harmony prevailed. Miss Etta T. and Ella R. Swing became teachers, one in the Bank Street, the other in the Second Ward public school of Bridgeton, where they have remained for several years in succession.

Following in the footsteps of his industrious father, Leonard R. Swing became a successful navigator himself, and is well acquainted with the shoals, bars, sounds and inlets along the Atlantic coast. He has been engaged in the coasting trade for the past twenty years, and spent most of his life on the water; is half owner of the "Richard Vaux," a substantial and well built vessel, sailing between Maurice River cove, Philadelphia, Cape May City, and New York, where cargoes of fish, oysters and other merchandise are usually sold.

There are now 422 licensed vessels, manned by 1700 men, engaged in oystering in Maurice River cove. The average cost of working a boat for the season is $1200 to say nothing of the "plants" purchased. This feature of the business is an immense drain upon the resources. The cost of oysters purchased for planting alone runs from $700 to $1000 a boat. Besides the men engaged on the boats, there are hundreds of others engaged in taking up, sorting and shipping the oysters to market.

CHAPTER XIX.

B. F. SWING.

THE ancestral homestead of Benjamin Franklin Swing stands along the banks of Cohansey river, in Cumberland county, N. J. The township in which this historic homestead is located was named Fairfield, in honor of the salubrity of its climate and the richness and fertility of its soil. Nothing could be more delightful in spring and summer and more picturesque in winter than the scenery along this useful and historic stream, which passes through broad, cultivated fields, with here and there a farmhouse or an elegant country seat in view, then rushes madly onward past busy manufacturing towns and wild marshes on its way to the ocean.

Benjamin was numbered among the youngest of a large family of children who have made their native place renowned as themselves, and there may be those who would like to read something of his birthplace and the brief story of his life.

In marriage Mr. Swing was united to Miss Hurf, a lady residing in one of the adjoining towns, who did not object to becoming a partner in his joys and disappointments.   Years rolled on ; he became a family man, and in the process of time an interesting company of sons and daughters gathered around his family table.

Besides cultivating his farm, he was interested in mercantile pursuits, sold country produce, general merchandise, horses and cattle.   In the way of freight and passenger traffic he was a good patron of the railroad and steamboat companies.   On account of his unusual size and splendid personal appearance he was the admiration of the " small fry " and men of limited genius. Throughout his life, from childhood to old age, he had great physical strength and power.   His massive head sat upon a strong and muscular neck, and his chest was broad and capacious.   His strength was great, his hand and foot large and well made.   He never knew the feebleness of youth, that unlucky check to many a promising career; nor the weakness of old age.   In walking he had a firm step and a great stride, without effort.   In early manhood he had abounding health, a good digestion, a hearty enjoyment of food.   His excellent physical condition gave him a placid and even temper and a cheerful spirit.   He was a man whose appearance, language and demeanor bear out the fact that he came of a race of gentlemen.   He was tall and august in stature, of conservative tastes and habits, with great veneration for established institutions and pious regard for his honorable ancestry, of whom, in addition to those mentioned, his parents were famous among the pre-revolutionary clergymen of New Jersey for their religious zeal and good works.

He never was a politician in its ordinary sense, and avoided both the legislature and congress, preferring to acknowledge no political favor. He was a most delightful companion. In conversation he was never controversial, never authoritative and never absorbing. In a multitude his talk flowed on sensibly, quietly, and was full of wisdom and shrewdness. He discussed books with wonderful acuteness, sometimes with startling power, and analyzed men, their characters, motives and capacity with great penetration. Nine times out of ten a big man finds it easier to gain the reputation of being great than does a little one, and wherever seen Mr. Swing was acknowledged to be a big man.

During the year 1876 centennial celebrations were held at Pittsgrove, Bridgeton, Burlington and Trenton in commemoration of our revolutionary struggle in 1776—the building of churches, school houses, and other interesting events which had transpired one hundred years before.

Many of our people visited the Centennial celebration at Fairmount Park and Independence Hall, Philadelphia; some visiting the room where once were gathered the signers of the Declaration of Independence, while others made a pilgrimage to Mount Vernon and the tomb of Washington. In our educational report and school statistics gathered that year many interesting facts abound. At this moment we recall to memory the names of many distinguished men, and some of our largest and most prominent citizens then living in New Jersey:

Herman D. Busch, Hudson county . . . . 445 pounds
Benj. F. Swing. Cumberland county 440   "
W. S. Whitehead, 6 ft. 8 in., Essex county 380   "
John Husted, Cumberland county 330   "
Hon. Jas. Nightingale, Passaic county 300   "
Saml. Wentz, Esq., Camden county 319   "
L. B. Smith, Mercer county 296   "
Barclay Haines, Burlington county 394   "
E. S. Packard, Gloucester county 285   "
Hon. Isaac Newkirk, Salem county 250   "
J. F. Sickler, Salem county 285   "
Thomas Garrison, Cumberland county 320   "
Charles G. Meyers, Esq., Cumberland county 328   "
Average weight 336   "

The second person named in this list of illustrious
men—B. F. Swing—and sons have been engaged for
many years in mercantile pursuits in the county of Cumberland. They were also farmers, drovers and dealers
in cattle, purchasing large droves of York state and
western stock. By the introduction and sale of improved
breeds of Ayrshire and Alderney from Herkimer and
Duchess counties, N. Y., for dairy and breeding purposes, together with the Holsteins, short-horns, and
black Galloways. (famous for their excellent beef and
celebrated for many good qualities for both flesh and
dairy use); by the introduction of these varieties among
our native stock the quality and value of cattle in New
Jersey have been greatly improved.

The Alderneys are celebrated for their rich, yellow
milk, cream and butter, as many of our citizens can
attest after purchasing these articles from a wagon pass-

ing daily through the streets of your city, having the name "Alderney" inscribed upon it.

The Ayrshires are said to have originated in Scotland, taking their name from the county of Ayr, where they attained great celebrity. It is the most popular breed of milk cows in that country, and long held pre-eminence in this, especially for milk and cheese.

The Hereford is one of the oldest of the thorough-breeds, and is noted for beef and for large working oxen. This stock grows larger than the Jersey, and resembles them somewhat in color, red predominating with inter-mixture of white. A farmer can put his money into no better investment than good cattle. They are a neces-sary companion to good farming, and always accompany it. The dairymen and butter-makers of Pittsgrove, including a large majority of those engaged in this industry in Salem and Cumberland counties, now pro-duce an article of great value and demand in our markets equal in taste and flavor to the celebrated York state butter.

Double rows of buttons were needed on the vests of those who accompanied B. F. Swing to the drove yard or to York state, to assist him in purchasing stock or driving a herd of cattle. Among cattle dealers and the droving fraternity he was extensively known as being lively and humorous, and well thought of by all his associates. Not slow and tedious in making a bargain, he could soon fix upon a price and tell at first sight if the steers were fat. Some of the best cattle owned at the present writing by prominent farmers in the counties of Salem and Cumberland were selected and purchased from droves of the late B. F. Swing.

To illustrate the manner in which some farmers get through the world, I may relate that some years ago a friend of mine went out with Mr. S. on a cattle-buying tour. He found a hundred head or more for sale in the hands of an old farmer who lived in Ohio. He owned a thousand acres of land, mostly in pasture, and enclosed by a high rail fence. Away back from the road was an old log house with two rooms—kitchen and bedroom— a small garden patch, and ninety to a hundred acres in corn or other crops. In the rear of the house stood a log stable for the accommodation of horses ; everything else was out of doors. The swine grunted and rooted about the grounds, and the turkeys and chickens roosted high in the trees. There lived the man and his family, a large one, composed of his wife and six full-grown boys and girls, contented and happy. As far as husking corn and out-doors work were concerned, these females could excel " our Jersey girls."

After purchasing stock we went into the house to pay for them. Needing a light, the farmer went to a shelf in the room and took down a saucer filled with lard ; a small stone tied up in a rag lay in the center, the fuzzy end of the rag sticking up by way of a wick, which he lighted at a fire on the hearth. With the aid of this glimmer they sat down to the table, figured up the amount of the sale, and the money was counted out. After being carefully recounted by the farmer—for he knew the value of bank notes as well as any one—he "made his mark" at the bottom of a receipt. That being done, Mr. S. got up, put on his hat, and as we were leaving the room the old farmer blew out his light and bade us good-night.

Among the droves of cattle coming from the west, a few wild Texas steers are sometimes found. One of these excited animals became detached from the drove while passing down Market street, ran through the Market House, near Dock street, Philadelphia, upsetting boxes and barrels of fruit, and causing a general stampede among the huckster men and women in that vicinity.

Cattle not fattened or sold to the butchers for immediate use were sold to the farmers and stock-growers in South Jersey. Halting the drove for a few days, he made sales at Woodbury, Mullica Hill, Pittsgrove (Pole Tavern), Deerfield and Bridgeton. While driving between Mullica Hill and Pittsgrove, in the fall of 1868, we remember two Texas steers that became unmanageable and refused to keep the road, or "turn to the right as the law directs." In the cedar swamp at Pineville, Gloucester county, they disappeared, and remained for several days enjoying their freedom in a wild state, all attempts at capture for a time being unavailing. The late John D. Smith, then proprietor of the hotel at Pole Tavern, William B. Brown, Isaiah Conover, John W. Janvier, the writer, and several gentlemen of leisure, visited the swamp alluded to, with dogs and shot-guns, and reconnoitered round about. The beasts became excited at the approach of man, pawed the ground, snuffed the air, bellowed and chased the dogs. Some of the party climbed up into the high trees, taking refuge therein. For a time the excitement was very great, exceeding in interest the " memorable bear hunt" in the cedar swamps of South Jersey, in which the writer participated in later years.

It is popularly supposed by those who knew him that Mr. Swing got more fun out of this present life than any other twenty cattle drovers that could be found in Cumberland county. As a man, he was kind and benevolent, strictly honest and temperate, and as a friend he would do to anchor close to in a high tide of prosperity or in the storm of adversity.

A young minister who traveled through Cumberland county on horseback many years ago (Rev. Willis Reeves) recently informed the writer that when first he arrived at his new appointment he hitched his horse for the first time in front of the church at " Harmony." Not having in his pocket the correct time of day, he had arrived in advance of the congregation. When he ascended the pulpit there were only two persons present —the sexton and another " big man." A moment later the portly form of Benjamin F. Swing came walking leisurely down the middle aisle, taking his seat near the front of the stand, on the right. Brother Reeves looked up for a moment and surveyed the newcomer with satisfaction and surprise, and while a genial smile illuminated the countenance of this eminent divine, he quietly remarked to himself, " Bless the Lord, the conference has sent me this year among the giants." And when the first hymn was announced the speaker was again pleasantly surprised to hear the same big man strike up the tune of " Old Hundred," and sing it beautifully.

When at home Mr. Swing usually drove a team of fast horses, and could appreciate a joke as well as any of his neighbors. Dividing his time with everybody he has managed to keep busy, and more than promises to honor and keep up the credit of his family name.

Peace to his memory.

CHAPTER XX.

OUR RELATIVES IN THE WEST.

IT is related of Uncle George, who was the only brother of Michael Swing, and born at York, Pa., in 1766, when quite a young man, he made frequent visits among relatives in New Jersey, and that he subsequently became greatly charmed with the appearance and beauty of his cousin Sallie, who had been raised a quiet country girl on her father's farm.

In the process of time this romantic courtship terminated in marriage, and some years later they purchased a farm in Deerfield township, to which the family removed, his name being found recorded in the clerk's office among the chosen freeholders of Cumberland county. The name of George Swing also appears among the list of grand jurors in 1802.

Mr. S. was regarded as being a very ambitious man, and the subsequent life of this great " pioneer of civilization " fully bears out the assertion that he from early youth manifested a spirit of perseverance and sagacity far beyond ordinary mortals.

By industriously cultivating and improving his land it had more than doubled itself in value in the space of ten years.

After a residence of sixteen years in Pittsgrove and Deerfield townships a sale of real estate and personal property was effected, and in the spring of 1804, he, with his wife and family of five children, two servants and one hired man, emigrated to Ohio by land. Each of the boys packed a blanket in the wagon, some provisions and cooking utensils, a rifle and shot-gun, in order to somewhat vary the monotony of beans and pork with a rabbit and quail along the road. The owners were men who could use the guns to keep peace if necessary, and also to afford protection to themselves during the journey.

After the arrival of the family in Clermont county, the first purchase of land was five hundred acres a short distance from the Ohio river and about twenty-five miles above the place where Cincinnati now stands. Everything went on in the same prosperous way as before, and while the emigrant went to work with a brisk step, felling the trees and cultivating the land, a happy light shone in his eyes and satisfaction beamed forth in his countenance.

For several years after, George Swing was the most prominent white man or inhabitant of this region, and only occasionally visited by a wandering cattle trader, trapper or missionary. The nearest trading post to him was the village of Cincinnati, some twenty-five miles across a densely timbered country toward the south. All supplies from abroad came by water, and the early settlers lived a far more isolated and truly frontier life than it is now possible to do anywhere in the United States.

When we remember the thrill of emotion caused by bidding adieu to friends and kindred and taking up our abode in a new country, how it stirs the current of life in the most sluggish heart; when we remember the log house, the first clearing of land made near the running stream, the first years of destitution, and the comfort and plenty which an earnest faith and a stout arm has finally won for the hardy pioneer—all these crowd upon our memory as we see the emigrant with his face resolutely turned in the direction of the setting sun.

The removal of this family to Ohio in these early days, when considered in connection with its results and the future prosperity of their children, was perhaps one of the most important events of his life. It served to wake up a sleeping spirit of enterprise in our people, opened extensive fields of labor and new sources of industry and wealth. It led to the discovery of valuable tracts of prairie and timber land, gave a new impetus to colonization and improvement, and prepared the way for the advantages of civilized life and the blessings of Christianity to be extended over vast regions which before were the home of Indians and wild beasts.

Some years later people from Connecticut, New York, and the eastern states, settled in Clermont county, and society began to improve. A demand was created for bread and provisions of various kinds; the markets improved, and money began to circulate more freely.

Mr. Swing purchased more land; his children grew up to manhood; they married and settled around him, and during all the years of his eventful life continued to increase and prosper. A large amount of work was accomplished in the space of a few years, the improvements being in the clearing of land, erection of houses and barns, and shelter for sheep and cattle.

Although the sudden acquisition of wealth by inheritance or through a mere caprice of fortune can scarcely be regarded as an unpleasant experience in the history of any individual, yet we are of the opinion that the proudest and most abiding inheritance is that which is built up into large and absolute independence by the sturdy right arm of the brave and honest youth who had stood penniless on the threshold of his career. And so, also, are we satisfied that one of the most benign dispositions of providence is the hiding of the book of fate from the ken of man, or the dropping before his eyes of that curtain whose impenetrable folds shut out from all the mysteries of the future.

When the subject of our sketch, over three-quarters of a century ago, had turned his face westward and, leaving the east, settled in a part of Ohio that was then little better than a wilderness, dotted with a few log cabins, could he have but lifted a corner of this curtain, his soul would have expanded with unspeakable pride and happiness. He would have seen that the sparse settlement around him had become concentrated into flourishing towns. But as this reading of the stars was denied to him, and wisely, he sought not to build castles in the air, but like a good man and true, turned in cheerily to hew and to plow, to sow and to reap his way to fortune; and that he accomplished his task in a man-

ner worthy the most exalted love of independence, and
the respect and confidence of his neighbors, is a fact that
is well authenticated and gratefully remembered.

In 1810 the price of merino wool, in Boston market,
was one dollar per pound; and it continued very high,
especially about the time of the war of 1812, some of
it selling at $2.50 per pound. A mania for growing
sheep and wool sprung up throughout the north and
west, and the growth of wool as an article of production
appeared next in importance to our bread. In all ages
has the sheep been a prominent representative of rural
husbandry. The great antiquity of this business is sufficient evidence of its profit. We read in the Bible of
the shepherds who figured in the early history of the
world. Abel is represented as being a keeper of sheep;
and the shepherds of Judea for centuries had trained their
flocks to follow their keepers into " green pastures and
by the side of still waters."

Many farmers seek relief and large profits by a varied
agriculture; industrious pioneers, many miles distant
from navigation or a railroad, seem to practice the most
obvious principles of domestic economy in raising on
their farms those products which can be taken to market
for the smallest per cent. of their value. Among the
great staples of Ohio, wool possesses this requisite in the
greatest degree; nor can I think of anything produced
in a more limited space. As far as transportation is concerned it is no great objection to live fifty or one hundred miles from a railroad, for a farmer can haul eight
hundred dollars' worth of wool with one pair of horses,

and fifteen hundred dollars' worth with four yoke of oxen. The expense of hauling a crop of wool a distance of two hundred miles, as was often done in the west, is a mere trifle. The driver of the team camps under the wagon at night, cooks his own food, and baits his cattle on the road.

The early settlers labored under many great disadvantages to the successful raising of stock. The winters were often long and severe. Deep snows lay upon the ground, and bears, wolves and wild beasts, prompted by hunger, often attacked the sheep-fold at night. Hearing a great noise in the stock yard upon one occasion, Mr. Swing sprang from the bed on which he was sleeping, and shouted at the top of his voice: "Call Wesley and Lawrence, and let the dogs loose; I cannot have my sheep destroyed in this way." Major Higgins, another old resident of Clermont county, relates that about fifty years ago himself and two boys were husking corn in a field near the banks of Sugar Tree creek. In the afternoon of the third day the ox-team was brought out and used in hauling loads of corn into the barn. Just before sunset a panic ensued among the cattle, and presently they became unmanageable and ran away at full speed. "I ran out around the wagon to see what the matter was," said Major Higgins, "and right before me, on the banks of the creek, stood the largest black bear I had ever seen. He was close by and standing so still I could scarcely believe my own eyes. A moment later, when the animal advanced towards us, the boys and myself retreated in the same direction the ox-team had gone. During the following night a light snow covered the ground. The water in the creek was very low, so that one could easily wade across it by carefully stepping on the rocks. On the other side the face of the country was covered with a dense growth of large timber, and our little party of four men and two boys lost but little time in crossing the creek and taking up the trail on the other side. After going about three miles we came into a thickly wooded valley leading down toward the Ohio river, and following on in this direction discovered the bear sitting beside the carcass of a sheep. Startled by the barking of the dog, and the unexpected approach of man, the bear ran away, and such was his speed and activity that we failed to overtake him. Reconnoitering the valley we found the paths well trodden by the footprints of wild game, and could rely on their return to the carcass. Our leader next ordered the digging of a long, narrow pit, six feet wide and ten feet deep, and very carefully concealed it with dry branches and dry leaves. Wild beasts are regarded as being both cunning and wise, so the pit was not dug beside the carcass of the sheep, but twenty-five yards away, and directly across the path leading out of the valley. Next morning, on going out to investigate the trap, we found that two half-grown bears had tumbled into the pit and were unable to escape. No hunters in Clermont county had better luck in securing their game alive. The agents of John Jacob Astor were then in Cincinnati buying furs, and offering premiums for living curiosities to be exhibited in the zoological gardens of New York city."

After some years of experience Mr. Swing found it a very uncertain way to make a fortune by engaging in the sheep business. Next he tried hogs and cattle. The raising of pork and beef has always been profitable, and consequently a favorite department of farming. The rich harvest yielded by the oak, beech and hickory in the forest formed, to a great extent, excellent food for swine, while natural grasses and roots in the woods supplied subsistence during the spring and summer months; so that the expense to the farmer in raising hogs was mainly during the feeding and fattening for market. Before the building of railroads in Ohio, Indian corn would little more than pay the cost of transportation to market, and therefore hardly entered into consideration in the cost of raising hogs. Taking into view the prolific character of the animal, and the amount of labor invested in its care, it was the general impression throughout the west that it cost a farmer nothing to make his own pork, and after being fattened brought little or nothing in market. For many years vast quantities of hogs were sold in Cincinnati at prices ranging from $1.50 to $1.75 per hundred weight, and little demand at these prices except when steamboats were loading for some distant port.

A retired Philadelphia steamboat captain relates that he lived in Cincinnati, Ohio, in his younger days (from 1825 to 1835), and was employed as a deck hand on the steamboat "Tecumseh," Capt. MacLaughlin, and afterwards fireman for Capt. Bill Swing, who was the commander of the steamboat " Corsair." These were then the largest freight and passenger boats on the river; they ran down to Louisville, Ky., and other towns along the Ohio, and later established a route between Cincinnati and New Orleans.

Captain Bill Swing was a man of commanding presence. He understood navigation, and was in favor of quick time and speedy intercourse with remote points of the country. In the furnaces dry wood was used, and sometimes rosin, pitch and turpentine were included to increase the heat and the speed of the boat.

CHAPTER XXI.

NOTES OF TRAVEL.

SOME years ago the writer enjoyed a trip through the western states, including a visit among relatives in Ohio and Indiana. During that year a series of letters were written for the *National Standard*, only two of which we select:

STEAMER " STAR OF THE WEST,"
OHIO RIVER, May 8, 18—.

MR. EDITOR.

Dear Sir:—With your permission I propose offering the readers of your paper a few rough " pen and ink sketches" taken by the wayside, while travelling toward the setting sun. From Pittsburg I went down the Ohio river, passing Economy, Beaver, Liverpool and Steubenville. There are many pleasant towns and villages scattered along its banks on either side. Rafts of lumber float leisurely with the current, and the " everlasting hills " look down in quiet dignity upon the splutter and hurry of the steamboat and railroad train.

In the vicinity of Newark the banks are steep and rocky; the hills are covered with large ash, walnut

and live oak timber. The land in many places can
never be brought under successful grain cultivation on
account of the steepness of the hills, but it is said to be
excellent sheep-grazing land. A line of steamboats run
regularly between Pittsburg and Cincinnati, carrying a
large amount of freight and passengers. There being
many stopping places, our boat makes slow progress. At
Wheeling, W. Va., the boat discharged part of her cargo,
and then took on more freight and passengers for Cincinnati. Some of the passengers are getting uneasy,
having been on the steamer three days and nights. They
begin to inquire of the captain when he will arrive at the
end of the journey. He informs us that the distance by
river is 480 miles; the boat is making good time, and he
will land the passengers at their destination on the following day.

While passing the flats below the mouth of the
Muskingum river large flocks of wild ducks and geese
were seen. Two of the passengers on the boat amused
themselves greatly by shooting rifle balls at these birds
in the distance. The game did not appear at all concerned for its safety, as the balls took no effect.

We passed Brown's Island, a great summer resort,
six miles above Steubenville, containing two hundred
acres of land, with large shade trees, beautiful lawns and
extensive boarding-houses erected upon it. This is one
of the most beautiful islands in the Ohio river.

On Saturday afternoon the boat arrived at Cincinnati.
A strong cable rope made the boat fast to the shore, the

gang planks were made ready, and while the bell tolled
and the whistle blew off steam, the writer and the other
passengers went ashore to spend the Sabbath.

G. S. S.

BETHEL, Ohio, May 22.

The city of Cincinnati presents to the eye of the
traveller a lively and business-like appearance. Many
large stores and business houses were noticed here that
will compare favorably with those seen in Philadelphia
and New York. Crowds of people were promenading
the streets, and along the levee men were loading
vessels, wheeling boxes, bags and barrels on board the
steamboats for Louisville, Cairo and New Orleans. The
" Jacob Strader," a large freight and passenger boat, loading for the last named city, is already loaded down almost
to the water's edge; but the men were piling on " more
goods." This steamer is one of the largest and most
beautiful I have yet seen—a regular floating palace.

We left Cincinnati on Monday morning, the 9th of
May, in the old stage coach, for Bethel and " the Swing
settlements," stopping first at the residence of Merrit J.
Swing, whom we found ploughing in the field for corn.
His farm is located near Poplar creek, on the north side
of the turnpike road, and embraces some of the land
originally purchased by Uncle George. At first sight, a
Jerseyman would say, " This is goodly land"—" a land
flowing with milk and honey." At the next farm, on
the opposite side of the road, we found the home of

Lurinda C. Swing, and further on the residence of Lawrence Swing. The latter person informed us that he was born in Salem county, N. J., September 11, 1790. He had lived in Clermont county for a period of over fifty years, and was then able to recall many interesting events connected with the early history of our family and their settlement in the "Miami country," as it was then called.

In the village of Bethel we visited the home of Zachariah Riley, who informed us that he was united by marriage to Mary Swing in 1816. They had then enjoyed a married life of forty-four years together, were in good health, and he had no occasion to regret his choice in selecting his partner for life. Their family consisted of eleven children, nine sons and two daughters. Most of them were married, and all had left home to carve out for themselves a name and do honor to the land that gave them birth.

Upon our arrival we found the old people occupied the house alone. The next morning the horses and carriage were ordered, and three days were pleasantly enjoyed with this venerable couple in "spying out the fullness of the land and the fatness thereof."

Some of our relatives, he said, were located "over the hills and far away" from the home of their childhood. One of his sons, Rev. Edward S., was a Baptist minister, then stationed at Veva, Indiana. On the way we passed the highly cultivated farms of J. D. Covert, one of the Ohio pioneers who went out from New Jersey in 1807, three years after the emigration of George Swing from

Salem county. In relating incidents of the journey he said that at Chautauqua, N. Y., his team of horses gave out, and he and his family walked on the rest of the way. Only a few dollars in cash remained in his possession when he reached Ohio. He has been very industrious, working steadily for fifty years, and is regarded as one of the wealthiest farmers in the township. In his family were eighteen children.

We admired his productive farm, looked at his noble herd of cattle, and visited a neighbor three miles distant, stopping on the way to look at a large tract of timber land, then offered for sale at three thousand dollars, some of the trees being very large, two of them standing near the main road measuring twenty-eight feet in circumference.

A WESTERN MARRIAGE CEREMONY.

[The following is the marriage formula in a German settlement out west :]

> (You will please join your right hands.)
> You bromise now, you good man dere
>   Vot sthands upon de floor;
> To dake dis voman for your vrow,
>   And lub her ebermore;
> Dat you will feed her vell on sourkrout,
>   Beans, buttermilk and cheese,
> And in all tings to lend your aid
>   Vot will promote her ease?
>   —Yah!
>
> Yes ; and you goot voman, too—
>   Do you pledge your vord dis day,
> Dat you will dake dis husband here,
>   And mit him always stay?

Dat you will bed and board mit him,
  Vash, iron and mend his clothes;
Laugh ven he smiles, veep ven he sighs,
  And share his joys and voes?
                    —Yah!

Vell, den, mitin dese sacred halls,
  Mit joy and not mit grief,
I do pronounce you man and vife—
  Von name, von home, von beef.
I publish now dese sacred bonds,
  Dese matrimonial ties,
Before mine Got, mine vrow—mineself,
  And all dese gazing eyes.
And now, you bridegroom standing dere,
  I'll not let go your collar,
Until you dell me one ding more,
  And dat ish : "Vere ish mine dollar?"

Our communication being longer than usual, I will
close for the present without telling all I know, or all
we have seen and admired in the highly cultivated and
beautiful county of Clermont.

                    G. S. SWING.

THE HARD-WORKING FARMER.

You may envy the joys of the farmer,
  And fancy his free, easy life;
You may sit at his bountiful table,
  And praise his industrious wife.
Ef you worked in the woods in the winter,
  Or followed the furrer all day,
With a team of unruly young oxen,
  And feet heavy loaded with clay;
Ef you held the old plough—I'm a thinkin'—
  You'd sing in a different way.

You may talk o' the golden-eyed daisies,
  An' lilies that wear such a charm.
But it gives me a heap o' hard labor
  To keep 'em from sp'ilin' my farm ;
You may pictur' the beautiful sunsets,
  An' lanscapes so full o' repose.
But I never get time to look at 'em,
  Except when it rains or it snows.
You may sing o' the song birds o' summer,
  I'll attend to the hawks and the crows.

You may long fur the lot o' the farmer,
  An' dwell on the pleasures o' toil ;
But the good things we hev on our table
  All have to be dug from the soil ;
An' our beautiful, bright, yaller butter,
  Perhaps you may never hev learned,
Makes heap o' hard work for the wimmin ;
  It hez to be cheerfully churned ;
And the cheeses so plump in our pantry,
  All have to be lifted an' turned.

When home from the hay-field in summer,
  With stars gleamin' over my head,
When I milk by the light o' my lantern,
  And wearily crawl into bed ;
When I think o' the work o' the morrow,
  An' worry, for fear it might rain ;
When I hear the loud peal o' the thunder,
  An' wife she begins to complain—
Then I feel ez if life was a burden,
  With leetle to hope fur or gain.

But the corn must be planted in spring-time,
  The weeds must be kep' from the ground,
The hay must be cut in the summer,
  The wheat must be cradled and bound.

Fur we are never out of employment,
 Except when we lie in our bed ;
Fur the wood must be hauled in the winter
 And patiently piled in the shed,
While the grain must be took to the market,
 The stock must be watered an' fed.

You may envy the joys of the farmer,
 Who works like a slave for his bread,
Or, mebby, to pay off a mortgage
 That hangs like a shade o'er his head.
You may sit in the shade o' the orchard,
 Nor think o' his wants or his need ;
You may gaze at his meadows and corn-fields,
 An' long fur the life that he leads ;
But there's leetle o' comfort or pleasur'
 In fightin' the bugs an' the weeds.

But the farmer depends upon only
 The things that he earns by his toil,
An' the leetle he gains is got honest,
 By turnin' and tillin' the soil.
When his last crop is toted to market,
 With a conscience all spotless and clear,
He may leave the old farmhouse forever,
 To dwell in a holier sphere ;
And the crown that he wears may be brighter,
 Because of his simple life here.
       —American Agriculturist.

CHAPTER XXII.

OUR FAMILY IN THE WEST.

BY GEORGE L. SWING, ESQ., BATAVIA, OHIO.

DEAR COUSIN:—

About the holidays I promised to write you a brief sketch of what we might be able to call to mind touching the history of the family in the west. My grandfather, George Swing, married his cousin, Sarah Swing, of Pittsgrove, Salem County, N. J., a sister of your great grandfather; so that we are of kin to you in a double sense. My grandfather left New Jersey some time in 1804, with his family and household, consisting of himself, his wife, and the following named children, to wit: Michael, Samuel, Lawrence, Wesley and Polly. He also brought with him two servants, a girl by the name of Maria Lawrence and an apprentice boy by the name of Josheets Ireland. They came by the way of Fort Pitt (Pittsburg). At Pittsburg he bought a flat boat, upon which they came down the Ohio river, family and horses, bag and baggage; and very early in the spring landed on the southern borders of Clermont county. My grandfather, the same year of his arrival, purchased a tract of land of about five hundred acres,

near Bethel, between Poplar and Sugar Tree creeks, on
the east and west, extending from one creek to the other,
all densely covered with heavy timber; and there in the
spring of 1805 he built a cabin, and commenced clearing
out a farm. Being strong handed, he made rapid progress in clearing; and I remember to have heard him
say that by the first of June, 1805, he had several acres
cleared and planted in corn and vegetables, and
raised considerable stuff that year. Several years, however, passed away before any considerable number of
people located in this vicinity. The country was new
and wild. They struggled long with the difficulties
and hardships incident to all new settlers; remote from
civilized society, and from the means of procuring assistance in case of sickness and disease. All these impedi-
ments were gradually overcome by perseverance, industry and enterprise, aad the family began to flourish and
increase in wealth and prosperity. In three or four
years after he had a large farm cleared. The ground
was rich and produced abundantly of everything that
was planted, often yielding fifty bushels of wheat and
seventy-five bushels of corn to the acre.

The first settlers made great havoc with the timber,
the only object being to get it out of the way. In
springtime large tracts of timber were girdled by cutting
through and stripping off the bark near the ground, thus
preventing the sap ascending into the tree; the trees
died; in a few years they became dry and were easily
destroyed by fire without cutting them down. Cattle
and hogs did well in the woods. Mast being abundant

it cost little or nothing to raise pork, and worth but little after it was raised, often being obliged to sell at $1.50 per hundred, and frequently for much less. In those days a good cow could be bought for $10; a horse for $20; a pair of working oxen for $18; a set of rawhide harness for $4, and a wooden mould-board plow for $5, and a man was ready to commence farming.

When our people first settled here Southern Ohio was densely covered with timber, and one of the grandest forests in the world. As years rolled on the navigation of the Ohio and Mississippi increased; men were engaged in loading flatboats with grain, pork and various articles of commerce, trading it off at New Orleans, payment received in sugar, coffee, tea, rice, molasses and Mexican dollars. This made the markets for our people somewhat better. The boatmen were a jolly set of fellows; they seemed to love the river, and cared but little for the danger attending their business, several boats usually starting in company together. When the cargoes had been sold, and payment received, some of the men would purchase a lot of horses and make their way up through Louisiana, Mississippi and Kentucky by land. Most of this route was then a wilderness, inhabited only by Indians and wild beasts. In some portions of Indiana and Ohio there are yet to be seen vast tracts of timber land, in many places extending for miles without a tree amiss except those blown down by the wind, or fallen to the ground through decay and old age.

Many years ago I remember a large poplar tree growing upon the land of my grandfather, in Clermont

15

county.   Upon examination it proved to be hollow.   A
tenant by the name of Graham, who lived in a cabin near
by, cut a door into it and used it for a long time as a
stable for his horse, and a few sheep.

In 1828 my grandfather built a large stone dwelling
house, which he occupied for many years.   He was a
remarkable man in his day and generation.   He was of
commanding presence, and his life was one of great
purity.   His piety was deep toned and decidedly demon-
strative in its character.   He was devoted to his church
(the Methodist), and his seat was never vacant when it
was possible for him to be there.   He liked sharp, earnest, pointed preaching, and was not slow to signify his
approbation of such preaching by crying out "amen!"
"preach on."   When the preaching did not suit him he
used to scratch his head with a sharp, quick scratch.
He was liberal in his contributions to all benevolent
objects, and especially in his contributions to the church
in all its enterprises.   He took great interest in the
American Bible Society, and for many years was its
agent for his township.   He was ever careful to see that
every family in the township was supplied with a Bible.
He visited the sick all over the neighborhood, and often
beyond the township limits.   He often conducted funer-
als when it was not convenient to procure a minister.
Many a time have I seen him standing at the head of a
new-made grave and talking to the little company that
was gathered there.

My grandmother was one of the excellent of the
earth.   I have never known a better woman.   After a

few years my grandfather gave to each of his sons a farm, embracing his original purchase and some that he subsequently added to it. Michael Swing occupied his only a short time, and then removed to the neighborhood of his wife's people, near Milford, in this county, and died on a farm the family owned there.

I will now give you briefly a list of the names of my grandfather's children by their families. Michael Swing was united in marriage with Ruth Galch, and the issue was eight children—Betsy, George S., Sarah, Mary, Ruth G., Philip B., Aaron H. and Martha. Samuel Swing, the second son of my grandfather, was married to Miss Lydia Dial in 1815, and the names of their children were Michael W., Sarah, Abraham, Eleanor, Jeremiah, David and Shadrach D. Again he intermarried with Nancy Osborn, and they had two children, Lydia A. and Harriet W. Samuel lived to be past seventy years of age. He died in Ohio. Michael Swing, Abraham and Shadrach emigrated to Illinois in 1840. The first named was elected a member of the Illinois legislature, and became a very prominent person in the state. Abraham became a dry goods merchant, was successful in business, and in his old age was nicknamed " Honest Old Abe." Wesley married Miss Nancy Crane. Five children were born to them, George W., John Collins, Elizabeth G. and Merritt J. My father, Lawrence Swing, intermarried with Sarah Light, and they had seven children, namely : Ruth, John S., George L., Eliza, Sarah, Charles W. and William L. Father outlived all his generation, and died in 1872. When I was a small boy

I happened to be at my grandfather's house when a letter was brought from the post office to him. It came from New Jersey. He broke the seal and looked at it silently for a moment, then said to my grandmother, "Abraham is no more." It was the announcement of the death of your grandfather. He was a brother of my grandmother. Then he said, "We remember Abraham as a good man; it is well with him." This little incident made an impression upon my mind that has never faded. The history of our family in the east and west is an interesting one to you, and to me, and to our kindred. My grandfather was a grand old man; mighty in word and in deed. His emigration to Ohio was a success alike to himself and to his family; they all fared well in a pecuniary way, and were honored, respected and useful in their day and generation. They were Methodists, but their posterity have not all adhered to that denomination.

My grandfather had considerable means when he came to Ohio. His first purchase of land he bought for $2 per acre, and often wished that he had invested more than he did in land. He deposited one thousand dollars of the money he brought with him from New Jersey in the Farmers' and Mechanics' Bank of Cincinnati. His confidence was inspired in the bank by the fact that it was controlled by Methodist brethren, chief among whom was the late Rev. Oliver M. Spencer. But the Methodist brethren managed the bank badly and grandfather's thousand dollars were lost. I saw his old certificate of deposit among his papers after his death.

When our people came to this county it was new and

wild. The settlements were "few and far between." The forests abounded with deer and wild game of many kinds. The streams of water were full of fish, but my grandfather never ceased to long for sea-bass, haddock, Jersey shad and the fish that were caught from the ocean. The roads were little more than cow-paths. Cincinnati was only a village, twenty-seven miles from our settlement, and a trip there and back generally occupied about three days, with a loaded wagon and team.

Great changes took place in his day, and much greater changes have taken place since that time. My grandfather preserved his mind and memory well until the very last. In old age his sight failed; the last year of his life he was entirely blind. This great affliction did not seem to affect his cheerfulness; it rather caused him to look with greater desire toward the world of light and the final home of the blessed in heaven. His death occurred in the eighty-second year of his age. My grandmother survived him about two years. You may have seen the family graveyard when you visited our people some years ago.

I must not omit to give some history of another branch of our family and of yours. Near the close of the last century, Samuel Swing, a brother of your grandfather, came from New Jersey with his wife, Polly Murphy, and such of his family as were then in being, and settled on the Licking river, in Kentucky, not far from where the cities of Covington and Newport now stand. The Licking empties into the Ohio directly opposite Cincinnati.

Samuel was engaged in building barges and keel boats, with which the western rivers were then navigated. Steamboats had not yet come into use. He died before my recollection; but his widow (Aunt Polly) survived him many years, and I well remember her visits to our people. She was a tall, dignified old lady, and was a member of the First Presbyterian church of Cincinnati, so long ministered to by Dr. Joshua Wilson. She was an esteemed Christian lady.

The children of this family were named Samuel, Betsy, Jeremiah, Mary Ann, David, Phœbe, William and Abraham S., all of whom, I believe, have passed away. But they have left many descendants who are now scattered far and wide over this continent.

Rev. Professor David Swing, a distinguished minister of the Presbyterian church, Chicago, Ill., is a grandson of this Samuel Swing and a son of David Swing, before mentioned. Once, when he was a boy, he was a pupil of mine at Williamsburg, seven miles east of here. He was a very bright, thoughtful and interesting little boy, and a good student. I had the control of a scholarship in Miami University at Oxford when David was growing up, and gave him the benefit of it. He graduated with honor, and soon after entered the ministry. He is a good speaker; there is a freshness and sparkling originality about his thoughts that give them a charm and makes them interesting. The multitude gather about him, and listen with unflagging interest to his discourses.

Dr. Charles Swing, of Salem county, N. J., was out

here once in his time. I remember hearing our people frequently speak of him.

Captain John Swing was here not far from 1845, perhaps a little later, and visited our people. It was said long ago, by one who knew him well, that " he was a noble-hearted man, and his life was crowded full of exciting episodes." He was a large man, and, if we remember correctly, weighed about 250 pounds—a real jolly, social kind of person, and interested us very greatly by relating " his experience of life on the ocean wave" and a " home on the rolling deep." He had been for many years engaged in the coasting trade, and finally became a celebrated navigator of the sea. He was a very fine-looking man, well proportioned—not fat, but large and strong.

Some years later, Nathaniel G. and Gilbert S. Swing visited Bethel, Ohio. On their arrival our people formed a very pleasant acquaintance with these relatives, and since that time this acquaintance has been renewed by letter and greatly improved by correspondence.

The two brothers that came over from Alsace, as your father wrote me, have now a large posterity scattered clear across this continent. Some of our people are in California. Our family name in the west is an honored one.

I have lived in Batavia since 1847, and shall probably remain here. Our lives are in God's hands ; He directs our way and orders our steps. It often occurs to me, and more of late than formerly, that life in this world is very brief, quite too short to accomplish anything worth speaking of, either in the way of labor or enjoyment. We have to hurry through so fast that we have only time to recognize and hail each other as we pass. It will not be so in the next life. We shall have time then to tell the whole story, and if we shall be so fortunate as to secure a place in our father's house of many mansions, it will be no matter of regret then that we had not a longer stay in the world through which we are now passing.

I love our family name in the United States. I believe we have a common origin, rather humble at the beginning, but that is nothing to be ashamed of; and it is a source of gratification to know that no one of the members who have borne our name for successive generations has cast much dishonor upon it, while not a few, by lives of integrity and uprightness, have made their mark in the world, and our name an honored one.

CHAPTER XXIII.

CORRESPONDENCE WITH CAPTAIN G. P. RILEY.

YORKTOWN, Virginia, Nov. 3, 1863.

DEAR UNCLE:—

Your kind favor of the 25th duly received, and was much pleased with its contents; have never enjoyed a happier week than the one recently spent with relatives in Salem county.

Our regiment (the 6th United States colored troops) started for this place the day after we left Pittsgrove. We left New York on Wednesday on board a new steamer called the "Conqueror," with fifteen hundred troops, including officers; five hundred cavalry horses, and a large cargo of rations and government supplies; and arrived at Yorktown, Va., on Sunday evening, after a very rough and disagreeable voyage. The wind was high, the sea rough, and I was never before so seasick in all my life; most of the officers and two-thirds of the men were the same.

When we arrived at the Breakwater, mouth of Delaware Bay, our captain lay to for some hours, on account of a heavy storm, and when the steamer started out on Saturday morning we were compelled to return again and wait for the wind and sea to subside. Through the mercy of an over-ruling Providence we arrived here safe without the loss of a man or a dollar's worth of property.

After landing we formed in line and marched through Yorktown (which consists of fifty or sixty houses, surrounded by a large and well built fort) on to our camping grounds, one mile and a half down York river.

Our regiment is encamped close by the house in which Lord Cornwallis surrendered to General Washington. History informs us that this event took place October 17, 1781. I have just been over to the house where this surrender took place. It is a large two-story log building, weather boarded and ceiled, and now belongs to a rich rebel, who has fled to Richmond, as many in this vicinity have done, leaving their farms and slaves behind.

This place has been the scene of important events during this war, as well as in the Revolution. Here was McClellan's siege, and some fighting. This whole country is cut up with fortifications, rifle pits and military roads, and presents the picture of desolation—not a rail or fence of any kind have I seen. Surrounding our camp is a vast plain of thousands of acres, once in a high state of cultivation. The timber (and there is some very good) is being cut by the soldiers to build their winter quarters. I suppose this place will be garrisoned with troops all winter.

The Sixth is a good regiment; I am pleased with it; am senior captain. Most of our officers are from the regular army; those who are not have passed a rigid examination. Out of eleven hundred applicants at Cincinnati, not more than forty passed.

From our position here I suppose, when Richmond is attacked, we shall be there; many of our boys are anxious for it. There are four regiments of white, three of colored and two of artillery encamped near us. It has been very sickly through the hot weather, and still deaths are frequent among us. We get plenty to eat, have good meat and bread; sweet potatoes are sold to us for $2 per basket, and Irish the same. I am getting quite portly and much heavier than when you saw me last.

On our way to Philadelphia we happened to fall in with Mrs. Lydia Swing, widow of the late Captain John M. Swing, of Fairfield. After a brief, yet pleasant acquaintance, my daughter Antis went home with her. I received a letter from her last week, and she is having a good time.

While strolling along the wharf, looking at the large and beautiful ocean steamers and the thousands of vessels collected in the port of Philadelphia, I noticed the schooner Geo. M. Swing, of Fairfield, N. J., unloading oysters at Dock street wharf for the firm of Swing & Corbin, commission merchants of that city, and dealers in fish, oysters, country produce and salt water terrapin.

Philadelphia is a very handsome city. We left here the same evening for New York with a few car loads of enlisted soldiers, *en route* for some Southern port.

Yours truly,

CAPTAIN GIRARD POLICARP RILEY.

United States Christian Commission "sends this as
the soldier's messenger to his home. Let it hasten to
those who wait for tidings."

CAMP OF THE 6TH U. S. C. T.,
Before Richmond, Oct. 28, 1864.

DEAR UNCLE:—

Your communication gives me much encourage-
ment, and I am always glad to hear from friends and
relatives in New Jersey. Since last we wrote our regiment has been called to pass through many scenes of
blood and carnage. On the morning of the 29th of
September our brigade, only about nine hundred strong,
charged on the rebel line of works, where we met over
two thousand of the enemy. As you have doubtless
heard, our little brigade was almost annihilated. But
the works were carried and the rebels routed. Our
regiment went in with three hundred and came out with
only seventy-two. Our officers were nearly all either
killed or wounded. I was in front of the line of battle
with my company deployed as skirmishers. Out of
thirty picked men we lost twenty-two; but through the
abounding mercy of God, and, as I think, in answer to
prayer in my behalf, no bullet pierced my flesh, though
many passed through my hat and uniform; one bullet
cut my coat collar, another went through my canteen on
my right side, and another through three thicknesses of
cloth under my left arm. We can but feel thankful to
God and grateful to all his people who pray that our
life may be spared. I have thought that God sent me to

defend my country, and believed it was a Christian duty to stand in the foremost of the fight.

I once heard a pious lady say that she never could reconcile the idea in her mind of a Christian going into the army to fight; it was so inconsistent with the Christian character that she was tempted to doubt the piety of all fighting men. I beg leave to differ with the lady's views upon this subject, for I believe that a man can serve God and his country just as acceptably in fighting the enemies of liberty with the musket down South as he can in the halls of legislation or the quiet pulpits of the North, and I am inclined to think he can do so much more effectually in the former place. My own observations are that Christian men make the best soldiers and the most zealous and ardent defenders of our national independence.

Our troops are still at work at the canal at Dutch Gap, but it will be spring before this great undertaking can be completed. Since leaving the "Gap" our brigade has advanced, and is now six miles below Richmond, on the river; a small force of men holds the line of works here. There was considerable cannonading and a general movement last night, and we are expecting orders to advance upon the city in a few days.

Two colored soldiers belonging to our regiment informed me that they enlisted from Salem county, and that they were formerly acquainted with and employed by Dr. Charles Swing, of Sharptown, and Leonard Swing, of Pittsgrove, and while in the employ of these gentlemen had dug thousands of loads of marl from the beds at

Woodstown, N. J. Their names were Bond and Sullivan.

Prices here are very high; potatoes are $2.50 per bushel, butter 75c. and 80c. per pound, and eggs about the same a dozen. I would like to know the prices of butter, eggs, home-made cheese, etc., in your market, and if we should winter here I might save considerable by sending you the money, and have boxes of provisions expressed to us. We notice the express charges on boxes sent from New Jersey are quite reasonable, while those sent from Ohio amount to the full worth of their contents.

G. P. R.

HEADQUARTERS 3D DIVISION 10TH ARMY CORPS,
DISTRICT OF BEAUFORT,
NEW BERNE, S. C., June 24, 1865.

MY DEAR UNCLE:—

It has been a long time since I have heard from home, and quite as long perhaps since you have heard from me. For the last four months I have been on General Paine's staff, have had a great deal of writing and some business outside the office, such as settling difficulties between former masters and slaves; but amid all our cares, dangers and excitement, have not forgotten our relatives and friends.

You, no doubt, with all other good people, rejoice at the close of the war. How wonderful the workings of

Divine Providence; to Him be all the praise, honor and glory!

I am going home in a few days, and our troops will soon be mustered out of service. I have not heard directly from Captain George W. Swing for three months. I saw one of the officers of the 9th New Jersey a few days ago. He said he was at Greensboro, N. C. I cannot write, for all my thoughts are homeward; will be there in ten days. Write to me at Bethel, Ohio.

P. S.—I wrote the above at New Berne a few days ago, and " receiving leave of absence," we are preparing to embark for home. We go on a steamer by way of New York city. Amid the strains of martial music, the hum of industry and the excitement of landing two thousand troops, I forgot to mail my letters while passing through New York. Will mail this at Cincinnati.

The war is ended. Blessed be God; and at this moment I can subscribe myself one of the happiest of living men.

G. P. RILEY.

CHAPTER XXIV.

NOTES OF THE GETTYSBURG CAMPAIGN, BY GEO. W. SWING, CAPT. 12TH REG. N. J. VOLS.

ALL was beautiful in nature on the morning of June 14, 1863, when the long roll sounded and the Army of the Potomac was once more aroused to do active duty in the field. The rest enjoyed after the battle of Chancellorsville was rudely broken. Though in the quiet repose of that lovely Sabbath morning everything around spoke of peace and rest, yet the stirring sounds of the trumpet, the bugle and the drum, mingled with the stentorian commands, " Pack up," "Fall in," and "Forward, March," proved conclusively that there were still battles to be fought and victories won.

Intelligence had reached headquarters that Gen. Lee and his army were crossing the Potomac. They had manœuvered behind the Blue Ridge Mountains and had nearly gained the Maryland side before their intention was fully understood by the Union commander. Our regiment, the 12th New Jersey Volunteers, belonged to the Second Army Corps. Passing rapidly through Dumfries we hear heavy guns in the direction of Manasses. Soon the Occoquan creek was passed and we hasten in the direction of Centreville, Gen. Hooker's headquarters. A vast number of men and ambulances were concentrated at this point. Our route lay over the Bull Run battlefield and through Gainesville to Sebley Spring and Edward's Ferry, where we crossed the Potomac on a pontoon bridge on the morning of June 27th into Maryland, and rested for a time in a large wheat field. It was a grand sight to see the troops in motion. Our train was twenty miles long, and occupied several parallel roads, well guarded by the infantry deployed on either side of the teams, as these were rapidly urged forward. Poolsville and Urbania, beautiful towns, were soon left behind, and Frederick City was in view.

The next day, June 29th, the troops marched thirty-three miles, passing through Liberty, Johnstown, and other small places. June 30th Uniontown is reached. The troops rested for a short time, and the train is parked.

It was muster day in camp, and anxiety and a stern determination were depicted on the countenances of officers and men alike. We knew that the army of Lee, in strong force, well equipped, was in front, and that in a short time we would be in the midst of a tremendous conflict, which might decide in a great measure the issues of the war.

The *morale* of our troops was splendid. Everyone, as far as we could judge by words and actions, expressed a firm determination to conquer or die in the impending conflict.

There had been on the march a great deal of racing by the various corps to be first, if possible, on the field.

16

Once the 12th New Jersey was aroused from rest at midnight, and made a rush with fixed bayonets to prevent our road being crossed or occupied by a rival corps. These bloodless conflicts for the right of way were by no means pleasant to be engaged in, but, as incidents, illustrated the zeal and ambition of our officers and men to rival each other in devotion to their country's good, and to be first, if possible, to meet the enemy.

We did not, any of us, have long to wait. July 1st the train was in motion. We passed through the lovely town of Trebania, a place of considerable wealth, with fine houses, barns, mills, etc.; also Tarrytown, where we halted in a woods to rest a short time, and then passed over the state line, near the little town of Harney, into Pennsylvania, where we had our bivouac for the night on the road side, and rested well in anticipation of the impending conflict.

July 2d, a day never to be forgotten while memory lasts. The rebels are in heavy force a few miles distant in our immediate front. The fighting had already commenced, and the various corps, as they arrived on the field, were assigned positions at the nearest point where they could be of immediate service.

The Union line extended about ten miles in length, cavalry, artillery and infantry. It was a strong position, the wings right and left receding, making it a formidable line for defence, as most of it occupied a ridge of low, uniform hills, well protected by sugar-loaf peaks at either end, densely clothed with timber. On the left was the Fifth corps. The Third, First, Second, Eleventh and

Twelfth extended in the order named from left to right of the line, which was flanked by heavy squadrons of cavalry.

The brigade was aroused early in the morning, and went with a rush into the field. Our position was near the centre of the line. Our regiment was placed obliquely to the first line of battle, and the men dropped on the ground for a rest. The enemy's shells were beginning to fly over and fall around us.

General Smythe, Major Hill and a part of French's staff are near us, awaiting the development of events. The battle-ground is on a beautiful, well cultivated country. The harvest fields are trampled under foot. Thus far the Union army have the advantage in position and artillery practice.

About half-way between the Union and rebel lines are a farmhouse and brick barn, occupied by rebel sharp-shooters. They are shooting at our mounted officers with long-range rifles, and must be dislodged. There is a hasty consultation among the officers. General Smythe said he had a regiment that would do it. In a few minutes an order came for four companies of the 12th New Jersey to attack the house and barn. We were lying left in front.

The men sprang to their feet and prepared for the onset. We numbered about one hundred and forty men in the storming party when we started. General Smythe, our brigade commander, rode with us a short distance, and then resumed his former position, where he could witness the charge. We soon changed from a double-quick into a rapid run, and as we neared the house the rebel rifles made fearful havoc in our ranks. One poor fellow, I remember, begged to be left behind when we started on the charge, on the plea of being too sick to keep up with the men. There appearing no good reason for doing so, he was not excused, but was ordered forward with the rest. He was killed at the first fire that struck our ranks.

The men faltered not, but leaping over their fallen comrades as they advanced, rushed with fixed bayonets upon the sharpshooters, two companies advancing on the barn and two companies surrounding the house. As we closed up around the house we found an open hatchway or cellar door, down which the rebels poured pell-mell to get out of the way of our bayonets. Many threw down their arms and surrendered at once, while others waved their hands or handkerchiefs in token of submission ere we reached them. Two of our men went into the cellar and drove the prisoners out, while others scattered through the house and opened fire on the retreating fugitives.

A door in an upper room was apparently fastened on the inside. On forcing it open a rebel soldier was found inside, unhurt but nearly scared to death.

Our prisoners taken numbered eighty-seven men, including seven commissioned officers. This was a hard fight, as it was a hand to hand struggle, and many of our brave comrades were numbered among the fallen. About thirty-five or forty were killed or wounded in that fearful charge. Capt. Horsfall, commanding the detachment, was killed near the house while gallantly leading his men. Many brave soldiers, some of them my own personal friends, shared the same fate. The men were black with gunpowder, and suffered much from the intense heat of the day. Some of our number, after the prisoners were secured, bathed their aching brows in basins of water found standing around, already stained with rebel blood.

There was in rear of the house a number of apple trees, and lying among or behind them were many riflemen from whom we were subjected to a constant fire, we returning in like manner the compliments of the season with buckshot and ball. After holding our position for a time, no reinforcements appearing, the detachment returned in good order to the first line of battle on a full run, where we rested on our arms. And truly rest was required for our weary men. Some had been knocked down insensible during the fight, but eventually revived, while others received slight wounds, enough to take them away from further danger in the field. One of our men collected a basket of eggs from about the barn after the fight, which he brought into our lines and kindly shared with his less fortunate comrades.

After resting through the night, with picket lines well advanced in front, the Army of the Potomac, strong in position and in the justice of a righteous cause, awaited the pleasure of the enemy. Early in the morning a first detachment of men from our regiment charged again on the house and burned it to the ground. The barn could not be destroyed so readily, and its walls continued to be a cover for the rebel sharpshooters during the remainder of the day.

General Lee had been foiled on both his right and left flanks in the battles of yesterday, so that the morning of July 3d opened with an apparent hesitancy on the part of the rebel commander where to strike.

A decisive blow at once, or retire from the field, was, from his standpoint, a " military necessity." In a short time his plan developed itself. His skirmishers, thrown out early in the morning, for several hours continued to press up close to the Union lines, feeling the strength of the various fronts and positions of the corps. The point of attack was a matter of uncertainty to General Meade; but everything was in readiness.

A large amount of artillery, in reserve, was quietly concentrated near our lines, and all was eager expectation. Soon, like a whirlwind, the storm broke upon us. With about one hundred and fifty guns, drawn from the right and left of his line, a terrific cannonade was opened on our right centre, held by the Second and Eleventh corps. This was continued for about two hours. Shells and bullets of all sizes and descriptions flew over, around and among us as we lay close to the ground behind our stone fences, or such temporary works as could be hastily constructed.

The air was full of shot and shell. Our artillery horses, as they brought the guns into action, were killed in large numbers. One fine battery, a little to our left, lost nearly all their horses, sixty-four out of seventy-two falling in a short time after fire opened. I could not but notice how patiently those noble animals bore their wounds when stricken down in their harness.

In a few minutes the caisson was blown up by a well directed rebel shot with a report louder than thunder, and making the earth tremble for a long distance around. The men of the battery who found themselves alive after the explosion were soon on their feet, and the clear, ringing voice of their captain called them anew to duty, while he, coolly sighting one of his pieces in person, successively blew up two of the rebel caissons in return. The smoke from them arose like an immense sheaf of wheat over the battlefield.

Railroad iron, stones, and missiles of all kinds, which they could cram into their guns, were hurled from the rebel cannon. It seemed as though pandemonium were let loose, and that the very rocks around would be rent to their foundation. Vengeance, hate and fury were concentrated in a remarkable degree in that terrible cannonade. With each repeated crash, carrying death and destruction into the Union ranks, their hopes grew higher until the climax came. All at once the rebel artillery ceased firing—an apparent calm after a storm, but a calm that was to usher in one of the most terrific infantry battles of the war. All was expectancy, as the artillery duel was but the prelude to the final charge.

Soon dark masses of troops were seen collecting on the left, front and right. They began to advance. The skirmishers were bold and numerous, they having three lines in front of the main body.

We were confronted by about forty-five thousand of the best troops of the South. The view we had of them as they advanced rapidly towards our position was truly grand. We could not but admire their martial array. Such a sight was probably never seen before of the same magnitude on our continent. Their step was firm and quick; the guns were, most of them, carried at a trail. They have about three-quarters of a mile to march, over an open space, before reaching our position, with five common rail fences to obstruct their march. Most of these fences were leveled by the first line. A strong post and rail fence a little in our front served in a slight degree to check their final dash, as our artillery, at point blank range, opened on their solid columns, making gap after gap in their ranks. Then the small arms opened also with a rattling roar as loud as Niagara, and so stunning to the sense of hearing that many soldiers could not distinguish the report of their own rifles, the general crash was so great. The oldest officers present had never before witnessed such a scene.

As the rebel column advanced its impetus increased, and for a time it appeared as though they would break through our ranks and sweep the field before them. But the discipline, drill and indomitable courage of the Army of the Potomac were too much for them. Every one of our men, from the highest to the lowest in rank, fought as though the salvation of our country depended on his individual effort. We had on our immediate brigade and regimental fronts Pickett's division of Longstreet's corps, and he led his troops with the reckless bravery of a Murat, and they rent the air with hideous yells as they charged on the Union lines.

The storm of shot, shell, canister and spherical case fell thick among them. Fresh guns were brought forward, and double or treble charged for use at close range. The smoke at length became so dense on the field that we could scarcely distinguish anything before us, and there was a slight lull in the firing. Soon the smoke lifted, and we had the pleasure of seeing the rebel army in full retreat, leaving behind them multitudes of dead, wounded and prisoners that thickly strewed the ground in our front

Captives came in by hundreds, and there was a rush made by many of our men on to the field to capture flags and drive in the prisoners, and although the loud voice of command restrained somewhat the impetuosity of our troops, it was impossible for a time to keep the men in line, the desire to advance was so great.

The scene at this time was inspiring to the highest degree; a glorious victory had been won. The fight was nearly over on our part of the line. Their repulse had been complete. In other quarters the conflict appeared to sway back and forth for a time; but soon the plain before us was cleared of all except the dead and wounded.

At this point, while random shots were yet being exchanged at long range, a flag appeared from the rebel line. It was a very large white flag, and with it were some twelve or fifteen men. As the firing was not en-

tirely over, the impertinence of a truce at this time was
apparent to all, and as they advanced a well directed
shot from one of our cannon near by scattered them like
chaff and sent them reeling back to their own lines.

With this repulse the battle was over for the day, and
the tired soldiers rested on their arms. It was a beautiful moonlight evening after the battle. About 9 o'clock,
finding I could not rest or sleep while there was so much
suffering around and near me, I took a walk to a
part of the field in our immediate front. Here is where
Pickett's troops charged us with such infinite fury, and
were hurled back in wild disorder. The dead were
in quiet repose, while the suffering among the wounded
was indeed sad to contemplate.

A fine looking South Carolinian attracted my attention.
Stopping to converse with and aid him, if possible, I
found him wounded in five or six places, and could see
no hopes of his recovery. He asked for water, which,
such as we had, was promptly furnished from a ditch
near by. It was muddy and impure ; but as soon as possible good water from a spring was procured, which
gave him great relief for the time. In return he kindly
gave me a part of his provision, which was acceptable
indeed, as few of our men had anything remaining of
their rations, as in hastening to the field provisions were
left in the rear.

The whole scene around was enough to make angels
weep—men with an infinite variety of wounds, and their
misery no tongue can tell. But soon, in mercy to them,
the skies were overcast with clouds and a kind Providence

sent a heavy rain during the night, which was a blessing indeed to the poor, fevered sufferers.

We found the prisoners well supplied with three days' rations, consisting of cooked meat and two or three large cakes, about the size of a common dinner plate and over one inch thick. Their boots and shoes were nearly new and their clothing good. When asked where they had procured their outfit, they answered that the goods had been sent from Europe and ran the blockade. The personal intercourse had with our prisoners and the wounded after the battle, as far as I could see, was of a kind and friendly nature.

Early on the morning of July 4th our regiment was sent forward as pickets to the field, where we lay close to the ground for several hours, among the wounded and dead, and were subjected to a sharp fire from the rebel picket line. It was a trying ordeal; but our men faced it nobly, without being able to do much in the way of reply, as we were armed with smooth-bore muskets, which would not reach them, but were terribly effective at short range with their buck-shot and ball.

On returning from the picket line, bringing our wounded with us, we were greeted with the joyful news of the fall of Vicksburg.

Next day—the holy Sabbath, clear and beautiful—was devoted to the burial of the dead of both armies, the enemy in their haste leaving theirs on the field. By noon this sad work was completed, and the Union commander again turned his face to the south in pursuit of the army of fugitives from the bloody field.

P. S.—Of the writer of the Gettysburg Campaign Notes the author has this postscript to add, the perusal of which may assist the reader in forming a more intimate acquaintance with the captain:

George W. Swing was born at Pittsgrove, Salem county, N. J., May 19, 1830, a son of Jonathan L. and Rebecca McQueen Swing. He was a farmer and school teacher in his younger years, and very attentive and devoted in his work; was greatly interested in the study of vocal and instrumental music, and the reading of books of travel and history. His blood, however, was too ardently patriotic to calmly sit in a country school house teaching children and youth, while the war drum was sounding in his country. Throwing down his books he assisted in the formation of a company of men, hastened to the front, and served three years in the war of the rebellion. Returning to his native place at the close of the war, he was married, and subsequently settled at Vineland, N. J., where himself and family have continued to reside. His occupation was a dry goods merchant, an insurance agent and farmer. He was a member of the fire police, the board of health and the Society for the Prevention of Cruelty to Animals.

After his return from the war he was chosen a justice of the peace, and also appointed commander of Lyon Post, No. 10, Grand Army of the Republic, in this place Like his father and many of his kindred before him, he is an elder in the Presbyterian church, a member of the board of trustees and one of the most efficient officers in that body.

In speaking of himself recently he said: " The language of my heart is—

" ' I am a poor sinner, and nothing at all,
But Jesus Christ is my all in all.' "

In stature Mr. Swing is tall and slender, his features are regular, and his bright, expressive eyes light up his face as he recognizes and salutes a friend. He is very temperate and domestic in his habits, genial and pleasant in conversation, and in all the glories of his success he did not forget the companions of his youth or the associates of later years.

CHAPTER XXV.

WESTERN CORRESPONDENCE.

MASON CITY, Ill.

DEAR SIR:—
Yours of the 20th instant received, making further inquiry concerning our family in the state of Illinois. In reply, I wish to state that I am a son of the late Samuel Swing, was born in Clermont county, Ohio, in the year 1821. Am one of a family of seven children—four brothers and three sisters. My father came from New Jersey when a small boy. My grandfather also came from the same state, and settled in Ohio at an early day.

Nearly forty years have passed away since my first purchase of prairie land, and settlement in Illinois, our time mostly being occupied in agricultural pursuits, and in raising hogs, sheep, horses and cattle. In this department of work we have been very successful. Our state has become one among the larger states, and thickly settled with people. Some are selling out and emigrating farther west, notwithstanding there is room here to make a living and work only half the time. Since our settlement here my brother and two sisters have died, only two in our family remaining, David and myself, the former named being the owner of a large amount of property.

I have a family of five children, four of whom are married; one is engaged in the dry goods and another in the hardware business. One of my daughters married the missionary, Rev. W. P. Paxson, of St. Louis. He frequently goes to New York on business connected with the book concern and the missionary work in the West, and stays there from two to three months. I have requested him to call, the next time he goes East, and see our relatives in New Jersey. Our soil is varied, and mostly good for agricultural and grazing purposes; yet we have long since learned that the soil will wear out without proper care and attention.

Earth has many grand places for the few years of this life—places where the sunshine falls on rich land and is transformed into fruit and flowers—places where spring comes early and where the winters are short. For our three score and ten years, New Jersey, Ohio or Illinois is good enough.

Your communication went further back in the family history than I had ever before been led. Among our relatives in the west I mention the name of Professor David Swing. The well-known preacher, who addresses in Central Music Hall every Sunday an audience of from 2,500 to 3,000 people, was born in Cincinnati, Ohio, August 18, 1830. His father died in 1832, and his mother married again, removing to Readsburg, Ohio, when David was seven years old. Three years later his family removed to a farm near Williamsburg, Ohio. At eighteen years of age he entered Miami University, at Oxford, Ohio, graduating in 1852. He studied theology at Cincinnati for one year, when he was appointed professor of Latin and Greek at the Miami University. Here he remained thirteen years, occasionally preaching till 1866, when he was called to the new Westminster church, of Chicago, which soon united with another (old school) Presbyterian church, retaining him as pastor. The fire in 1871 destroyed his church, and he preached in McVicker's theatre until the completion of Central Music Hall, where he now preaches.

[*Extract from the New School Presbyterian.*]

The Westminster church, Chicago, presented Professor David Swing, their pastor, on the first day of January, $500, and raised his salary from $3,000 to $3,500.

A great change had come over the face of the country since our settlement in Illinois in 1840, when the prairie was everywhere marked with cow-paths, made by cattle passing to and fro in search of water. Occasionally the bleached skeletons of cattle were seen, white and decayed. This section was formerly the " cattle ground," where vast herds were turned loose in spring and summer to shift for themselves. Look where we might, in either direction, there was always cattle in sight, and fences were almost unknown. To-day fields of grain, farmhouses, and numerous villages, dot the plain, and remind us of our boyhood days in eastern states.

In politics, as a family, we are divided. There are but

few, if any, " Free Soilers," and no " Barn Burners," among us.

By the blessing of Providence we enjoy good health, and finally hope to reach the Port of Peace.

Yours truly,

SHADRACH D. SWING.

In the Mason City *Independent*, published February 13th, we find the following item:

" Last week a sale was made between Shadrach D. Swing, of Illinois, and C. L. Stone, who bought one of Mr. Swing's farms, at Swing's Grove, three miles from Mason City, 240 acres, at fifty dollars per acre ($12,000). Mr. Swing takes the brick storehouse on Main street at $6,500, and a dwelling-house in the north part of the city at $1,500, and a mortgage on the farm of $4,000. Mr. Stone is going to sow hayseed and be a granger."

17

MERRITT J. SWING.

CHAPTER XXVI.

MERRITT J. SWING.

IN presenting to our readers the name of the gentleman whose name heads this chapter we are, of course, sensible of the fact that many of our people will be gratified to read a few "items" regarding the life and occupation of a prominent "Western man," and one of the living representatives of our family. His mother's maiden name was Nancy Crane. His parents were Wesley and Nancy Swing, both of whom were born in Salem county, N. J. Our hero was the fourth child born to them, and his parents, being persons of culture and refinement, undertook the education of their own family. These educational methods were highly practical; to know was made the incentive to do; hence the advice, "Whatsoever thy hand findeth to do, do it with thy might."

His thoughts soon turned to the business of life, to striking out for himself, and being in a farming country naturally took to that occupation. Most of the farms in this section had to be cleared by cutting down large trees, and this required hard work, chopping wood, hauling logs with oxen, and pulling up stumps. He mowed grass with a scythe and grain with a sickle then, and one acre was considered a fair day's work.

As he grew up his life was as peaceful and happy and free from discontent as the home of a country lad could be. In the meantime he had met and courted the fair Maria Carruthers, believing woman to be the helper and counsellor of man. Soon after their marriage they established themselves on a good farm in Clermont county, Ohio.

He is now in the meridian of life, not far from sixty years of age, but looking younger. As a man he is full grown, standing six feet in height, perfectly innocent himself, and walks erect, with one foot before the other, is somewhat dignified and rather handsome, with a remarkably full, sonorous voice, but so kindly in manner and disposition that the admiration and respect of women, and even little children, were attracted.

He was twice married, and raised a large family, the most of whom were daughters, who have already grown to womanly stature, married well, and settled down in life around him. After the death of his first wife he retired from the farm, entrusted its management to his eldest son, and removed himself into the village of Bethel, where a wider field of activity and usefulness awaited his ambition.

For the past eighteen years the wholesale dry goods and notion trade claimed his attention. His motto has been ' Quick sales," with fair and honest dealing. He has made his own money, and carries about him the general air of a good common-sense business man. In

FOX CHASE.

all his habits he is methodical ; in his plans, deliberate and conscientious ; chaste in expression, and seldom embellishes his forms of speech with either flowers of rhetoric or the exuberance of poetical delineation, but expresses things which the people can understand without the use of a lexicon. In conversation he is pleasant and self-possessed, and when among friends delights in hearing good stories, of which he himself is well supplied.

The demand of a western town of moderate size in a rich farming district is now so much larger than in former years that it exceeds the possibilities of the old assortment methods of former days, and looms up into double and treble proportions.

By careful attention Mr. S. has founded an industry much wider and attractive in its range, and the people manifest a disposition to buy. His notion house (on wheels) perambulates the streets of our country towns regardless of mud, and reports business lively. Long may he persevere and continue to sell sound notions to his customers.

In political views he is a staunch Republican, and during the war a consistent Union man, although the close attention paid his own business leaves but little time for participation in political life. He is proud of his ancestors, as he may have reason to be, but at the same time loves to dwell upon the difficult problems and stern realities of life which brought the family to its present eminence.

Some years ago he visited the writer in Salem county,

and was delighted with the kind-hearted people found in
the state.   He became acquainted with the late George
M. Swing at Fairton, and other members of our family;
visited the "old stone church" (Presbyterian) and the
M. E. church ; the graveyards, and also the farms of the
late Simon Sparks and Michael Swing, located on the
banks of the Cohansey river at Fairfield, N. J.

☞ I'll subscribe for a copy of the " Swing History,"
if it amounts to nothing but a primer.

OFFICE OF M. J. SWING,

WHOLESALE DEALER IN

NOTIONS, TRIMMINGS AND FANCY GOODS.

BETHEL, Ohio, Sept. 28th.

MY DEAR COUSIN :—

I write a line to inform you of my safe arrival home
after my visit to New Jersey.   We arrived at Bethel in
pretty good shape, the cold contracted while on the
journey having disappeared, and my health much improved.   The goods purchased in New York are coming every day, and we have plenty to do marking and
displaying them for sale.   Have just opened the box of
Duchess and Bartlett pears sent us ; they had ripened
while on the journey and were splendid.   Jersey soil
and air give fruit a peculiarly good flavor, if Jersey is
poor.

My trip throughout the Eastern states was very
enjoyable all the way ; not an accident or mishap of
any kind occurred.   Our people are anxious to hear

the report of my visit, and some description of the place where our ancestors first settled in America. A brief historical sketch of our family in the East and in the West would be very interesting; and as you are accustomed to writing and study, and enjoy a large correspondence with our people, I hereby propose that you proceed at once to write a biographical sketch, and "I'll subscribe for a copy of the 'history' if it amounts to nothing but a primer." Am glad at all times to hear from our people, and would be glad to see you again among the big trees growing around our settlement, some of which still survive the storms and axemen.

Here we can find quail, pigeon and prairie chicken. Almost every fall we go deer hunting to Michigan, West Virginia or Tennessee; have a new breech-loading Parker gun, weighing ten pounds, ten gauge, and have captured several deer and wild turkeys in my time. While tramping through the forest and over the mountains we usually have a guide, an old hunter, board with the backwoodsmen, and eat corn bread and bacon with great relish. Last fall our party was hunting on Walden's Ridge, within twenty miles of Chattanooga, Tennessee. I believe that any one who enjoys innocent amusement, hunting and fishing, will live longer and better. Such trips add ten years at least to a man's life, and make him more industrious, useful and happy at home.

SUCCESSFUL HUNTERS.

CLERMONT NIMRODS BAG THREE DEER AND COME HOME REJOICING.

Extract from the Clermont (Ohio) Sun.

CUMBERLAND MOUNTAINS, Nov. 30, '88.

Messrs. J. F. Knight, M. J. Swing and C. H. Homan arrived here Friday, the 16th inst., and have bagged to date one gobbler and three deer, one of them a fine large buck, It so happened that the whole party was together when all of them were killed. The first two killed were a large doe and her fawn. They intruded too close to where the party was sitting on a log resting. When they were discovered passing at our backs we turned suddenly and opened fire from the whole line, and the two fell dead in their tracks. Then, of course, we felt much proud. We got help and carried them in, dressed them, got a good warm supper at 'Squire Wm. Whittaker's, where we were stopping, talked deer during the evening and went to bed feeling first rate. To the eye and ear of experienced hunters there is no sight nor sound more grand and exciting than the music of a full pack of well trained dogs in full pursuit of game, and the sight of a noble stag running at full speed. One might suppose, from the long, branching horns that it would be difficult for them to force their way through the woods, but, in fact, its horns are a defense, as it lays them flat on its back and plunges through the forest with great rapidity.

In a few days after, the buck tackled us, when we

opened on him and downed him with only six loads. Then we grew a foot. It takes old hunters to down such game. Providence sent a young man to us with a strong mule, and as he offered to take our prize in for us, we loaded him on the mule, thereby making it easy for ourselves. Everybody in the mountains is just as clever to strangers as can be. We had many invitations to call upon persons with whom we met; in fact, it is the custom with all the mountaineers to invite anyone, though he be an entire stranger, to eat with them if they happen in at meal time. This is a very healthy country, and if it was not necessary to return to the land that gave us birth, would be glad to stay longer with those who have so kindly cared for us, but we expect to be in old Clermont ere this reaches the firesides of the readers of the *Sun*. Good bye, " my deer," till we meet again.

MERRICK.

CHAPTER XXVII.

ZACHARIAH RILEY.

A SOLDIER OF 1812 FALLEN.

ZACHARIAH RILEY, who has been a citizen of this county for more than sixty-five years, was buried in the Swing family graveyard, on the Ohio pike, on the 12th inst. His remains were taken into the M. E. church at Bethel, a large audience being present. The services were very impressive, consisting of scriptural reading, singing and prayer by Rev. G. W. Swing, after which the following was read by Rev. Chiney, preacher in charge:

Zachariah Riley, whose lifeless form lies before us here to-day, departed this life in peace on the 10th inst. at 9.30 A. M., at the residence of John Riley, his son, in Bethel, Ohio.

He was in his eighty-fourth year. He professed faith in Christ in early life. He was baptized—that is, immersed in water—in the name of the Holy Trinity, by Rev. John Collins, more than sixty years ago, by whom he was also received into the M. E. church, where he remained an acceptable member for several years, when he obtained a letter of good standing, and joined the Baptist church at Bethel, Ohio, in the fellowship of which church he remained until his release from his earthly tenement.

He was joined in marriage to Mary Swing (only daughter of George Swing) in 1816. Their family consisted of eleven children, nine sons and two daughters, eight of whom are still living, seven sons and one daughter. His wife closed her peaceful and quiet life in triumph over ten years ago.

He was a soldier in the war of 1812, and has regularly received the benefit of a pension as such. His eyesight failed him over twelve years ago, and though compelled to grope his way in gloom and darkness, abandoning forever many pleasures consequent upon the sense of sight, yet he was never heard to murmur or complain, or even deem his lot a hard one; but with an intellect vigorous for planning he found many avenues of pleasure and happiness to his mind that he might never have thought of if his sight had remained. From this loss he became more resigned, quiet and hopeful for the future, all vanity, worldly-mindedness and ambition were greatly abated, and in their stead more humility, charity and meekness, so that even this light affliction was greatly sanctified to his good. His memory, which was always good, was now greatly strengthened, his conversational powers much improved, and his love for old acquaintances greatly quickened. He delighted very much in talking with young people, giving his own experience and warning them of the dangers in their pathway. He was always peculiarly fond of children, and by kind talk, thrilling stories and many little presents and rewards he won them and bound their hearts to his so that they loved to meet him and lead and call him their own blind grandpa.

He was always fond of church privileges, and spent as many of his Sabbaths in the sanctuary of the Lord as almost any man among us. This was the habit of his life, and continued unto the last, having attended a series of meetings held here recently, in which he took an active part, giving of his joyful Christian experience.

For many years his desire, as expressed to his friends (and prayer to God as well), has been that he might not become helpless, or suffer much or long in his last illness.   It was even so; his sickness was only one short week and his sufferings very light, having quietly, gradually and painlessly breathed his life away, without a groan or struggle, or even a death frown.

His request was that no funeral sermon should be preached. A friend whom he had selected was to conduct the services with singing and prayer; he desired to be laid in his grave with as little trouble to any one as possible. His prayer in life was that he might die in peace, and his request to his children was that he might be buried quietly, and all to be free from the pomp and vanity of this world.   His pilgrimage has ended; his cloudy days are passed; his sufferings are over; his feet are through the journey, and may we not modestly hope that he has already realized the joy that is felt where there are no tears or troubles, no groans or graves, and where sorrow and sighing forever flee away?

CHAPTER XXVIII.

SAMUEL SWING.

SAMUEL SWING was born at Pittsgrove, Salem county, in 1810, and belonged to a generation whose active work is remembered only in the past. In early life he was interested in agricultural pursuits, the study of music and the military drill. One of his greatest triumphs was his ability to march in the military parades of the olden time, and handle the "drum sticks." Throughout the community he was known as the drummer boy, and from his youth up to middle age delighted in musical recreation.

In marriage he was united to Miss Elizabeth Van Meter, daughter of Deacon Erasmus Van Meter, a prominent land owner and stock grower of Salem county. After his marriage Mr. Swing removed to his farm, where they lived some thirty years, and his business activity ended only with his life. On Thursday, June 25th, he met with an accident; he was driving a pair of young horses into the barn with a load of hay, when his head and shoulders were jammed against the beam over the top of the door, causing his arms to be bruised and paralyzed, and fracturing the skull. After four days of

18

intense suffering death came to his relief. He died on
Monday, June 29, 1874, aged sixty-four years. He
leaves a widow and family of children, three of whom
survive him, to wit: Dr. E. V. Swing, of Coatesville,
Pa., Mrs. Ruth Dunham, and Mary Jane, the latter
named residing on the homestead farm.

In politics Mr. Swing was a Republican, a strong Union
man during the war, honest in his convictions, and withal .
regarded as a solid, substantial citizen. His sudden
death has left a vacant place in the home and family circle not easily filled.

> " If death our friends and us divide,
>   Thou dost not, Lord, our sorrow chide,
>   Nor frown our tears to see.
>   We feel a strong, immortal hope,
>   Which bears our mournful spirits up
>   Beneath their mountain load.
>
> " Pass a few fleeting moments more,
>   And death the blessing shall restore,
>   Which death has snatched away.
>   For us thou wilt the summons send,
>   And give us back our parted friend
>   In that eternal day."

[Extract from the National Standard, Salem, N. J.]

As we go to press we learn that the accident which
befell Samuel Swing has resulted fatally. The deceased
was driving a load of hay into his barn and his head
struck the beam over the doorway which rendered him
senseless, and paralyzed him so he could not move. He
lived until Monday about midnight, when he expired.
Interment and funeral service at the Presbyterian church,
Pittsgrove.

CHAPTER XXIX.

FREDERICK CARMAN.

MR. FREDERICK CARMAN, the subject of these remarks, was born in Deerfield township, Cumberland county, N. J., August 11, 1798. The name of his father was Frederick Carman. He was owner of a large farm near Allowaystown in Salem county, where he lived for many years. After this farm was improved, he sold it and bought another, near Woodruff's. His mother's maiden name was Catharine Fox. The names of his father's six children were Frederick, Mark, Margaret, Daniel and Polly; four of these are now living; two of them have finished their earthly course and passed away from the scene of earthly things. His first recollection of attending school was in a log school-house, near Woodruff's church. The names of our teachers were Mark Peck, John Rose, John Smith. Mr. Smith was a good teacher, a kind-hearted man; by his assistance he mastered addition, subtraction, multiplication and division. The names of many of his school companions are fresh in his memory, and the lessons learned in the old log school-house were never forgotten. In 1812 the war broke out between England and the United States.

FREDERICK CARMAN.

Father enlisted in the heavy artillery for eighteen months, and was stationed for a time at Fort Mifflin. He was absent in the service about one year. When he returned, his son Frederick, a boy of fifteen years, went with him to Fort Mifflin, and was examined by the recruiting officer, and enlisted May 11, 1813. A soldier's cap was placed on his head, a flint-lock musket in his hand, and he was assigned to duty on the outpost.

As the darkness of night began to gather around the place the boy examined his gun and assured himself that it was loaded, but was not sure that the flint was in perfect order. To test its good qualities he poured the priming out of the pan and snapped it, when, to his astonishment and surprise, the musket went off with a tremendous report. A few moments later the roll of the reveille sounded at camp, and an officer on horseback came galloping along the river bank. Halting at the post he inquired: "Did you fire that gun?" "Yes, sir," answered Frederick. "What for?" inquired the officer. Anxious to invent some excuse the officer was informed that the mosquitoes and green head flies were very troublesome, and in fighting them off his coat sleeve caught on the cock of the musket and the load was accidentally discharged. "You have no right to fire a gun without an enemy in sight," said the officer, "and I shall hereby order your arrest."

The next morning, Frederick, with two other offenders, were marched into the presence of Lieutenant Stewart and Major-General Beal, commanders of the fort.

"And what is the charge against this lad?" inquired

General Beal. "Firing off his gun and creating a false alarm on the outpost," said the sergeant.

The story of the flies and mosquitoes was repeated.

"Let's see your gun?" said the major-general, examining the lock. Handing it back to Frederick he said: "Show me how you were fighting the mosquitoes."

Then our hero went through the motions, but was unable in this way to spring the strong lock on the trigger.

"Ah!" said the major-general; "to the offence committed he certainly has added a lie. What shall be done with this man? We regret exceedingly to have him shot."

Then Frederick burst into tears and confessed to the truth. After some further conversation General Beal remarked: "We forgive the lad. Sergeant, take him away; give him another gun—one that is sure fire; and to-morrow night try him again on the outpost."

By strict attention to duty Frederick soon became a favorite among the officers, and being a good oarsman was often employed in rowing boats across the Delaware river to convey the officers to headquarters in Philadelphia.

After serving out the time of enlistment, they were sent to Philadelphia, received their pay and discharge from General Bromfield; the soldiers from Cumberland county returned home in a vessel. The young man's military achievements had made him deservedly popular among the young people, for he had lived in a time of extraordinary activity in the development of the country, and in the days that " tried men's souls" assisted to carry our banner through the storms of war to peace and freedom.

Mr. Frederick Carman and Miss Margaret Edwards were married November 11, 1821, by Rev. Holmes Parvin. The waiters were Mr. Ananias Edwards and Mary Fox, all of whom are now living. In 1821 Mr. Carman built a new house on the road to Woodruff's Mill, and commenced housekeeping in it. Here four children were born. In 1825 Mr. and Mrs. Carman joined the M. E. church during the ministry of Rev. Walter Burroughs. After living in this house eight years, he sold it and moved into Bridgeton. He did not locate along the creek, on the low ground, but purchased a lot on Laurel Hill, where the ground is high and the water runs deep and still. Here he built another house, and here three children were born. In 1834 he sold his property in Bridgeton, moved to the Lake, and purchased a farm there. Soon after his arrival, they both joined the M. E. church by certificate, and being the best singer in the congregation he was elected chorister, which office he filled for nearly fifteen years. He was also class leader in that church. The ministers who traveled Gloucester circuit during these years were the Revs. Abram Owen, Noah Edwards, H. S. Norris, S. Hudson, Joseph Atwood, Jonas R. Chew and L. O. Manchester; all these ministers were remembered and often entertained at Father Carman's house. He is a man who has always been active, industrious, a good citizen, kind neighbor and friend, useful in his family, in the church and in the community in which he lived. The father of ten children, he believed in the scriptural injunction, "Be ye fruitful, and multiply and replenish the earth." The names of the children were John, Eliza E., Frederick, Margaret, Mary, Rachel Jane, Gideon B., Lydia, Emily R. and Allen S.

It may be said that the religious life of Father Carman was not as a flashing meteor, but as one of the fixed stars, always in its place. He was relied on by his pastor, anxious to do his duty, and if called on to "testify" in meeting had not the inclination to refuse. At the Lake, and other places of residence, none was more respected and none took a livelier interest in the prosperity of the church and the welfare of the community.

His years increasing, and his family grown up, married and settled in other places, he again removed to the city of Bridgeton, where the family have enjoyed their annual reunions together, one of the largest of these gatherings being on Thursday, August 15, 1878, to celebrate the anniversary of his eightieth year. After partaking of a bountiful dinner, which was served in excellent style, the company assembled in the parlor at 2 o'clock P. M., and sung the hymn:

> "Blest be the tie that binds
> Our hearts in Christian love."

Prayer was offered by John Carman, of Vineland, and an address delivered by Gilbert S. Swing.

In closing this sketch of Mr. and Mrs. Carman, I

would just say, you have enjoyed a married life of nearly fifty-seven years together. Ten children are now living; they sit within the sound of my voice; they are all here to-day to unite their voice and their song in thanksgiving and praise.

Fifty-three grandchildren and thirteen great grandchildren, rise up "to call thee blessed." You have been acceptable members of the M. E. church for more than fifty years; you have chosen the better part which never can be taken away; you have fulfilled the duties of a long and useful life, and are now almost in sight of our Father's house in heaven.

EIGHTY YEARS OLD.

THE CARMAN FAMILY GATHERING.

The third annual gathering of the large and well-known family of Frederick Carman, met at his late residence, in this city, June 3, 1882, to celebrate the anniversary of the eightieth year of his surviving widow, Mrs. Margaret Carman.

Carriages from the country and passengers on the early trains reached the city at 10 A.M., some of the representatives residing at Newfield, the Lake, Vineland, Williamstown, Atlantic City and Cape May.

After enjoying a good dinner, the company was called to order by Charles Jepson, Esq., and addressed by Gilbert S. Swing. The speaker commenced by saying there were four things necessary to make a family gathering a success, to wit: A good reception, a good dinner, good music and a good speech. The reception, dinner and singing have been all that could be desired, but the address, it was feared, would be the least entertaining of all. Since coming here and looking upon this assembly of distinguished men, women and children, we have tried to escape this ordeal, but have been unable to effect a sale.

In the Bible we read, "In six days God created the heavens and the earth, and on the seventh day ended his work, rested from his labor and pronounced it good." Commemoration is natural to the heart, and therefore the usage of renewing the recollection of great events is commendable and worthy of praise. The degree of interest is in proportion to the character and value of that which is remembered. The birthdays of individuals are often celebrated, and marriage days as well. States and nations commemorate great events, such as William Penn's treaty with the Indians, the signing of the Declaration of Independence, July 4th, 1776, and the birthday of Washington. Thus it will be seen that days of commemoration have been observed through all periods of time, and ordained by our Creator from the foundation of the world. One of the most pleasant things connected with family re-unions is the coming home of the boys and the girls, who often continue to be boys and girls, even though their heads be tinged with the scars of life's battles.

We are coming home to-day to visit again for a little while the old familiar scene, to sit by the accustomed fire-

side and renew the companionship and the fraternal greetings of youth. Father and sons, mother and daughters,
sisters and brothers, parted in search of education, in
the struggle for wealth, are coming together again at
this time, and the vacant places at the table will be filled.
Like the patriarchs of old our people have killed the
fatted calf, and make merry with family and friends.
The delight that everyone feels while preparing to gratify, or even to surprise friends by kindly gifts; the satisfaction that comes to those who have contributed to the
happiness of others, brings with it so much amusement,
good feeling and personal enjoyment that it might be
well to keep the spirit of family reunions alive.

One of the ways in which our esteem is manifested is
in presenting gifts, and this will make us more disposed
to charity and better able to appreciate the happiness of
others.

It has been said by one of the ancient writers of the
olden time that true happiness consists in the following
sentiment: " Love to God and love to man, love to one
woman,—and the possession of a good hired girl."
(Laughter and applause.)

Coming down to later events, we meet together to
celebrate the anniversary and birthday of Mrs. Margaret
Carman, who was born in Deerfield township, Cumberland county, N. J., June 4, 1802. You may look upon
this venerable lady, moving around among her posterity
with a firm step and loving spirit, and in the enjoyment
of reasonable health ; surrounded by all the attractions
of home, by relatives, friends, and everything that con-

spires to make life agreable and existence a charm.
To Frederick I would say, "Your mother welcomes you
again to this family circle and to the home of your
father, and not only yourself, but the remaining nine
children from the storehouse, the farm, the factory and
the mill.   And our mother rejoices to know that among
her daughters were those whose comeliness and personal
charms were sufficient to allure young men into the
marriage relation, and thereby the family embraces not
only the illustrious name of Carman, but also those of
Kirby, Dougherty, Jepson, Swing and Johnson, and
these were the men who hope to make their names honored."

> " Lives of great men all remind us
>   We can make our lives sublime,
> And, departing, leave behind us
>   Footprints on the sands of time."

I now come to what may appear to you a more interesting and appropriate theme—the presentation of useful
and ornamental presents—among which I notice that of a
pair of gold spectacles, composed of glass and gold;
and through these glasses you may look upon the hearty
complexion of your daughter, may admire them as
patrons of neatness and household economy, or look
with eyes of love and wonder upon their gorgeous bon-
nets, and through these glasses read the Psalms of
David and the promises recorded in the Bible to the
Christian of the life that now is, and of that which is to
come.

It will be remembered that nearly four years ago a gathering, somewhat similar to this, convened in this house, it being the anniversary of your father, when in his eightieth year, and since that time deceased, and also one of his daughters, Mrs. Rachel Johnson, who died recently at Cape May, and passed away to the scenes of a brighter and better life.

When we leave this place and journey toward our distant homes, may we remember this occasion as being a day well spent, and memorable in the history of our lives.

CHAPTER XXX.

MICHAEL POTTER.

VISIT TO WILLOW GROVE—DESCRIPTION OF THE PLACE AND
PEOPLE, BY G. S. SWING.

ONE of the oldest villages in Salem county is Willow
Grove, located near the eastern part of the county
line, at the head of Maurice river navigation, twenty-
four miles from Salem, the county seat. Before the Revolution a few hardy pioneers and lumbermen located here and
engaged in cutting pine and cedar logs, and making
shingles for building purposes. These were floated
down the river in large rafts, finding a good market in
Philadelphia, Baltimore, and other cities.

For the first one hundred years of its history the place
was known as Fork Bridge, and obtained its name from
the circumstance of two large bodies of water coming
together at this point, one stream from Porch's Mills and
the other from Malaga, and both entering at the head of
the pond. Just below this was constructed a mill-dam
one-quarter of a mile in length, and a long bridge crossing the stream. This immense body of water is used for
driving two mills—one for sawing lumber, the other for
grinding grain and feed—while the waste water, of which

there is a vast amount, passes with a rumbling sound over the gates into the river below.

The date of the first building of those mills is unknown to the writer, but most of our older citizens will remember the names of the early settlers who resided here for three-quarters of a century. John Richman, James Edwards, Michael Potter, Richard Langley, Rev. John Clark, and his son, Rev. James Clark, both of whom in their day and time became eminent preachers of the gospel; Matthias and Adam Kandle, MacKendey Richman, Joshua Lacy, Reuben Langley, William Bowers, Felix English, John Wesley Potter, Rev. Samuel Woodford and David Garton, all of whom resided in this vicinity and owned mills, farms and tracts of timber land, raised large families of children, and lived to see almost the entire community grow up around them. Some of the industrious men herein named still linger on the shores of time, while others have solved the mystery of death and passed away, leaving brilliant records behind them.

The post-office is Willow Grove, named in honor of those majestic willow trees surrounding the water-course, one ancient mother tree measuring fourteen feet and ten inches in circumference. The village contains a couple of stores and a post-office, Michael Potter, Jr., being the postmaster; a church and school house, and several residences, around which are a number of well-tilled farms.

A large amount of ice is generally gathered here and

housed along the shore, and shipped in the summer to Vineland, Atlantic City, and other places.

Richard Langley & Son, the present owners of the mill, do a flourishing business, their brand of flour being in demand throughout the country. We found the miller, Z. W. Dare, who has long been engaged in this occupation, at his post of duty, and who richly deserves the position which he fills. He is a good-natured, portly gentleman, now in the meridian of life, with bright, piercing eyes, which scan the *Dollar Weekly News*, and keep well-posted in the price of corn, and enjoys life to its fullest extent.

Longevity appears to be one of the leading character-istics inherited by this people. Meeting a noted octo-genarian, living on the road from Porch's Mills to Willow Grove, a Salem county physician said to him: "Mr. Langley, I think you have the consumption." "What me? No, sir; nothing ails me. The doctors would like to get after me and make me sick. I never took much doctors' stuff. My wind is good, and I can out-chop all the doctors in Salem county." The good man then related how, in order to keep his teams going, he had caught cold while chopping in the woods in damp weather, and did not feel as well as usual. Another old resident informed me that he cast his first vote in 1806, and was out on last election day and voted for the seventy-seventh time. In his younger days he shot about one hundred deers, and on one occasion, with rifle balls, killed two at one shot.

Here was a sportsman's paradise, amid scenery of the most beautiful description, the forest abounding in game, and the pond and river teeming with fish. All the forest. to the south of this locality afforded good sport, and the hunter could take his choice of going a long or a short distance. Fifty years ago partridges and squirrels were very numerous. When a weak or lazy man went after game he took a boy with him to carry the load home, which they divided with friends and neighbors. The country that in his younger days was covered with a heavy growth of timber is now occupied by hundreds of valuable farms, and the game then abundant has almost disappeared from the busy haunts of men.

Half a mile from the village we pass the Richman farm—the flower garden of this locality. The dwellings were literally surrounded by climbing plants, sunflowers, clematis, Duchess of Edinburgh and Bourbon roses, dahlias, etc.

> "There woman reigns ; the mother, daughter, wife,
> Strew with fresh flowers the narrow way of life."

As we mused upon the scene before us, we thought it no sad fate to be a farmer, or a school teacher either, in such a corner of the earth.

For several years past it has been the custom of the descendants of Michael Potter, Sr., to celebrate the anniversary of his birth. Wednesday he reached his ninety-ninth birthday, and the event was celebrated by a family reunion which embraced nearly the whole settlement of

19

Willow Grove and many other persons besides. The residence is about three hundred yards west of the church. He built the house in 1811, in which year he was married, and here he has continuously resided. It is his boast that he has never moved since he married.

He visited the Centennial Exhibition in 1876, and is well known all over this and adjoining counties, but was never farther away from home than Philadelphia and Cape May. He is still hale and hearty, and goes into the woods with his axe to chop a little. He enjoys telling a " yarn."

A large table was spread under the oaks near the M. E. church, on which the ladies placed the best the market and farm could produce. At noon the older members of the family, with the invited guests, sat down to dinner, when the whole party joined in singing, " Praise God from whom all blessings flow," after which grace was said by the pastor of the church, Rev. J. G. Edwards. At this table were seated sixty-one persons. The table was loaded " with all manner of food "—roast chickens, roast meats, vegetables of all sorts, a dozen or more varieties of cake, fruit, confections, pies, coffee, tea, chocolate, rolls, butter, sauces, puddings, everything the appetite could desire. Near the upper end of the table, and between two of his sons, sat the aged patriarch. Any one looking at him or listening to him would take him to be about eighty years of age. He was dressed in a blue coat, with dark satinet pants and vest. He is a small man, and quite hale and hearty. He ate heartily and with as much relish as any young man at the table, of chicken, beef, vegetables, cake and pie, and drank two cups of coffee. While eating a piece of cake a young lady approached with a plate of cake, and said: "Grandfather, will you have a piece of this cake?" He replied, pleasantly, " No, I've got enough."

Mr. Potter is the father of eleven children—seven sons and four daughters. Eight of them are still living, two sons and one daughter are dead. All lived, however, to have families. He had the pleasure yesterday of having all his living sons present, a circumstance which has not occurred before for a number of years. One daughter, Mrs. Ambrose Pancoast, of Pancoastville, has been many years an invalid, and could not be present.

Mr. Potter is quite a local celebrity. He was a militia officer in the third company of the Salem brigade during the war of 1812. He still has his epaulettes and sword. He says : " I was the ensign of the company, and was afterwards made its captain. I have one of the handsomest swords there was in the regiment—the hilt is solid silver."

He married in 1811, his wife dying June 25, 1863, twenty years ago last month. The names of his children are John W. Potter, deceased, Matthias R. Potter, Jacob Potter, Henry Potter, Emeline Pancoast, Hannah Kandle, deceased, Ephraim K. Potter, deceased, Charlotte Sharp, Lydia A. Clark, Michael Potter, Jr., and James K. Potter.

After the first table was served, a second table of sixty-two persons were seated, and after that a third table of forty-three, and after that a lot of stragglers. There was an abundance of food for all.

The old gentleman likes to talk, and he talks intelligently and in a very sprightly manner. When Miss Leavitt approached him to shake hands she said, " You don't know me, do you ? " "Oh, yes," he replied, "but my eyesight is a little poor." He does not use glasses, but he can see to tell the time on a watch.

He said : " My father's name was Henry Oxinbaker ; he was a German, and came from Germany. He was a potter by trade, and people used to call him ' old Henry the potter,' and that is how we came by the name of Potter. My mother's name was Christine Mooney, and she came from the Blue Mountains in the northern part of the state. My parents died at about sixty-nine or seventy years of age, but my old Grandmother Mooney was pretty old ; she used to say she was over a hundred, but she wasn't, for towards the last she used to forget and gain ahead and think she was older than she was ; but she always remembered that she was just twenty years old when her son, Adam, was born ; so I got the old Dutch Bible and saw what year Adam was born in, and then I added twenty years to that and that made her ninety-seven years old when she died."

" You have always been very healthy, have you not?" was asked him. "Well, yes ; I never took $10 worth of medicine in my life ; I never had much doctor's stuff in me." He related how he was taken sick once and how he got his mother to put on the big pot to sweat it out of him, and how he ate a piece of pig-tail tobacco to induce vomiting. He said he never used tobacco and was never drunk but once in his life, and that was when he was between boy and man. He said: "I never saw but one man who could out-jump me. He was a little fellow and could jump thirty-six feet forwards or backwards. I could jump thirty-two feet. John Hankins used to think he was a great jumper, but I beat him at Port Elizabeth. He was jumping off the tavern steps, and had great holes where he had jumped. I out-jumped him three or four inches. Very few men could throw me wrestling. Jim Creese and Joe Dallas and others came here to Fork Bridge to put up a mill; they were millwrights, and Joe Dallas wanted to know who was the bully of Fork Bridge, and when they told him I was, he said, what, that little fellow? Well, I'll be the bully now. When we come to wrestle I threw him twice out of three times, and the last time he tried to jump over me and catch the 'crotch lock' but I threw him over my head, and when he came down it hurt him; he did not wrestle with me any more. This was before I was married, and became a meeting man. I built my house then and moved into it, and I've never moved since. I followed floating lumber from here and from Malaga to Millville and Port Elizabeth for forty years. I floated for Sam Downs, Aquilla Downs, Bill Chew and others. There is not one of them living now. I used to go with Polly Stewart, Betsy Stewart and Nancy Stewart, who lived about Tuckahoe. I used to court Betsy Stewart. They are all dead, all passed away, gone home ahead of me."

Mr. Potter was for more than sixty years the sexton of the church of which he was and is still a member. He was born in 1784 and consequently has lived through the term of every president of the United States but the present one; he has seen the administration of the twenty-one presidents. He was born three years and two months before the adoption of the constitution, and he still has a quantity of continental money. The remark was made that he had voted a good many times and it was supposed he voted a good Democratic ticket. The old man smiled and said shrewdly, " They give me a ticket and tell me that it is the right one," but he added, " I voted for John T. Nixon when he ran for congress. I was a judge of election then and the other man was a ' no heller,' and carted the men around and gave them rum, so I wouldn't vote for him. I voted for Nixon because I thought he was the best man." In politics he has always been a Democrat, and yet, strange to say, the greater portion of his male descendants are Republicans, which goes to show that they did not follow the old gentleman's political teachings.

All the relatives present collected on seats together to the number of 175, to be photographed; Grandfather Potter in the centre, with his sons and sons-in-law and daughters-in-law at his side. Then the three oldest persons in the company were photographed together, Mr. Potter, aged 100, Bartholomew Cole, 99, Mrs. Hosea Joslin, 89.

After dinner the assemblage repaired to the church, filling it completely, where a service of song was held, and speeches made by Revs. J. L. Roe, J. G. Edwards and Samuel Woolford, Mr. Potter also expressing his obligations to those present in a very neat speech. He said: " I am very thankful that God has taken care of me until this time. I have a goodly number of blessings and I am glad to see so many of my descendants and friends here to-day. I have been spared many years to serve God, and I feel very thankful that so many of you have come here to-day. I am ninety-nine; I don't wish to live a hundred years. Whenever I get so I cannot take care of myself I want to go home. I now understand what old Daddy Long used to say when he was preaching, ' Or the silver cord is broken, or the golden bowl is broken, and the windows became darkened,' &c.; I did not understand it then, but now I understand it all. I am ready to go home. I am glad you are here and I hope you will all enjoy yourselves." Mr. Ambrose Pancoast made a few remarks in which he said that the father and all the children and most all the grandchildren were Methodists, and that in all this large family there were none who drank liquor or who used profane language. The old man's hearing seems to be still perfect, and his voice is clear and distinct ; he says he feels signs of decay in his eyesight, and in his toes; in all other respects he feels as well as he did a year ago.

THE CELEBRATION AT WILLOW GROVE.

INCIDENTS OF THE LIFE OF MICHAEL POTTER.

Yesterday morning dawned bright and clear, and at daybreak, almost, people began to congregate at Willow Grove to join in celebrating the 100th anniversary of the birth of Michael Potter. By 10 o'clock there were 500 people at the Grove, and every hour thereafter augmented the number, until 5 o'clock in the afternoon there were fully 3000 people on the grounds. As he is a well-known citizen in this end of the state, the occasion was made one of great festivity. Every road leading to Willow Grove was lined with carriages and wagons, and scores of people from Bridgeton, Millville, Vineland, Pancoastville, Salem, Woodstown and other places were present. It is estimated that there were 500 vehicles on the grounds during the day. People flocked there from all parts of South Jersey, and were anxious to see the old man, and to shake his hand. The old gentleman bore up bravely all day, and did not show any unusual fatigue when night came. The Vineland Cornet Band furnished the music for the occasion, and right good music it was, too.

This patriarch was born and has always lived at Willow Grove, where he has spent a quiet, pious, uneventful and happy life. He is the father of eleven children, having married Lydia Richman, who was born in 1793, and died in 1863. They were united in Willow Grove on the 31st of July, 1811. All of their eleven children grew up and married, and seven of them are still living, besides nine children-in-law. The total number of the descendants of the venerable centenarian is about two hundred and fifty, most of whom are living to-day.

When the couple went to housekeeping they had two rooms 18x16, one above and one below. The family increased and every time a new arrival would put in an appearance, Mr. Potter would make a division of the 18x16 room, and he continued making divisions until he had four rooms made out of the original one. The family continued to increase, so he converted a shed into an addition to his house, which contained two rooms, a dining-room and a bed-room. The usual arrival came, and it was necessary to divide this bed-room into two rooms. Just about ten years before his wife died he built another addition to his house, and the house stands that way to-day. It is two stories high, and is only a short distance from the church. His children all lived to grow up and marry. Mr. Potter never married again. He was faithful to his first and only love. He says he has been a granddaddy a great many years. His wife's tombstone can be seen in the M. E. cemetery. She died at the age of seventy years and five months.

TWO OLD MEN.

While Michael Potter was the chief attraction, there was still another gentleman there who crowds him pretty close in age. This gentleman was Mr. Bartholomew Coles, who lives near Harrisonville, in Piles Grove township. Mr. Coles turned his ninety-ninth mile stone the 7th inst., and says he celebrated his birthday by mowing. Mr. Cole appeared in very good health and held himself quite upright. He was born near Cole's mills, which was named after him, and was one of a family of eleven, all of whom he survives. He has several great-great-grandchildren living. His hair is perfectly white, and his eyes are dim, but he is not bald, and his erect carriage makes him appear as if he might live ten years to come. Mr. Potter is able to walk by using two canes, and Mr. Coles is able to "go it alone." It was entertaining to listen to these old patriarchs talk over "ye olden times."

Some characteristics: Mr. Potter says he never used whiskey to any extent. He said he used to take a little "applejack" when he worked in the harvest field, but he never made it a practice to drink anything in the way of intoxicants. He has never used tobacco. He has never taken a dose of medicine in his life, and never employed a physician but once. He related that he had cut his leg and the physician upon whom he called to sew it up made such a bungling job of it that he vowed he would never have anything to do with doctors again, and he has scrupulously kept his vow. He regarded doctors as humbugs; was in the habit of going to bed early, and getting up at five o'clock. He used to weigh 144 pounds when young, and butchered hogs with the best of them. He was a shoemaker by trade, and also a farmer and lumber merchant. Up to two years ago he could read a newspaper. He can hear distinctly, and he possesses all his other faculties.

There is nothing childish about him, and he knows by name nearly the whole long train of Potters. He sat yesterday in a chair perched upon a dry goods box, where he was at all times hemmed in by a curious crowd. Hundreds of his acquaintances shook hands with him. The old gentleman is brimful of interesting reminiscences, and was a great deer hunter in his younger days. He killed ten deer in Salem county, and a good many in Gloucester, Atlantic and Cumberland. At one time he shot two deer with one shot, an old flint lock being used.

"I kept up my hunting until about three years ago. One day I took the musket and followed the boys out. I tried to use it, but my sight and my strength failed me, and I had to come home and hang it on the rack for the last time. The last deer I shot was when I was ninety-four years old. I haven't seen a deer since that time."

He has owned the old flint-lock ever since he was a boy fifteen years old, an eighty-five-year old gun.

This was the thirteenth reunion of the Potter family, as it has been their custom for several years to hold one on "grandfather's birthday." Over two hundred of the Potter family, descendants of Michael, were photographed in a body. The old gentleman ate a hearty dinner of chicken, bread and butter, coffee, etc.

A service was held in the church, at which Rev. Dr. Charles H. Whitecar was the orator. At half-past 10 the services in the church were announced. Only a quarter of those present could crowd into the little edifice. "His mercy endureth forever," with Miss Addie Smith

at the organ, was the opening of the programme. A
scripture selection was then read by Mr. Pepper, editor
of the *Christian Standard*, of Philadelphia. Rev. Mr.
Matthews, a former pastor of the church, lead in prayer,
thanking God that the good old man who had brought
them together sought and found the Lord in his early
days.   Rev. Dr. Whitecar opened his discourse with
the remark that the aroma of other occasions made the
place fragrant for the present morning. They had not
forgotten the distinguished men who had made previous
celebrations pleasant.   He told an incident connected
with Mr. Potter's history. Three years ago, while in
charge of the Foundry church, the preacher went to
speak at a camp meeting. There a youth was converted,
and he called upon Father Potter, who was present, to
come forward and lay his hands on the boy's head and
give him his blessing. The scene was worthy the pencil
of a Raphael.

July 18, 1784, which witnessed the birth of Michael
Potter, was an interesting period. Washington had just
resigned his commission as commander-in-chief of the
American armies. Our country was without a constitution, and Methodism had no organization. Michael
Potter had paralleled his country. He had watched its
growth from three to fifty-two million population. He
was born in the age of rushlights, open fireplaces and
rugged roads, and he lives in this age of steam and electricity.

The doctor concluded with a poem composed for the
occasion, commencing :

> " Hail!   Chieftain of one hundred years.
>   Nobly you stand amid your clan ;
>   Your age and virtue still endear to all,
>   Most venerable man."

---

101 YEARS OLD.

CELEBRATION AT WILLOW GROVE—HOW MICHAEL POTTER'S 101st
BIRTHDAY WAS COMMEMORATED—WHO WAS THERE AND WHAT
WAS DONE.

All was beautiful in nature on the morning of July 18,
1885, as the sun arose and reflected its bright and cheerful rays upon the sparkling waters in front of the ancient
village of Willow Grove.   At early morn the people were
astir in anticipation of the gathering multitude to witness
the celebration of Michael Potter, who had now attained
the remarkable age of 101 years.   The centenarian was
found to be quite feeble in health and not sufficiently
recovered from his recent sickness to attend the celebration.

During a part of the day he sat in his invalid chair,
received company, and also had his photograph taken.
In the same little room at the farmhouse, to which he
took Miss Lydia Richman, his bride, in 1811, the centenarian still sleeps, calmly and peacefully waiting the
approaching end and the dawning of immortality.

The old patriarch, though feeling the weight of his
years, is still perfectly rational and hopeful, and until
within some eight weeks Mr. Potter was able to do some

work and build the fires for his son. He told us he had thought at times he was going home, but, to give his words, it all fell through and passed over, and the old man can't see why he is spared while others were taken. He said his faith in his Father above was strong, and that this religion was good enough for him to die by if he was 101 years old. Who would not crave for such a sustaining faith as this, that makes the way bright in youth and brighter still in old age.

About a quarter of a mile north of the farmhouse is located the mill, the school house and the church. Beneath the shade of these venerable trees, which perhaps have withstood the storms of a hundred years, and beneath whose shade Rev. John Clark, Michael Potter, Kay Richman, Adam Kandell, Reuben Langley, and other patriots have played in their boyhood, long rows of tables were spread and amply supplied with all the good things of this life. Among the assembly were some of the prominent and aged citizens of Cumberland, Salem and Gloucester counties.

In the afternoon the guests were invited into the church near by, and as the speakers passed down the aisle the choir sang the hymn in which occurs the beautiful verse :

> " Still hold the stars in Thy right hand,
>   And let them in thy lustre glow ;
>   The lights of a benighted land,
>   The angels of thy church below."

Speeches were then made on the subject of family reunions by Rev. J. P. Connelly, of Willow Grove;

James Coombs, of Pittsgrove ; G. S. Swing, of Bridgeton; Samuel Woolford and Rev. J. G. Edwards, of Gloucester circuit.

Mr. Swing also read a letter from President Cleveland, offering his congratulations to Father Potter on the advent of his 101st year. He also stated that the aged centenarian cast his first vote in 1806, and in 1809 voted for James Madison, the fourth president of the United States, and had voted at all of the presidential elections since that time.

THE PRESIDENT OF THE UNITED STATES WRITES TO A BRIDGETON GENTLEMAN CONCERNING WILLOW GROVE'S CENTENARIAN.

Druggist Harry Camm, of this city, in reply to a letter sent by him, received the following answer, tendering through him the congratulations of the chief executive of our country to "the oldest Democrat extant." This is a rare honor, and Mr. Potter may indeed feel proud upon obtaining the letter. Its phraseology is exquisite, and it will no doubt be widely read, and with great interest.

EXECUTIVE MANSION,
WASHINGTON, July 9, 1885.

H. V. CAMM, ESQ.

Dear Sir:—I cannot resist the temptation to comply with the request contained in your letter of the 7th inst., and tender through you to Mr. Potter my congratulations upon his attaining the age of 101 years.

I am sure that he can justly claim to be the oldest Democrat extant. The fact that adherence to the principles and faith of that party has not, in Mr. Potter's case, been inconsistent with wonderful longevity, ought, I think, to reassure those of our fellow citizens who believe (if their professions are reliable) that American institutions are in danger from Democratic supremacy.

It is fitting and proper that the neighbors of this aged man should, on the anniversary of his birth, cordially demonstrate their esteem and veneration for one who lived before the constitution and who had seen the growth and progress of the country from the beginning.

But in the midst of their congratulations they may well renew their pledge of devotion to the cause of American freedom and the perpetuity of our government under the constitution, with gratitude to God who has thus far preserved our national life, and with devout acknowledgment of the power of Him who holds our destiny in the hollow of his hand.

Yours sincerely,
GROVER CLEVELAND.

[Extract from the address of James Coombs, Esq., at the Potter Family Reunion.]

Having been requested by the family to make a few remarks, I would just say that I have known Mr. Potter for more than half a century, and can cheerfully bear testimony to his industrious habits and good citizenship.

We notice that most of this assembly are farmers, and agriculture is the largest and most important interest in Salem county. Let us look for a moment at the condition of things when Mr. Potter first settled here. But few horses were then owned in this part of the state, and when cows were bought they were fed on coarse wild grass, and often became lost in the woods and died from exposure. The horses and cattle of that day were not to be compared with the beautiful animals now seen in our fields, and the ox was small and inferior.

Mr. Potter had lived, I might say, in the time of the spinning-wheel, the sickle and the flail. In those days the farmer and his family wore homespun, and the spinning-wheel and loom were a part of the household furniture. The grain raised was principally rye and corn, and when we remember that no attention was paid to the cultivation of grass, and very few vegetables now existing were then introduced, it is difficult to appreciate fully the changes which have been made within the past hundred years. The fact is, I well remember myself driving all over Broad Neck, looking for harvest hands to cradle wheat and mow grass, and occasionally found a man who thought he could not work in the harvest field without whiskey or applejack.

In 1833 a mechanic named Schnebley, of Maryland, obtained a patent for a machine for mowing grass. Obed Hussey, of Baltimore, patented another machine soon after for reaping grain. The last-named has been used from that time to the present day, and has furnished, in fact, the basis for the most successful reaping machines

20

in this country. Some years later McCormick, of Virginia, and Manney and Atkins, of Illinois, appeared on the field with their inventions, but none of these machines attained perfection until within the past ten years.

The improvement in schools and medicine should also be noticed. I remember, when a person was sick, it was formerly the custom for the doctor to bleed, and blood was drawn for the cure of almost every disease. There is no more important branch of science to the human race than how "to preserve the health of the mind and body," nor any in which more advance has been made within the present century. Old things and theories are indeed passing away, and new ideas, born of closer observation and more practical results, are taking their places. Blood-letting, once so popular, is resorted to only in very rare cases, and the use of calomel for all the "ills that flesh is heir to" is largely abridged. The accepted limit of three score years may be reached by many mcre, if people would use moderately the good things of life.

For fourteen years Mr. Potter has held public "birth-day celebrations," and the life of the patriarch has been long and eventful. I am gratified to attend this family reunion and offer congratulations. His great age speaks well for the longevity and healthfulness of a citizen of Pittsgrove township.

G. S. Swing was next introduced, and said:

Ladies and gentlemen, our acquaintance with Father Potter began some thirty years ago when I was

stationed near this place as a teacher in the public school.
The memories of " Good Hope," Lower Neck, Center-
ville and Willow Grove will never fade away from
memory. In these places we have known the names of
hundreds of children, and striven to train them up for
usefulness and honor. The coming home of the boys
and girls is one of the most pleasant things connected
with family reunions, and we rejoice to-day that you have
lived to see so many birthday anniversaries. We also
rejoice to know that so many good and useful men were
born and lived in Pittsgrove township, and you have
been led to honor the names of Potter, Parvin, Richman
and Clark, and a host of other illustrious sons. We
meet here to-day not only to honor the living, but to
pay a passing tribute to the dead—to those whose lights
have gone out along the shores of time. And then,
here is another fact worthy of mention: ever since the
days of the Revolution, honest men and good-looking
women have been found in Salem county; many a gay
couple have indulged in a grand, pompous swell. Some
have made their first public appearance here on the marriage day; and you know, when a young man is looking
for his intended, he is looking for a perfect woman:

> " A perfect woman, nobly planned
> To warn, to comfort and command;
> And yet a spirit still and bright,
> With something of an angel's light."

(Applause.) In coming to this place again, we are gratified to notice many improvements—a new school house,

new church, and those large, majestic trees, under whose wide-spreading branches this company have enjoyed their entertainment to-day. Do not cut down those large trees, friends, for they are among the "ancient land-marks" of Willow Grove and should never be destroyed.

In reviewing the life and history of this good and useful man and his record of one hundred years, there springs up within my heart a feeling of admiration, and I rejoice that a citizen of Pittsgrove township has attained the age of one hundred and one. This community honors and respects him, not only for himself, but for his character, for his integrity, and judgment and iron nerve. Be content to follow the path marked out by providence. " Keep a stout heart, a clear conscience, and never despair."

To my mind, there is nothing more grand and inspiring than to look upon the countenance of an aged man like Mr. Potter, who is well preserved in health and strength, standing on the battlements of truth and nearing the shores of a well-spent life. Oh, that this may be our happy experience! And may we finally enjoy a grander and better family reunion—if not in this life—in that blessed country where the stars never set, the eye never grows dim, and the river of waters shall never run dry. (Applause.)

[Extract from the address of Rev. J. G. Edwards, of Gloucester Circuit.]

I would just say that I remember Father Potter very well. He was sexton of this church, I think, about sixty years, and has stood by the open grave of many of our people. To-day, while in feeble health, he is resting and calmly waiting to be called home—anxious to see "the King in his beauty." While I was pastor on this charge his religious expressions were bright and encouraging, and he was enabled to look beyond the cares and perplexities of this present life, in anticipation of the dawning of a brighter day. At one of our last extra meetings on this charge he gave a testimony something like this:

"I have great cause to bless God for his goodness to me. My father and mother told me to be a good boy, and God would take care of me. He has done so all these years, and is able to keep me to the end. Some nights I felt weary and faint, and thought I might die; but it all passed over. I am with you to-day, and trust that our religious experience will be brighter and better further on."

Rev. Samuel Woolford, of Willow Grove, was next introduced, and said:

"Friends and Fellow-Citizens, I have some acquaintance with these old settlers, having spent a portion of my life among this people. I did not expect to be called upon to address this assembly, and feel reluctant to speak, but cheerfully respond, however, to say a word for Mr. Potter—one of those old-style, good-natured, reliable men whom this community delights to honor."

And then he poured forth a torrent of eloquence which had rarely been equalled before. At this point the eyes of the reporter became dim, and the pencil fell from his grasp.

Rev. J. P. Connelly, in closing his remarks, by way of pleasantry, said :

"The Democratic party is now in the ascendency ; we have just heard from the President ; but over in another part of Salem county we have another centenarian, a Mr. Coles, a Republican, who is vigorously strong, and may yet win in the race of longevity. This is caused by leading a temperate, industrious and religious life. Father Potter neither chewed tobacco nor drank rum. Long life is not attained through politics; if it was, we might all turn Democrats. (Applause.) We have enjoyed a grand time here to-day, my friends, and, as regards myself, I feel like spending the next one hundred years among the good people of Willow Grove."

The long metre doxology was then sung, and the company dispersed. Thus ended the one hundred and first anniversary.—*Extracts from Evening News.*

JAMES COOMBS.

The funeral oration recently pronounced in the Presbyterian church marked the close of the career of James Coombs. It was notable from the fact that many

oi his employees attended the service as a tribute to
their late master, while numerous mercantile, insurance
and banking institutions in which he was interested when
alive also sent representatives, for the deceased had been
favorably known. He was born in Salem county, N. J.,
in the spring of 1804, and his ancestors were numbered
among the first families of that name who settled in that
portion of the state, and extensively engaged in agricultural work. During his early years he was engaged in
teaching, was also employed as a surveyor of land, and
drifted then into agricultural pursuits. Besides superintending the cultivation of a large farm he was teacher at
the Washington Seminary. He subsequently resigned
teaching and became a business man in the full sense of
that word; had the spirit and courage of Stonewall
Jackson, and all through life his motto was "onward."
"If you upset your cart and spill your milk, drive on,
for the world is full of life and activity; and in Uncle
Sam's country there's room enough for every man to
own a farm."

Mr. Coombs was one of the noblest looking men of
his time. He had a massive head, a splendid blue-grey
eye ; and there was a frank, kindly look in his face and
an expression of dignity in his whole appearance. He
always had an affinity for good horses and stock, and
was a large man in every sense of the word, large heart-
ed, large intentioned and never did things by halves.
He was the owner of a good farm of nearly 600 acres
and it was not unusual for him to market a thousand
bushels of wheat and two thousand bushels of corn a

single season.   He raised large beeves and plenty of
them; had large droves of sheep, and slaughtered mammoth porkers, sending to market some of the handsomest stock produced in South Jersey.

The deceased was married but once, to a Miss Henrietta DuBois.   Six children were born to them, four of
whom are still living.   In politics he was an active Republican, popular among his neighbors and frequently
elected to office.   As a man he was instructive, social,
temperate, industrious, and kept business moving on.
With a strong, sympathetic face, a warm, generous enthusiasm of manner, a friend to the laboring man and
the poor, his likeness will be missed in the house of his
friends.

[*Extract from the Daily Morning Star.*]

THE LATE JAMES COOMBS' FUNERAL.

The funeral of the venerable James Coombs, a well-known and highly respected Salem county farmer, who
died in the eighty-second year of his age at his residence near Shirley, August 19th, 1886, was an interesting occasion.

The day was a most lovely one, the ride to the residence of the deceased being through one of the richest
sections of this part of New Jersey.   Taking all things
into consideration, we very much doubt whether a finer
agricultural country can be found anywhere in the
United States than is the greater part of the land lying
along the route from Bridgeton to Daretown.   It is an

astonishing feature of the landscape how many handsome structures have recently been erected where formerly stood plain buildings of no architectural adornment whatever. The land, of course, is under a proportionately high state of cultivation, showing general thrift in the management and ownership.

We arrived before the great body of attendants at the funeral; carriages were seen coming one after the other from various directions, and by the time specified for the movement of the cortege to the burial ground, several hundred of the sturdy and substantial neighbors of the deceased, with many old friends from a distance, had gathered at the house, all intent in showing their high regard for one they so much respected during life. In the absence of the pastor, who was on his vacation, a former pastor of the Daretown church, Rev. William A. Ferguson, now of Ohio, being on a visit, officiated. The church was filled in every part and by an audience rarely to be seen in any locality.

Mr. Ferguson read a chapter from Matthew, then the choir beautifully sang "Jesus, lover of my soul," being accompanied by the fine organ, when, after prayer, the text from II Kings 11:11 was discoursed from in the most fitting terms, and in a style but few ministers of the day could surpass. At the close Mr. F. spoke most touchingly and in eulogistic terms of the character of the deceased, especially referring to his great kindness of heart, integrity and earnest patriotism. It is impossible for us to give even an abstract of his remarks, which were so appropriate to the occasion, and in this instance true to the very letter, as everyone within the sound of his voice could assent.

At the conclusion of the sermon the body was exhibited in the vestibule of the church for the last time on earth. All who had not seen his placid and natural features at the house took occasion to momentarily gaze thereon. In the meantime the organ played "Nearer my God to thee." The carriages moved thence to the old burying ground a few rods beyond, where the body was deposited by the side of his wife, who had preceded him to the better world beyond the grave. Next to the mother lies the son, Albert, a member of the 12th New Jersey vols., who died in the service of the Union.

Mr. Coombs had been for forty years a director of the Cumberland (National) Bank and for thirty-five years a director of the Cumberland Mutual Fire Insurance Company. Messrs. William G. Nixon, president, Charles F. Elmer, Jonathan Elmer, Richard Lott were present and represented the directors of Cumberland bank. Messrs. D. P. Elmer, president, Dr. George Tomlinson, Charles S. Fithian, Ephraim Lloyd, secretary, represented the Cumberland Fire Insurance Company. The pall bearers were James Hurst, James Summerill, Henry DuBois, Harmon Lawrence, Elijah Eastlack, John M. Swing.

CHAPTER XXXI.

REMINISCENCES OF MY LIFE.

BY A. R. SWING, OF WASHINGTON CITY, D. C.

THE eldest son of Leonard Swing, Abraham R., was born in Pittsgrove in the year 1826. The early years of life were spent on the farm, in going to day and Sunday schools, and in learning the carpenter's trade with my mother's brother, David Shough, at Allowaystown. In the schoolboy days there was more pleasure in such books as Riley's and Bruce's " Narratives of Travel and Adventure " than in arithmetic. Mungo Park had a warm sympathy : his sufferings and captivity among the Moors ; the compassionate African matron who rescued him, half starved, weary and dejected; took him to her hut, fed him and then sang a sweet, plaintive chorus:

> "The poor white man, faint and weary,
>   No mother has he to bring him milk,
>   No wife to grind his corn."

To instill patriotism in one's soul there was that grand martial lyric, by Fitzgreene Halleck :

A. R. SWING.

> " Strike till the last armed foe expires,
>   Strike for your altars and your fires,
>   Strike for the green graves of your sires,
>   God and your native land."

At home we, "like our uncles and our cousins and our aunts," were natural born singers. There were religious books and newspapers. The " Pilgrim's Progress " was the best, I think; Baxter was rather unmerciful and harsh; Edwards, I thought, was awful; would prefer the Bible to the old theologians always; in it wrath is always tempered with kindness, love and mercy' There was something awe-inspiring in the ministers of those days. It was somewhat so of Rev. Mr. Janvier and Rev. Mr. Ker; especially was it thus of the Rev. Dr. Jones, of Bridgeton; his grand dignity, his noble physique, his solemn delivery, appeared something more than human. But that—ah! that was long ago. Intervening years have dispelled these illusions.

Political affairs did not have any attraction for the boys until the days of Harrison and Tyler, Tippecanoe and the Log Cabins. General Harrison must have been the most popular man ever run for president; no one ever before or since got so many electoral votes. He died in the White House just one month after his inauguration. Thus it was Tyler became president. Years after, he renounced his allegiance to Uncle Samuel and joined the confederates, and while seeking to destroy the government over which he had presided was taken sick and died in 1862.

In those years of struggle for, or to retain, political power, "death loved a shining mark." General Taylor was president but one year and four months, when he died suddenly in July, 1850. Along these years literature was improving and more diffused. Greeley and the *Tribune* became a power in the land; William Cullen Bryant edited the New York *Evening Post*. "Thanatopsis," that exquisite, solemn strain of blank verse, with its tender reveries of the woods, attested the great charm of Bryant's genius. There was also Henry Wordsworth Longfellow, with the delightful "Voices of the Night" and the "Song of Hiawatha." Then, to the delight of old and young, comes Captain Marryatt with "Jacob Faithful" and "Midshipman Easy." In retrospective, "distance lends enchantment to the view."

In November, 1849, I married Letitia Gilman Smick. The children were : Anthony W., Ella Josephine, Clement L. and Lenora Maud. I had a pleasant home and surroundings in Salem county; put up buildings in the neighborhood, some in Cumberland and Gloucester counties; was engaged two years on public buildings in Salem ; the year following, on a row of stores and dwellings in Salem for Dr. Patterson; three years on some fine buildings in Philadelphia, and a season at Cape Island on the mammoth hotel work.

In November, 1869, moved to Heathsville, Northumberland county, Virginia; was engagad in farming, building, wood and lumber operations. In the following year the state had an election under the new constitution, previously adopted. Military rule ceased, to the joy of the people. I was elected county clerk ; had an office in the court house.

The people were pleasant and social. I had a large acquaintance, having business with a great many people. Schools were established for colored children. One I built myself; it was twenty-five by sixty feet, two stories ; others, not so large. We got up some cottages for the teachers on the Gothic order, side to the front, door in centre, roof very steep, a high, steep gable in the roof over the front door, pediments, hoods, etc., one and a half stories high. They were much admired, and will grow in favor.

General Howard, of the educational department of the Freedmen's Bureau at Washington, furnished one thousand dollars for school buildings. Checks of princely donations came from the North. My plan was to engage a vessel to take five hundred cords of wood, more or less, to Baltimore, dispose of it to the best advantage, get my checks cashed at the bank, load up the craft with flooring, shingles, sash, doors, nails, builders' hardware, and whatever else was wanted. The publishers of Webster's Unabridged donated all the dictionaries needed, sent funds and supported teachers in the work for years. They were all white ladies from the North, mostly Massachusetts, well educated and accomplished.

I built a county bridge over Coan river, said to be the best bridge ever built in that region of country.

The climate was pleasant. The old, wornout soil responded generously to fertilizing ; great place for vegetables and fruit, oysters and game. Through my own plantation, north and south, there was a large stream and some meadow that afforded pasture all the year round. There were two hundred acres in timber, part original growth, oak, chestnut, poplar and pine. The wood on both sides of the stream was part of an un-broken line of forest from the Rappahannock to the Potomac rivers. Deer were numerous on the range; they pastured on my wheat in spring time, and nibbled at the growing corn in summer. One or two could be seen often; one Sunday we saw five. One day a large one leaped over the fence into the garden; another time, just at dusk, I shot a young one, weighing a hundred pounds, out of the door-yard.

Being correspondent to the agricultural department at Washington I was furnished with quantities of seeds for distribution, reports, documents, etc.; sent monthly re-ports of crops and prospects and experiments with seeds to the department. I corresponded with the New York Farmers' Club and some newspapers, and received mail matter semi-weekly by the arm-load.

It ought to have been said those school buildings were also for church purposes. The colored people appre-ciated them greatly on that account. Many of them, though ignorant, had a good Christian experience. Happily for the Christian religion, it does not depend upon the extent and accuracy of one's knowledge. If their preaching was mediocre, their songs and exhorta-tions and prayers were effective. Their old slavery songs retain much of Egypt and bondage. That, however, applies as well to the bondage of sin. When they sing of " Christ among the lilies, born across the sea, glory hallelujah !" they get happy. One old man I knew was wonderfully gifted in prayer; with his faith and trust, in tender sympathy, he cast himself upon the fatherhood of God. In listening to him one would feel the world receding, a rending of the veil between time and eternity, and almost catch a glimpse of the glory that is to be revealed. The white people never interfered with their meetings nor with their voting; and yet the gravest mistake in reconstruction was in not disfranchising the leaders in the rebellion, and obviating the years of removal of political disabilities, and in not giving the colored " *pater familias* " " the forty acres and the mule," instead of leaving them to the mercy of their old masters, to terrorizing, bulldozing and death.

At the time of emancipation there were millions of acres of government land in Texas and Florida, a congenial climate, not to speak of the millions of acres in the territories. There they would have become producers and more self-sustaining, and thus avoided all the wrongs and oppression they have had to endure. Besides, they have had to flee to the cities for protection, and every town in the middle, border or southern states is overrun with them, eking out a precarious existence, non-producers and thieves for want of work.

After two years of sickness and suffering occurred the death of our eldest son, Anthony W. Swing, when in the twenty-third year of his age. He was a young man of

21

much promise, and passed away in the hope of the resurrection and the life.

> " There is no flock, however watched and tended,
>   But one dead lamb is there ;
>   There is no home, however well defended,
>   But has one vacant chair."

Three years of summer drought succeeding, we sold
the plantation and lumber lands at Heathsville, Va., and
removed to Washington City, getting the daughters into
the excellent public schools, where they obtained a good
education.   Lenora was employed by General Walker on
the clerical work of the census of 1880, also by Commis-
sioner Loring of the agricultural department, on their
fine clerical work.

For three years I was engaged in the building of the
hospital at the Soldiers' Home, under Mr. Clark, the
architect of the capitol.   It is one of the largest and best
hospitals in its sanitary and all other appointments in
the country.   It is located north of the city on beautifully
laid out grounds of a thousand acres, overlooking the
city and the Potomac river.   Near by was the cottage
formerly occupied by President Lincoln.   Many a conference was held there by the president with those other
great men, Stanton, Chase and Seward.   But that historical building has been removed.

I never saw President Lincoln living, only in his coffin,
lying in state in Independence Hall, Philadelphia.   In
that historic fane I saw, for the first time, General

Grant, and shook hands with him on the New Year's day preceding his first inauguration. The fourth of March, on his second inauguration, was the coldest day I ever experienced in any latitude. Thousands were here from every land and nation, half perished with the cold. At night the ball building was obliged to close early owing to the intense cold, and even then the work of death had already begun, for several soon died from that night's exposure.

General Grant was a wonderfully reticent man. But if one did get into his likings and confidence, he would stick to him through thick and thin. Mrs. Grant never was *ultra* fashionable, but a good, kind, motherly soul.

The children, brought up mostly by the mother, turned out splendid. Miss Nellie, whom the queen of England delighted to honor, was a grand type of a quiet, ladylike, educated American girl. Soon after the inauguration of President Hayes I was employed in fitting up a summer residence for their use in the Soldier's Home grounds. There was some very nice work done. They frequently drove out to see the work as it was progressing, and were very pleasant, social people. I was afterward at their receptions, and saw them frequently at church and elsewhere. The Hayes administration was a good one, quieting down the excitements of the election, and the results of the electoral commission. At the White House, with Mrs. Hayes, if she was at home evenings, it was to all who called; she introduced people to each other, laughed merrily, had something pleasant to say to all; no restrictions to enjoyment, yet had the most unexceptionable of both sexes to call. She would receive in walking dress, or whatever dress she happened to be wearing when cards were brought to her, and by her sweet, gracious manner won all hearts. After the work was finished at the Soldier's Home, in the second year of the Hayes regime, he appointed me on the Washington monument work, and the new state department building. This great structure has been ten years in building, and is not completed yet.

From time immemorial when a great pageant was to pass in review upon the avenue there have been large stands erected on speculation. In preparing for the Garfield inauguration the committee resolved to have one for their guests and friends free, especially for the governors, state legislators, their senators and friends. I superintended the building of their stand along the park from Fifteen and a half to Seventeenth street, directly in front of the White House. The morning of the fourth was ushered in with a snow storm. By 8 o'clock it slacked up a little. Getting one hundred men we shoveled and swept off the snow. By 10 o'clock the sun came out, the escort to the president formed, going to the capitol. The whole mass of the participants did not form in line until after the ceremonies at the capitol. Then it was led by a splendid carriage, four-in-hand, containing the president and ex-president, Gen. Sherman and Gen. Logan ; at the gate of the White House the carriage passed into the grounds. The gentlemen alighted and joined the ladies on the stand. Then the whole grand parade for hours passed up the avenue in review, thousands upon thousands. I had seen and heard General Garfield many a time, but never saw him look so well and happy as on that day. It seemed to be the supreme moment of his life. To Mr. Hayes it appeared like a happy time, surrounded with friends, wife and children. The enthusiastic cheering of the passing multitude, the inspiring music; the dark clouds of the morning rolled away, the bright, sunny afternoon came ; statesmen and patriots confident of the future. Everything appeared auspicious. The formation of a new cabinet was not done to please everybody. Senator Conkling especially was displeased. Himself and his colleague resigned, expecting, however, to be returned by the state legislature and obtain a triumph over the president, whom he charged with not acting in good faith. He retired himself, by his own act, to private life.

In June and July I was making repairs on the officers' quarters at the Washington barracks, and was horrified when word was flashed along the lines, "The president has just been shot at the Baltimore and Potomac depot." There was a moment of wild excitement, and mounted cavalry rushing away, a company of infantry following; one party was put on guard at the president's house, where the wounded man had been removed ; other troops were stationed at the jail, where the assassin had been taken. Before night tents were put up in the grove of the mansion, and the soldiers guarded the place day and night until his removal to Long Branch. The following day, Sunday, was one of grief and sorrow. Monday,

Independence Day, was one of gloom and anxiety; all the usual observances of the day were suspended; and so in hope and fear the summer passed, until the sad end came, and he

> " Beyond the parting and the meeting,
> Beyond the farewell and the greeting,
> Beyond the pulse's fever beating,
> Beyond the frost chain and the fever,
> Beyond the heart-waste and the river,
> In rest, and love, and home."

Of the funeral it might be said, as it was of the burial of Moses by Nebo's lonely mountain: That was the grandest funeral that ever passed on earth.

President Garfield was a tall, noble looking man; he had a full, firm, sympathetic voice; he was one that always looked as though set apart for a high destiny. Mrs. Garfield had lived in Washington more or less a long time. She was a very quiet lady, with but little taste for fashionable society. She could speak the French and German languages fluently, and had the name of being the first president's wife able to talk with the foreign diplomats in the court language of Europe.

Having been in the habit for years of going to the New Year receptions, it was quite natural I would wish to see how President Arthur would compare with his predecessors. They always receive first the diplomatic corps, the judges of the supreme court, the army officers then the citizens. Amongst the foreign ministers there was Mr. Allan, from the Hawaiian Islands. After he shook hands with the president, and gave him his new year greetings and good wishes, he seemed about to faint. He was quickly placed upon a lounge, where he died in a few moments. The doors were closed immediately. The grounds were full of people, and they kept coming for an hour, but no more obtained admission. Mr. Allan was a native of Massachusetts. It was a great shock, and many a one in the crowd felt that " in the midst of life we are in death."

Senator Charles Sumner, "one of the few immortal names that was not born to die," used to attract large audiences to the senate chamber when it was known that he was going to speak. His soul abhorred oppression, injustice and wrong. On one occasion he said : " Aloft on the throne of God, and not down under the trampling feet of the multitude, are to be found the laws which should govern our conduct."

> " His life was gentle, and the elements
> So mixed in him that nature might stand up
> And say to all the world :
> This was a man !"

Horace Greeley was in the senate one day while some great event was transpiring. One of the other reporters, who was writing it up, and about the visitors also, said : " And there was Horace Greeley, sleeping sweetly." When the *Tribune* came out, however, it had the brightest, best and most wide-awake account of the proceedings of any of them.

That great American traveler, Bayard Taylor, was a

man I delighted to hear lecture. He was a very interesting speaker. Some of his books are charming. There are a dozen or more volumes of his works, and one at least of poetry. His books, "Hannah Thurston" and "The Story of Kennet," have some of the most unique, original, purely American and patriotic characters. In Mrs. Harriet Beecher Stowe's "Old Town Folks" and "The Minister's Wooing" are somewhat similar characters.

Another great lecturer is Rev. Joseph Cook, of Boston. I have seen a thousand people lean forward, eager to catch every word. His knowledge of ethics, science, cosmos and—well, there is no use to try to tell what—he is a regular encyclopedia, apparently inexhaustible.

A correspondent of the Boston *Traveler* relates the following amusing incident of another hero from the same state :

A WAY-BACK ARISTOCRAT.

CONGRESSMAN LAWLER EXPLAINS HIS PEDIGREE TO SECRETARY ENDICOTT.

[From the Boston Traveler.]

Congressman Frank Lawler, of Chicago, is a man of the people. He has climbed up to a position in Congress from the lowest rounds of the social ladder. He has been a laborer, a letter-carrier, a keeper of an influential gin-mill, a ward politician, a Chicago alderman and a congressman successively. Mr. Lawler recently had occasion to call on Secretary Endicott, and he found that gentleman surrounded by a frozen halo which displeased him. Mr. Endicott appeared to be somewhat bored by the persistency of the member of the legislative branch of the government, and was not at all disposed to pay much attention to him. Lawler stuck to him, however, and at last gained his point. After that the august secretary thawed out somewhat towards the congressman, and proceeded to give him a few points on the history of Massachusetts, especially on the Endicott family. He spoke of the glories of the old colonial days, and incidentally mentioned that his ancestors were among the foremost in Massachusetts. Warming up to his theme—and this is about the only subject that will warm him—he proceeded to trace the family back until he had passed down to where the Adamses first arose on the genealogical horizon, and wound up by saying :

"Why, Mr. Lawler, we have succeeded in tracing the Endicott family back to the earliest stage of the Norman conquest of England. In fact, the Endicotts were known before William the Conqueror was heard of."

"William the Conqueror the blank," replied Mr. Lawler. "Dooring the pasth summer, whin my legislative dooties have not been so pressing, I have paid a good deal of attintion to the airly history of the Lawler family. William the Conqueror! Why, he's nowhere. I found that the Lawlers were a prominent family on earth even before the flood."

To say that Mr. Endicott was astonished would scarcely express his feelings. He almost gasped for breath ; but at length a happy thought struck him.

" Mr. Lawler," said he, with withering scorn in his voice, " if you can trace the Lawlers back before the flood, how is it that we never heard anything of the family in the ark."

For a moment, and for a moment only, the Chicago man hesitated.   Then he recovered himself, and instantly replied :

" Mr. Secretary, I would have you to understand, sir, that the Lawlers were a respectable family.   They had yachts and horses, and everything else that was necessary for gintlemen in the antediluvian days.   The Lawlers, sir, had a boat of their own, and didn't have to go into the ark."

The New York Avenue Presbyterian church has the largest congregation of that denomination in the city. President Lincoln used to attend there under the ministrations of Rev. Dr. Gurley.   Gov. Shepherd, Col. Irish, judges of the Supreme Court and numerous noted personages worshipped there.   Formerly there was only a choir and organ gallery.   Recently the seating capacity has been enlarged to accommodate about four hundred more by putting in side galleries.   They had some extra nice work done.   I became acquainted with the pastor, Rev. Dr. Paxton, the building committee, and some of the elders as the work was going on.   I also remodeled and enlarged the home residence of one of the elders.   The church has two mission chapels that are getting in large Sunday schools and increasing congregations.

Dr. Newman, at the Metropolitan church, where Gen. Grant attended, was a splendid pulpit orator. No one with ordinary intelligence could fail to be interested in him. Bishop Simpson, who is often here, is another grand man to listen to; he is so earnest and eloquent few equal him in preaching, and in his gift of prayer he seemed like one conversing with God. The solemnity of the tones convinced one that he was conscious of an unearthly presence and speaking to it, and yet it was a prayer of deep simplicity. Bishop Haven and Bishop Andrews are bright and shining lights. Some prefer Andrews to any of them. When either of them are to preach and Chaplain McCabe is to sing there will be a shower of tears in joy and sympathy.

Sunday in Washington is a quiet, orderly day, perhaps as much so as in any city in the land; there is complete outward respect, at least. A great many public men attend church, and it is a respectable thing to do, and yet so many do not go one-half the churches are scarcely ever more than half filled.

Were it not that the Lord raises up some giant of moral power or of intellectual strength for an occasion, I should think we have already had the best of everything in this world. The greatest statesmen of the country have had their brilliant lights extinguished. The mighty, masterful souls of reformers and preachers who stood head and shoulders above their compeers have gone to their reward, except a few nearing life's sunset. Of the noted military men that passed through the fiery battles and saw the consummation of the late war, only a remnant remains. Of authors and poets, those of the past are surely better than any we now have. I have listened to all the great reformers and enjoyed the lectures of Rev. Mr. Murphy best of all. He was never rough or unkind, no matter how low and apparently lost a man was; he would say to him, "My good friend," or "My brother, the Lord needs you, and your family needs you," and then he would pour into his desolate soul the words of life, and the man was reformed by love. In art, in printing and in music the old masters stand pre-eminent. The old church music is a rich legacy from the past, and is a happy illustration of the survival of the fittest; like the songs of the sweet singer of Israel, they will afford comfort and joy to all that are struggling for a better life.

There are a great many wrecks and failures of life in Washington. Many a one is lured here in hope of a clerkship or some government office. For one that succeeds it is safe to say that a score fail. For one appointment now pending there have been a thousand applications, a great many of them ex-congressmen. The place is overrun with office hunters, mechanics and laborers. There are no manufactories except those of brick and gas. There are ex-congressmen and ex-senators, poor, seedy and dilapidated, ashamed to go back to the old home, but hoping to get office. Such is life.

Last fall I was engaged in the building of a house for the Rev. Dr. Hicks, the gentleman who obtained so much free advertising for visiting the assassin at the jail and of whom the papers have said so much nonsense about Guiteau's bones. The doctor's house has a front of twenty feet on B street, and sixty-five feet on Eighth street, a basement, two stories and mansard roof, bay windows, porches and gables, all press brick, black mortar joint walls, finished in oiled natural grain wood. It is a very imposing edifice. He has a little church around the corner hardly a hundred yards from where his future home will be in the new building. His congregation is mostly a split from a Methodist church that was aggrieved at an appointment of the conference. They are now Congregational. The doctor is counted the finest pulpit orator in the city. Liberal in his views, thinks men are pretty much alike, good and bad in all; that no creed does more than shadow one side of the truth; and when one sees this, he feels a pity for making a sympathy with his follies and his hopes, and that nothing but the divine pity is sufficient for the infinite pathos of human life.

The completion of the Washington monument was the occasion of an imposing demonstration at the national capital. The ceremonies opened with an address by Senator Sherman. The Hon. W. W. Corcoran made the formal presentation, and President Arthur the speech of acceptance. At the conclusion of the masonic rites a procession was formed, with General Sheridan as chief marshal, and reviewed by the president. Both branches of congress assembled in the House of Representatives. The diplomatic corps and many distinguished visitors were also present. After a brief address by Senator Edmunds, Representative John D. Long read the address of the day, written by the Hon. Robert C. Winthrop, of Massachusetts.

BRIEF HISTORY OF THE GREAT SHAFT.

In brief, the Continental Congress in 1783 resolved that an equestrian statue should be erected to Washington. In 1799 it was resolved that a marble monument should be erected, which should also serve as a receptacle for the remains of the *Pater Patriæ*. In 1800 a select committee reported in favor of executing both resolutions. The House passed an amendment to the resolution of 1783, requiring a mausoleum to be built, but the senate did not concur. The matter then rested for thirty-three years. In 1833 a voluntary association was formed for the erection of a monument, and funds were solicited. In 1848 the corner-stone was laid, and then, after the shaft had arisen 152 feet, work was suspended in 1855 for lack of funds. The war intervened, and it was not until 1876 that an appropriation of $200,000 by congress enabled the association to resume. The 6th of December, 1884, the great work was completed.

For nearly half a century it has been in course of construction on the banks of the Potomac, in the city of Washington, and not far from the White House. Its foundation is 126 feet square; height, 555 feet; 55 feet broad at its base, and it is the loftiest structure ever erected by man. It is a hollow shaft of granite, faced on the outside with blocks of white marble. In joining the blocks of stone every device that ingenuity could suggest has been used to prevent the possible introduction of moisture and the consequent danger from frost. The total weight of the monument amounts to the enormous sum of 81,120 tons. Since work was commenced it has settled about four inches. Four lightning rods protect the monument. In the pyramidion are windows. These latter are 504 feet above the ground. The interior of the shaft is lighted by electricity. Its cost has been $1,200,-000, of which $300,000 was raised by popular subscription. The interior contains a stairway and elevator, by which visitors can in a few minutes reach the summit.

This careworn old capital, that has seen so many heart-aches—so many of the ambitions that write wrinkles on the brow—that has echoed to the tread of armies, and worn mourning on its public buildings for scores and hundreds of the great men of the land, never looks so joyous as in the resurrection and the new life of spring.

WASHINGTON, D. C., 1885.

[Extracts from the Washington Chronicle.]

BRILLIANT WEDDING.

One of the most brilliant and fashionable weddings of the season occurred at the Congregational church, Washington, D. C., last evening, May 27, 1884, Rev. Dr. Rankin officiating. The contracting parties were Hon. Miles Fuller, the assistant chemist of the Agricultural department, and Miss Nora M. Swing, second daughter of A. R. Swing, of Washington City. Invitations were sent to friends in Bridgeton, Pittsgrove, Salem, and other places. The ushers were Messrs. Edgar Richards, Walter B. Grant, William H. Smith and Professor H. W. Wiley. Mr. and Mrs. Fuller left last night for an extended trip west.

Before going to press we learn from attending physicians, Drs. W. Prentiss and H. E. Leach, of the death of a well known architect, builder and contractor of this city, A. R. Swing.

In order to facilitate business he assisted the men, in rain and storm, in hoisting the joists and rafters of a new building to be used at the inauguration of President Cleveland. He also attended the dedication of the Washington monument on the 22d of February, and contracted a severe cold, ending in typhoid-pneumonia, from which he died March 24, 1885.

To the members of Federal City Lodge, I. O. O. F., the family extend their grateful remembrance for their untiring kindness during the last sickness of the deceased.

Rev. Dr. J. L. Mills pronounced the funeral oration at the residence, after which he was buried with the impressive ceremonies of the order of Odd Fellows, and laid to rest on a sloping hill in Glenwood cemetery, within sight of Washington's monument, and surrounded by the sleeping dust of thousands of brave men.

Among the accomplishments of the deceased was his

fondness for society, music, literature, and the splendid services of the church (Presbyterian). As a man he was finely developed, both physically and intellectually; he talked freely of business matters, and complimented his workmen, for excellent workmanship none more fully appreciated than he. Earnest, scholarly, refined, few men indeed have lived a more active life, or more nobly performed their life's work than Abraham R. Swing.

At the time of his death he left a widow and three children—Mrs. Ella Josephine Moreland, Clement L., and Mrs. Le Nora Maud Fuller, all residents of Washington City, D. C.

In writing of this sudden affliction his son Clement L. said: "Father was under the doctor's hands not quite three weeks. During this time it seemed impossible for him to take any nourishment. He seemed to break right down, was unconscious most of the time, and could not speak or say anything that we could understand.

"He had the typhoid-pneumonia, and died Tuesday night, March 24, 1885. Previous to this he was sleeping quietly, and in that sleep awoke 'beyond the golden gates.'

"To the members of Federal City Lodge, I. O. O. F. we shall always feel grateful for their untiring kindness during father's sickness. He was buried with the impressive ceremonies of the order, Rev. J. L. Mills preaching the funeral service at the house, after which we laid him down to rest on a little sloping hill in Glenwood cemetery at Washington, within sight of Washington's

22

monument, and surrounded by the sleeping dust of thousands of brave men.   Among the many accomplishments of the deceased was his great fondness for music and literature—a newspaper correspondent himself; fond of society and the splendid services of the church, instructive amusements, etc.   He enjoyed life, and always seemed active and young-looking."

CHAPTER XXXII.

GEORGE M. SWING.

THE people of Fairfield township are a noble, manly race; they have conquered difficulties by their courage and perseverance that would have driven others to the verge of despair, and I feel confident at this moment that we have a glorious future before us. Among the many examples of perseverance and honorable trading, leading to independence and the ownership of princely farms, fisheries and oyster grounds, stores, mills and vessel property, few are more successful than the careers of Trenchard, Whitecar, Westcott, Howell, Smith, Husted, Bateman, Gandy, Bamford, Sheppard, Michael Coates, Simon Sparks Swing, Diament, Ogden, Laning, Elmer, Duffel, Mulford, Willis, Tomlinson and Swing, all of whom were either natives of Fairfield, or spent their boyhood in it, and have, with many others equally worthy of mention, reflected credit on its history. In their day and time many of these were possessors of farms and gardens which Adam, in his innocence, might have coveted; barns, stables, buildings, agricultural machinery of the most approved style, fine horses, carriages and stock of expensive breeds.

"When, in the course of human events, it becomes

necessary;" no, no, that is not it. George M. Swing was born in Fairfield township, Cumberland county, N. J., in 1802; that is what we want. .

Let us look back over the space of fifty years to the humble period when the latter person named employed the early years of life as a teacher of the public schools. He was an inquisitive child, and succeeded in reading every book in the neighborhood before he was twelve years of age. From boyhood he was earnest, active and industrious, and in manhood fully sustained the reputatation wherever known of first-class instructor and disciplinarian. There yet survive a few old natives of Cumberland county that remember the light-haired, rosy-cheeked lad who, on Monday mornings, more than half a century ago, opened a school for the instruction of children and youth ; perched himself upon a stool behind a high desk, with forty scholars in front of him. These were days which the departed veteran, when in the height of his popularity, loved to recall, and he was never more enthusiastic than when picturing the boys and girls, and the surroundings among which he took his first experience in the duties of a teacher's life. Endowed with those natural gifts which constitute the essentials of success, he felt that his mission was destined to extend over a broader and wider field, and he began to see that there was but little money in teaching, however much fun there might be in it. Resigning his position as teacher he purchased some valuable tracts of timber land and subsequently engaged in the lumber trade, the shipyards at Mauricetown, Millville, Bridgeton and Fairton receiving from him a good supply of white oak plank, knees, keels, and boat building material.

Large forest trees were then found growing in great luxuriance in the vicinity of Newport, Herring Roe, Back Neck and other places in Cumberland county, thus affording employment for a large number of team drivers, wood choppers and laboring men, and in connection with this branch of industry he owned a large store in the centre of the village, and well filled with goods. Almost his entire life was spent in this locality, and he contributed greatly to the growth, prosperity and success of his native place, being engaged in active mercantile pursuits for a period of eighteen years; a part of the time the name of the firm was Swing & Tomlinson. With the inhabitants of the village and the farming community surrounding the place a large and prosperous business was transacted. They were also interested in cedar swamps and vessel property—the Joseph A. Clark, George M. Swing and other sailing craft. The vessels and oyster boats sailing from the port of Fairton, received their supply of provisions mainly from the store of Swing & Tomlinson. Many of these boats were engaged in the oyster trade; others were employed in carrying lumber, cord wood, country produce and general merchandise, and sailed direct for Baltimore, Philadelphia and New York, where cargoes of goods were usually sold.

In marriage Mr. Swing was united to Miss Harriet Whitecar, a prominent and estimable young lady of Fairfield. Four children were born to them, to wit:

Harriet, George M., Emma and Charles S. Of these, three are now living, one of the sons, Charles S. by name, being engaged in successful mercantile pursuits at the present time.

The death of George M. Swing takes out of the list of living men one of the most noted and influential citizens in his native place. He was more than a clever man socially, full of shrewd instances and plausible undertakings, a patriotic citizen, and like many others of our prominent men, self-made. Personally he was a high type of the American gentleman; cordial in his manners, warm-hearted in his methods, of suave and fluent address, and that universal kinship which springs from a kind and honest heart, made and kept for him many friends among all classes of people. To young farmers, merchants or mechanics who needed the advice and inspiration of an experienced head he was "guide, philosopher and friend," and ever ready to champion the cause of the weak and oppressed, and to aid every movement which seemed calculated to be of advantage to the great mass of people. While giving direction to matters of business there was little that escaped his notice, although he never had that busy and pre-occupied air of importance which some persons have with one-tenth of the work.

It is said of an eminent statesman of the present generation, that he has frequently declared that the most desirable condition of life was to have somewhat more to do than one could possibly accomplish. By this he did not mean far too much, but enough to supply a perpetual spur. Men that have been great benefactors of their kind, and have left great works behind them, have had to live under pressure with strained energies and the sense of having too much to do. A man can hardly become great under the condition of a calm, leisurely life. Man cannot run at his fastest or swim at his fastest under ordinary circumstances; he must be running an exciting race or swimming for dear life to do his best. Indeed, what a man is capable of rarely appears until he is put on his mettle.

What is true in regard to physical facts is equally true of our mental faculties; under pressure the mind becomes enlarged and quickened, and thus capable of producing results calm leisure never attains. But the evil of this is that it is so difficult to realize this happy condition. Men who are able to do much more are usually pressed to do too much.

George M. Swing used to say with great truth: "Don't go to men of leisure when you want anything done; go to busy men." Paradoxical as it may seem, it is nevertheless true that the busiest men are those who have the most time, or at least the most capacity for extra work.

Until the last ten years he enjoyed the best of health. His bright face and cheerful spirit brought sunshine wherever he went. He was a prominent and highly respected citizen, commanding an influence of which few are capable. His last years, however, were shadowed by business misfortune, including losses on land and by water, and also the destruction by fire of valuable tracts of timber land and hundreds of cords of wood already cut for market.   Thus he experienced success and reverse under circumstances of great trial, and his life struggles were heroic ; all, however, were borne with true Christian fortitude.   I would not do justice to my feelings without adding that I found it encouraging and profitable to visit him.   Indeed, his conversation was always entertaining and instructive, his voice, his vote, his influence being always found on the side of good morals and good government.

[*Extracts from the Bridgeton Evening News, February 20, 1879.*]

George M. Swing, Esq., of Fairton, a well-known and respected citizen of that place, died yesterday at the age of seventy-six years.   His health has been failing for some time past.   He was for many years employed in the store business as a member of the firm of Swing & Tomlinson.

The funeral of the late George M. Swing took place in Fairton on Saturday last, and was largely attended.   He was buried in the Cross Roads burial ground, near the site of the old church, founded by his father, the Rev. Michael Swing.

OBITUARY, BY REV. J. ATWOOD.

Mr. George M. Swing, of Fairton, N. J., departed this life February 19, 1879, in the seventy-seventh year of his age.   He had been a member of the M. E. church between forty and fifty years.

His father, Rev. Michael Swing, was a very devoted

Christian man, and a useful, strong and able preacher of the gospel. He brought up his family in the "nurture and admonition of the Lord," and they all embraced religion, and all the children that have gone have died in the sweet faith of the gospel. Thus we see the fruits of a godly training. Three sisters only are left of quite a large family.

Brother Swing was strongly attached to the church of his choice, aiding her most liberally with his pecuniary means; and his house was a putting-up place for the preachers and other religious visitors for many years, where they were cordially received and made welcome, and they all felt at home in the family of Brother Swing.

His wife preceded him to the spirit world some few years, and he was married to his second wife in the neighborhood of five years before he died, and she proved a most valuable helpmeet for him till he died, with all the attention and cheerfulness that always characterizes real Christians.

Brother Swing was a useful man in the community, and where he was known, which was quite extensively, he was esteemed as a man of excellent business habits, stern integrity and downright honesty in all his dealings. He was a man of considerable reading and information, and formed a judgment of his own. He had a keen perception of right and wrong in all matters of church and state. He took strong ground on the temperance question, and was much opposed to the license system as now prevailing in cities, towns and counties.

He took a lively interest in the religious prosperity of the church. When he was disabled by bodily infirmity, so that he could not attend the extra services, he would inquire how they prospered, who was forward for prayers, and who were converted. His heart and interest were there though his body was absent; and the last time I prayed with him, which was a day or so before he died, he was much engaged in prayer, and when I closed he responded audibly, " Amen."

My brother was always strong in faith all through life, and his closing moments were a triumph over death. About an hour before he died he was asked how his mind was in the near view of his departure. He replied that his spiritual sky was perfectly clear, not a cloud came between him and the sun of righteousness, and many other expressions of like import, showing the vigor of his faith and intensity of his love in his last battle with his last enemy—death.

A little over a week before his death he attended church, spoke in love-feast as one " waiting to go home." He said: " The Lord is my rock and my salvation; whom shall I fear?" And when his keel was ploughing the swelling floods of Jordan, with bowline at his feet and his hand hard on the helm, he said: " Though I walk through the valley of the shadow of death, I fear no evil."

He was quite a good singer himself, and a great lover of music, and the day but one before he died he broke out audibly and sang with a sweet voice, " We'll wait till

Jesus comes," etc. He is gone, we believe, to the home of the blest in heaven, to sing the high praises of the Redeemer in that bright world of light and glory.

"Precious in the sight of the Lord is the death of his saints."—Psalms 116: 15.

CHAPTER XXXIII.

CHARLES P. SWING.

HON. CHARLES P. SWING, who represented the First Assembly district of Salem county in the legislature during the year 1876, died at his residence in Sharptown on Monday evening last, March 24th, 1879, of pneumonia. The deceased was born in Salem county and passed all the active years of his life within its limits. He was seldom known to be sick or to employ a physician. Prior to his election he had a local celebrity and a popularity which made him known throughout the state. His ancestors settled in New Jersey before the Revolution, and by marriage and intermarriage is now widely spread through that and neighboring states, many of them clinging still to those strict Presbyterian ideas which have always been cherished by that society.

He was the son of the late Dr. Charles Swing, and was engaged in agricultural pursuits during the greater portion of his life, residing on a farm owned by the family near the village.

He was united in marriage to Miss Rebecca A. Gorden, of the same place, and at the time of his decease left a widow and the following named children: Lafayette W., Mary E., Clarissa, Belle, Edward, Charles Wesley, George W., Reine R. and Hannah—four sons and five daughters. The announcement of the sudden death and the funeral of our worthy townsman brought to the village a large concourse of relatives and friends. He was borne to the cemetery by his old associates, who, from long years of business relation, regarded him with the kindest feelings of veneration. As a gentleman of the most pleasing and social type, and as a member of society and the head of a family he will be greatly missed. At the time of his death he was proprietor of a livery stable and the Temperance Hotel at Sharptown, New Jersey.

MISS ETTA T. SWING.

The funeral of Etta T. Swing took place this morning from the residence of her mother, Mrs. Judith Swing, No. 80 Church street, and was largely attended. The principal and teachers of the First and Second ward schools were present. She had been suffering for several months from paralysis, and died suddenly on Thursday morning last. Miss Swing was for several years past a successful teacher in the secondary department of the Bank street public school, and was a young lady of rare gifts, pleasant, agreeable, and had a large circle of friends. As a teacher she had few superiors. In the school-room, where she was loved, her presence will be greatly missed, and at home her place cannot be filled. She was laid in white satin, and placed in a handsome black cloth casket, with silver handles and name plate. It was trimmed with beautiful headlining with a white satin pillow. The floral designs were a tribute of love from her numerous friends. At the head was a standing wreath, a sheaf of wheat and a floral design representing a pillow; on the right was one representing a basket; at the foot one representing a harp, and on her feet was placed a wreath. The pall bearers were A. E. Prince, principal of the First ward school, George W. McCowan, Augustus Cook, Charles Garrison, Benjamin F. Harding and Evan Wheaton. The services were conducted by Rev. Heber H. Beadle, who in the course of his remarks said: "From the olden time there comes a story of an ancient prophet, filled with the Holy Ghost, who was caught up to the clouds in a chariot of fire. A voice went up with it, crying, 'My Father, my Father, the Chariot of Israel, and the horseman thereof;' and his mantle fell upon him who stood by the banks of the Jordan." The soul has gone out of the waxen frame of her who lies in yonder room, and as it ascended it left its mantle behind. The soul cannot be buried, but will dwell in the realms of bliss while eternal ages shall roll their solemn round. In 1869 she stood before the altar and made confession of faith, and united with the Second Presbyterian church." Her pure spirit passed from its transitory world, reveling at the moment of its flight in a foretaste of its approaching bliss—catching a glowing beam fresh and warm from the fount of everlasting joy, picturing on the breathless clay a heavenly and matchless grandeur.

> " She died in beauty, like a rose,
> Blown from its parent stem ;
> She died in beauty, like a pearl,
> Dropped from some diadem."

The remains were taken to Swing's cemetery at Fairton for interment, and her pure spirit reposes in quiet with him who gave it.

———

ELIZABETH G. SWING.

[Extract from Cincinnati Gazette of May 21st.]

The funeral of Miss Elizabeth Gatch Swing, sister of Hon. Philip B. Swing, United States District Judge of the Southern District of Ohio, took place from the M. E. church in this place Sunday last. It was largely attended by the relatives, friends and old pioneers of this state, and for the information of many friends, and the pioneers of this valley that are scattered over distant states, we append a few brief notes of her birth, life, family history and death. Elizabeth Gatch Swing was born in Tate township, Clermont county, Ohio, March 1, 1808, and died suddenly at the residence of her brother-in-law, Mr. Hill Goodwin, near Bethel, the same township in which she was born, May 17, 1878, aged seventy years, two months and seventeen days. She was the first child of Michael and Ruth Swing, and on the paternal side granddaughter of George and Sarah Swing, and was the first born of the generation of Swings to which she belonged. In the maternal line she was the granddaughter of the late Rev. Philip and Elizabeth S. Gatch. When she was yet a child, with her father and mother she moved from Tate township to what was and now is the "Gatch" neighborhood in this (Miami) township, where a greater part of her useful life has been spent.

She united with the Methodist Episcopal church when quite young, and up to the day of her death has been a faithful and consistent Christian member of the same. Those who know her speak of her as a woman possessed of more than the ordinary graces of the Holy Spirit, seeming not to live so much for herself as for those around her, ministering to the wants and soothing the sorrows and lightening the cares and making glad the hearts of those among whom she dwelt, evermore laboring to bless and make others happy. A loving, dutiful sister, companion, neighbor, church member and friend, her departure is a painful severance of the most tender ties by dear friends and relatives, whose loss is her gain, and though dead she still speaks, and her memory will long be fragrant in the minds and hearts of those who knew her best. The Rev. R. K. Deem preached an eloquent and feeling sermon, being assisted in the service by the Rev. Mr. Powell, of the Baptist church. Her remains were deposited in the beautiful cemetery east of town, beside those of friends who have gone before.

CHAPTER XXXIV.

JUDGE PHILIP B. SWING.

DEATH OP THE EMINENT JURIST—BRIEF ACCOUNT OF HIS LIFE—
UNIVERSAL GRIEF IN CLERMONT COUNTY AND CINCINNATI
—TRIBUTES TO A CHRISTIAN JUDGE AND DISTINGUISHED
CITIZEN.

[*Extract from Cincinnati Gazette, October 31, 1882.*]

AFTER an illness of two weeks, Judge Philip B. Swing died yesterday evening at 6.15 o'clock. About the middle of last week his case began to assume a serious aspect, but his friends were not alarmed until Saturday, when his symptoms indicated that he was rapidly growing worse, and about 4 P. M. on that day he became partially unconscious. He afterwards rallied slightly, and remained easier during Saturday night. On Sunday he still grew worse, with sinking spells, when all hopes of recovery were given up by his physicians. He lingered in the most critical condition until about noon yesterday, when he rallied again slightly, and was able to partially recognize relatives and friends. During the afternoon he gradually sank until the above named hour, when death claimed the distinguished jurist. His complaint was kidney disease, with uræmia setting in at the

23

last.   His last judicial visit to Cincinnati was on October 12, when, accompanied by his physician, Dr. Ashburne, he went to open court, but his condition compelled him to return to his home the same night.   He was seen on the street but once or twice after this.

Funeral on Thursday at 1 P. M. from his late residence. Ceremonies to be plain and brief, consisting of remarks by Judge Baxter, of the U. S. Circuit Court, and by a member each of the Hamilton and Clermont county bars, the latter by Judge Ashburn, to conclude with a prayer by Rev. Dr. Walden, of Cincinnati, a valued friend of the deceased.

The Swing family came from Lorraine, one of the two provinces captured from France by Germany·in the late Franco-German war.   It was of Huguenot extraction and early identified with the doctrines and followers of the Reformation.   Before the American Revolution two Swing brothers emigrated from the father-land and settled in Salem and Cumberland counties, New Jersey.

In 1803, Rev. John Collins, "the old man eloquent" of the Methodist church, purchased a large tract of land in Clermont county, on the East Fork, and founded the "Jersey Settlement."   Another early settler was George Swing, a son of one of the emigrants.   He secured a fine tract of land on the Ohio turnpike, west of Bethel, and lived on the farm now owned by M. J. Swing until his death, when he was interred in the Swing cemetery on part of the homestead.

He was the ancestor of all the Swings in this region, among whom was the late Judge Philip B. Swing, the distinguished Professor David Swing, of Chicago, and Judges George L. and James B. Swing of this town.

He had sons, named Samuel, who lived in Tate township until his death, when his family removed to the West; Lawrence, who married the daughter of David Light, and died in Tate on the farm yet owned by the family (he was the father of Judge George L. Swing, of Batavia); Michael, who removed to Miami township; Wesley, who married Nancy Crane, and living on the homestead until his death, reared five children, among them George W. and M. J. of Bethel. George Swing had one daughter, Mary, who married Zachariah Riley, but both have deceased.

Michael Swing was married December 6, 1806, to Ruth, daughter of Judge Philip Gatch, and died in 1835, and his wife, Ruth, fifteen years later. Their children were: Aaron M., who died in 1840; George S., lately deceased; Philip Bergen; Sarah A., who married John Crane; Mary, intermarried with John Leming; Ruth, married to Hill C. Goodwin; Martha, married to President Matthews, of Hillsboro Female College; Elizabeth and Margaret L., who both died unmarried.

Judge Philip Gatch, the father of the late Judge Philip B. Swing's mother, was one of the most remarkable men our country has ever produced.

The Gatch farm, five miles out from Baltimore City, on the Belair road, has been in the family ever since it was purchased, in 1737, by the progenitor of the family in this country. He emigrated from Prussia and settled in this part of Baltimore county in 1725, obtaining from

Leonard Calvert, the Lord Proprietary, a passport permitting him to travel in part of the province. His son, George, and several brothers indentured themselves to obtain their passage to America, and were very cruelly treated by their masters to whom their services were sold.

Philip Gatch, son of George, was born March 2, 1751, and became the first American itinerant preacher in America. Before 1772 Robert Strawbridge, a local Methodist preacher from Ireland, had settled between Frederick and Baltimore towns, and he raised up three other preachers, Richard Owen, Sater Stephenson and Nathan Perigo. The latter preached upon the Gatch estate in 1772, and although the whole family were members of the established church he converted them to Methodism. Philip Gatch resolved to become a preacher, and went to New Jersey, where he served as an itinerant in 1773. In July, 1774, he attended, at Philadelphia, the second yearly conference of the Methodists in America, and was received into full connection as a minister. He and Rev. Wm. Duke were appointed the first circuit riders on the Frederick circuit, which comprised what are now the counties of Carroll, Frederick, Washington, Allegheny, Garrett and Montgomery. On one occasion his bold language drove upon him an attack from drunken ruffians. In 1775 he and Rev. John Cooper were ordered to Kent county, Maryland, to preach in place of Abraham Whitworth, who had been deposed for misconduct. Here he caught the small-pox, and was very near to death. Returning to Baltimore town he preached there and on the Frederick circuit. Between Frederickstown and Bladensburg he was assailed, after preaching on Sunday, by a mob who tarred and feathered him and treated him so savagely that he never entirely recovered his strength. Four weeks afterward, however, he had another appointment to preach in the same place, and he fulfilled it without molestation. In 1778 he was appointed to Sussex county, Virginia, and there he was once more made the victim of the popular antipathy to the new sect of Methodists or Wesleyans. Two bullies fell upon him and beat him so severely that his life was for a long time despaired of and his eyes were permanently injured. In addition to these sufferings his constitution had been broken by labor and exposure, forcing upon him a respite from duty. He was the more reconciled to this from the fact that the persecution of the Methodists was ceasing. On January, 14, 1778, he married Elizabeth, a daughter of Thomas Smith, of Powhattan county, Virginia. This family, like the Gatches, had forsaken the established church to become the disciples of Wesley. Although Philip Gatch never took another appointment, he had the superintendence of various circuits, and spent a considerable portion of his time in traveling and preaching.

He was one of the leading spirits in the organization of the M. E. church on the system which has endured to the present day, and was one of the three persons to whom the superintendence of the work in the Southern States was confided. In 1778 he removed to Buckingham county, Virginia, and October 11, 1798, he emigrated to what is now Clermont county, Ohio, fifteen miles from the present city of Cincinnati. Here he purchased the " Nancorrow Survey," a large tract of military reservation land, on which is now situated the thriving town of Milford. He also entered an extensive tract near Xenia. In 1802 he was a member of the convention which framed the first constitution of Ohio, and the next year he was chosen by the legislature, one of the three Associate Judges of the Court of Common Pleas. He was twice re-elected, and held this responsible judicial position for twenty-one years.

He died at his splendid residence in Clermont county, December 28, 1835, in the 85th year of his age. For a quarter of a century after removing to Ohio he occupied various pulpits as a local preacher, and he performed the marriage ceremony innumerable times, bridal parties coming long distances to be united by the patriarchal pioneer and minister. He was the close friend of Judge John McLean, of the U. S. Supreme Court, and that distinguished statesman commemorated his long and honorable career by writing the " Memoirs" of the Rev. Philip Gatch.

The descendants of this hero of early Methodism are found in Maryland, Virginia, Ohio and farther west, all prominent in their professions, which are the bar, the bench, the ministry, the press, and the chairs of collegiate institutions. At the old homestead on the Belair road are the lineal descendants of the first of the family in this country, and here stands the time-honored " Gatch Church," the first erected in this vicinity.

Philip Gatch came to the Northwest Territory with his brother-in-law, Rev. James Smith, his friend Judge Ambrose Ranson, and others (white and colored) to the number of thirty-six, making Newtown, Hamilton county, their objective point. Gatch and Ranson went to the McCormick purchase near Milford, and temporarily lived near Rev. Francis McCormick. In February, 1799, Gatch moved into his own cabin, which stood on the southern side of the present township cemetery, east of Milford, which he occupied for a long time, but afterwards lived in a large house on the county road, on the place lately occupied by George W. Gatch, near the place of his original settlement. Judge Gatch's pronounced hostility to African slavery led to his being chosen a member of the constitutional convention of 1802.

Judge Gatch had four sons and four daughters. The former were Conduce, Thomas, Philip and George. The daughters were: Presocia, married to James Garland and afterward to David Osborne; Martha, to John Gest; Elizabeth, to Aaron Matson, and Ruth to Michael Swing. Ruth was a woman of rare intellectual powers, and the impress of her strong individuality as well as that of her distinguished father was seen in her son, Philip B. Swing.

The latter was born October 14, 1820, in Miami township, this county. He was admitted to the bar at Dayton, Ohio, in 1842, having been examined by a committee whose chairman was Gen. Robert C. Schenck, then in large and noted practice. The discipline, flexi-

bility and ease which collegiate education is supposed to
best supply were in his case attained by self-culture,
quick observation, engrafted into the stock of native
good sense, superadded to such educational facilities as
the local schools afforded, and with a natural aptitude
for the practical adaptation of circumstances and means
to ends, he became like his illustrious grandfather, Judge
Gatch.   He soon achieved a deserved prominence at the
bar.   He immediately formed a law partnership in Batavia with his cousin, the late Hon. Moses D. Gatch, of
Xenia, Ohio, which continued several years.   The only
other law partner he ever had and with whom he was
long associated, was his father-in-law, Judge Owen T.
Fishback.

Judge Swing was married April 15, 1844, by Rev.
Edward Schofield, to Mary H., daughter of Judge Fishback.   The latter was born August 29, 1791,, in
Farquhar county, Virginia, and emigrated to Kentucky
when but a boy.   There he read law with Hon. Martin
Marshal, and, coming to Clermont, was admitted to the
bar at a term of the Supreme Court held at Williamsburg,
in 1815, by Judge William W. Irwin and Ethan Allen.
He was state senator in 1823 and 1824, representative in
1826, prosecuting attorney from 1825 to 1833, and presiding judge of the Common Pleas Court from 1841 to
1848.   He married Caroline, a daughter of Jacob Huber,
who had married Anna Maria, daughter of Dr. Christian
Boerstler, a Bavarian gentleman of much distinction, who
came to America on account of political oppression.   In
1806 Huber came to Williamsburg, accompanied by his

brother-in-law, Captain Boerstler. Mrs. Judge Fishback was a sister to the celebrated Charles Boers Huber and to Mrs. Major S. R. S. West, of Olive Branch. Of the large family of sons and daughters of Judge Fishback were George W., the late proprietor of the St. Louis *Democrat;* Hon. John Fishback, and Hon. W. P. Fishback, the eminent lawyers, both of Indianapolis. One of the daughters married Hon. H. N. Talley, of our town, father of Frank Talley, the postmaster of New Richmond.

Judge Swing leaves a widow and the following children: Capt. Peter F. Swing, an eminent attorney at Batavia; Carrie, wife of Judge James B. Swing, and Lizzie, an unmarried daughter, and one son deceased, Philip Bergen Swing.

Judge Philip B. Swing served as prosecuting attorney part of 1847, during Colonel Howard's absence in Mexico. He was a candidate at different times for prosecuting attorney, common pleas judge and representative to the legislature, but owing to his party being in a large minority was not elected. In 1859 he was defeated for the legislature by Dr. John E. Myers, the present state senator.

On March 31, 1871, he was appointed by President Grant judge of the United States District Court for the Southern District of Ohio, to fill the vacancy occasioned by the death of Judge Humphrey H. Leavitt, who had held that judicial position from July 10, 1834, the day of his appointment by President Jackson. Judge Leavitt was from Steubenville, and for twenty years was the sole

Federal Judge of the District United States Court in the state, and until Ohio was divided into the Northern and Southern districts, and Cincinnati made the seat of the latter's sittings.

Judge Allen G. Thurman, then in the United States Senate, remarked to us, "that Grant's selection of Judge Swing was the best appointment his administration had made, and he predicted Judge Swing would make a name on the bench that would add lustre to the Ohio bar."

As a lawyer there was nothing dramatic or startling in his career, but he kept right on in the higher levels of local practice, surrounded by a large and wealthy clientage, whom he served always with the utmost alacrity and scrupulous fidelity. As a judge his administration was able, pure and dignified ; giving him a well deserved reputation for his decisions. Coming of an honored lineage, celebrated in the pioneer annals of the county, born, reared and educated in Clermont, where he practiced for a quarter of a century his profession in a most successful and honorable manner, he maintained on the bench the character of an eminent and upright judge, "Untainted by the guilty bribe, uncursed amid the harpy tribe." He was a great student, and his literary tastes, although varied and quite ardent, seemed to incline more to modern history, which, it is believed he read more as a record of events than as showing a development of thought in a strict literary sense.

He was a man who, in the strong language of Napoleon, was "victory organized," who by the force of his own merits acquired high station ; yet he was not puffed up, proud or aristocratic, but remained plain, unpretending and true-hearted ; was easily approached, and always interested in the wants and purposes of the people.

For over two score years he was a devoted member of the Methodist Episcopal church, and a large part of that time a zealous class leader. In politics originally a Whig, he was identified with the Republican party from its very organization, and it can be well said, he was its chief head and front in this county.

Before going on the bench he contributed largely to the press, and his political articles were written with great force of argument, and in strong, compact, nervous style, showing not only a complete mastery of the subject, but a correct literary taste not usually expected in one whose studies for a lifetime had been solely legal and utilitarian.

His religious duties were to him of paramount obligation, and his ever-mindful kindness to those sick and afflicted is part of the noble, but unwritten, history of his life. Though he had naturally a high and quick temper, he kept it down under strong bolt and bar. No man ever set a more vigilant watch upon his own conduct, was more guarded in his language, or was more scrupulous as to what he believed was right.

The strong cast of his features, his heavy brow, his deeply set, sharp, and piercing eye, his firm mouth, and his look of decision and self-command indicated uncommon individuality, and gave the impression of a character somewhat severe and stern, yet no one had kindlier feelings, a more generous and forgiving disposition.

In judging men he habitually took the charitable view, and whatever his judgment might be, he was never censorious.

As a husband he was unremitting in devotion and kindness; as a parent, indulgent, yet steady in discipline; as a neighbor and citizen, kind and public spirited; as a church member, zealous and exemplary; as a politician, sagacious and liberal; as a lawyer and judge, honest, courteous and distinguished.

The character of Judge Philip B. Swing needs perspective, like a great building, which, standing near, we do not appreciate its harmony of proportions. He was not a man of society, yet society committed to him many of its most sacred public and private trusts, pecuniary and otherwise. A great part of his power was latent; he was an influence felt even where he did or said nothing. There was potency in his presence. He was often solitary, but never lonesome.

Although more than sixty-two years of age and subject during the past year to frequent indispositions, his eye was not dimmed nor his natural force abated; his tall form continued erect, his step elastic; his hair was but slightly tinged with gray, his spirits were buoyant and his whole mind alert and capable as ever up to a few days before death arrested the stroke of his mighty heart, and he sank away in the arena of his best achievements. " A gentler heart did never sway in court." Men of the bar suddenly realized that they were bereft of a courteous elder brother who had endeared himself to them as counsellor and friend, and that a standard of the court had fallen.

In English homelier than the inscription in the Roman Scipio's
    tomb ;
Of honest stock ; courage and wisdom crowned
The man who still good as he looked was found ;
Whom all its honors to his country bound ;
Best of the best in his dear Clermont home ;
A better consul from Patrician Rome
Was never carried to the Scipio's tomb.　.

"We cannot hold mortality's strong hand," therefore we leave his body to be placed in its granite mausoleum, fitting type of the solidity of his emulable qualities. May it sleep in peace, while "his blessed part" we trust to heaven. Philosophy can do no more.

His life, written by intelligent minds and practiced hands, would form a legacy to coming generations more and more valued as time passed along, far more interesting and durable than the short record of a marbled tombstone. In Clermont county and Cincinnati, where from his boyhood he has been so generally known, the estimate will be that many men have lived more brilliant lives than Judge Philip B. Swing, but rarely has any man lived a better one—one whose sweet impress pervades all society from the most humble to the most exalted, with its strong manhood set in pure heart-felt affections linked to intellectuality that commanded high esteem and veneration.

CHAPTER XXXV.

AUTOBIOGRAPHICAL SKETCH OF THE AUTHOR.

GILBERT S. SWING, the author of this volume, was born and grew to manhood on a farm in Salem county, N. J., about half a century ago. Without the advantage of wealth, he got his education in his native state, and was originally trained for an agriculturist.

Perhaps the most pleasing associations of early life were connected with the remembrance of school days and our quiet country home; its magnificent expanse of green fields and waving grain, clean, shady woods, brought us into a blissful sense of repose, and the welcome of nature was only surpassed by that of our school companions on the playground. The pleasures of youth, as he approached manhood, were exchanged for the studies of the school-room. This study was rewarded by a strong mind, quick power of perception, and his teacher said that " everything the boy learned he knew well."

His mother, who was somewhat high-toned, and could speak fluently both the English and German languages, encouraged the study of arithmetic, drawing, bookkeeping, music, penmanship and history.

During his student life he was a member of the "Washingtonian" debating society, a literary institution established for the benefit of young men, where many of the leading and most exciting questions of the day were brought up in public debate, and members found great pleasure in attending the weekly meetings of this society.

It was while attending a mathematical school that his mind turned toward the occupation of teaching, and soon all thoughts tended in that direction.

His first appearance as a teacher was in the winter of 1850, in a small country village containing about two hundred and fifty inhabitants and sixty school children. Here he met with merited success, and satisfied the demands of propriety. The trustees of the district said "the teacher understood his business fairly well and was very attentive to books." Being successful from the first he was subsequently employed in the following-named places: Good Hope, 1851; Deerfield township, 1852; Parvin's Mill, 1853–4; Jackson, 1855; Pine Ville, 1856; Fox Chase, Montgomery county, Pa., 1857; Franklin, 1858; Aldine, 1859–60; Fair View, 1861–2; Lower Neck, 1863; Centerton, 1865. In some of these places he "held the fort" for two years each, and escaped alive!

Nothing tests a man's backbone more than the control of fifty half-grown boys. If he can maintain discipline and the regard and respect of his pupils, combining both instruction and friendship, he may succeed. Courage and perseverance, he believed, were good, but grit and determination were needful to maintain order, truth and progress ; and early in life he nailed these colors to the mast-head, and stood by them bravely.

It may be said that he belongs to the type of quiet, prudent, energetic men, with firm grasp on any situation they might have to deal with, and whose lives are busy and active ones.

In marriage Mr. S. was united with Miss Emily R. Carman, of Gloucester county, a young lady of pleasing address and many accomplishments. The couple commenced housekeeping and mercantile pursuits in the county of Salem, and entered into work full of vim, life and spirit. Being attentive to business and generous in their natures, they soon rallied around them earnest and abiding friends.

During the administration of ex-President Andrew Johnson, Mr. Swing was appointed postmaster of Pittsgrove, and in connection with the office was proprietor of a store, and did a prosperous business in said village. Six years later he resigned the post-office and removed to Cumberland county, and engaged in mercantile pursuits, where by their united efforts and close attention secured to themselves their full quota of the business of the town.

In religious views the family are Methodists, and during the past sixteen years have been supporters and members of the old Commerce Street M. E. church, Bridgeton (founded by his ancestors in 1805), and worship with its congregation.

To-day, " life is real, life is earnest," with our joyous childhood and happy school days behind us.

Mr. S. is a tall and well-built man, five feet ten inches in height; weight, one hundred and eighty pounds ; and has the same temperate and industrious habits of his ancestors. He never wastes any time in bar-rooms or billiard saloons ; is regarded as a kind philosopher, whose chief delight is experienced in business, and his life has been an active and honorable one. He also delights in telling the struggles of his early youth and of the years when teaching a country school and earning forty dollars a month. He has gone through a greater variety and wider range of employment than many ordinary persons, is still capable of doing his share of life's work or enjoying its pleasures, and inclined to believe that the world is getting wiser and better and more desirable as a place of residence.

24

CHAPTER XXXVI.

RECOLLECTIONS OF A SALEM COUNTY SCHOOL TEACHER, BY
G. S. SWING.

THERE is a kind of pleasing sadness in the memory
of our youthful days. Like voices from some
distant land the dreams of youth return, each
fragrant with a thousand recollections. When I look
back to the days of my early manhood I am reminded
that

> "Life's but a dream,
>   Time's but a stream,
>   That glides swiftly away,
>   While the fugitive moment refuses to stay."

I remember the winter of 1854. In one of the rural
districts that lies inland the teacher found it almost impossible to arrange the classes. Sixty-six names were
recorded on the register, and many of the school-books
were old and wornout. Our first term of teaching expired at this place on the 30th of January, when the
trustees granted permission to purchase a new library,
and instructed their teacher to make the selection of
books, granting the children vacation for one week.
The writer engaged passage on the old stage coach (mail

LOG SCHOOL HOUSE.

line, Mark Lloyd, proprietor and driver) for Philadelphia, changed horses at the Pole Tavern, and also at Mullica Hill, and traveled all day through a blinding northeast snowstorm, a distance of thirty miles. The weather was intensely cold and the Delaware river frozen over. A short distance above Cooper's ferry, Camden, N. J., sleighs with passengers and heavily loaded teams were crossing to the city of Philadelphia on the ice.

The snow continued for two days and nights in succession, and when it ceased the streets and country roads were full, from four to six feet deep, and travel was obstructed for several days. At the end of another week the weather changed, and became warm; a great storm of rain came on, with thunder and lightning. The rain descended in torrents and the snow melted away. In attempting to reach our appointment we found the country flooded with water. At the Back mill the long bridge and gates had disappeared, and the rumbling sound of water could be heard for miles away as it passed over into the stream below. After waiting for two hours a man with a boat was hired to ferry us across the raging stream.

Arriving at the next village there was great excitement among the people on account of this flood. The hotel and public buildings were submerged and surrounded by water. Passing on in the direction of the "Little Jordan," a stream below the city, we found this bridge also carried away. Applying for assistance at the residence of a gentleman, his horse was offered on which to ride over the ford. Going to the stables we found the horses were all out, nothing left but one mule; and on

the back of this animal passed safely through the stream
—not dry shod, however, for the water was deep and
almost over the head of the animal.

On reaching the opposite shore the rider dismounted
in a half-drowned condition, thanked the owner of the
quadruped, who stood on the hill, for furnishing passage
through the stream so cheap and reliable. The sun had
already disappeared in the west, and the darkness of
night began to gather around the waters of the lake as
the teacher resumed his journey in the direction of the
school house. For the next half mile the road led
through a forest of large and stately trees, and just
beyond the woods was an extensive tract of cultivated
land. We called a moment at the dwelling to remind
the farmer's children that school would commence again
on the following day.

"Are you the schoolmaster at Little Jordan?" inquired a venerable lady in spectacles.

"Yes, ma'am."

"The scholars like you much better than your prede-
cessor of last year."

"Indeed; is that so?"

"Yes," she continued; "our children learn very fast,
and we do not have to drive them to school this winter."

Among the superintendents of Gloucester, Salem and
Cumberland counties, who filled the office acceptably for
three years each, and from whom I received certificates,
we recall the following named: Jonathan L. Brown,
William Null, Nathaniel G. Swing, Jonathan S. Whitaker,
David Shimp, Jr.; Thomas R. Clement, M. D.; John

W. Hazelton, Keasby Pancoast, James Coombs, Ephraim
B. Davis.

Before any person could be elected to a school they
had to attend an examination and obtain a license.
These examinations were conducted either at a private
office or in a country school house, and often attended by
half a dozen young men and maidens who had assembled
to go through the ordeal of an examination.

Upon a cold and frosty morning in November I remember driving eighteen miles into another county to
attend one of these inspections. Each candidate was
supplied with reading and writing exercises, while the
superintendent listened to a young man's reading

> "Oh, for a lodge in some vast wilderness,
> Some boundless contiguity of shade,
> Where rumors and oppression meet."

Next was the reading of extracts from an essay on
"Man:"

"Man, in his individual nature, becomes virtuous by
constant struggles against his own imperfections. His
intellectual eminence, which puts him at the head of
created beings, is attained also by long toil and painful
self-denials. It would seem to be a law of his existence,
that great enjoyment is only to be obtained as the reward
of great exertion," etc.

To the last person reading he inquired: "Who is the
author of this oration?"

"Blessed if I know," replied the young man, excitedly.

" Richard Rush," I replied, " a teacher, and member of the house of representatives at the capitol, Washington."

" Amanda," he said, " is there any h in sofa ? "

" Of course there is," answered Miss Jones. " S-o-p-h-a —sofa."

" How many n's in Cincinnati ? " he asked,

" Three," replied Miss Jones, casting a sly wink at her companions. C-i-n-c-i-n-n-a-t-i."

1st. Will each person explain the difference between learning and teaching ?

2nd. Define education, memory, discipline.

3rd. Recite the laws of the state of New Jersey pertaining to common schools.

4th. Write a specimen of your penmanship, and name the principles in the system you teach.

An elderly gentleman was asked :

1st. How is the earth divided ?   Into land and water ; one-fourth land, three-fourths water.

2nd. Name four of the largest cities in the world ? Paris, London, Peking, New York.

3d. Name the capitals of the states north of Mason's and Dixon's line ?

4th. How many states were represented in the first Electoral College ?

" Who were our three greatest men ? " was asked of an ambitious-looking youth.

Innocently, I replied : " People sometimes differ in opinion in reference to our greatest men, but I would suggest the names of George Washington, Andrew Jackson and Napoleon Bonaparte."

"Good," said the superintendent. " During what year was Washington inaugurated president of the United States ?"

"April 3, 1789, and continued in office, eight years," I replied. " What is your own age ?" " Past twenty-four, sir." " Have you taught before ?" " Yes, sir." " In what place ?" " Sodam and Gomorrah." " Indeed! and escaped from these places alive ?" " Yes, sir."

" What is the meaning of the word ' review ? ' " " To consider again, to carefully examine." " ' Rhetoric ? ' " " The art of speaking with propriety." " What is ' gossip ? ' " We answer, in a general way, it is talking about persons rather than books. " What is a fountain ?" " It is a spring, the source and head of a river." " Parallelogram ?" " Four sides whose opposites are equal." " How many sides has a circle ?" " Two," replied the student. " What are they " " An outside and an inside."

He turned away from me and began to question a young lady by asking her to name the longest river, the largest lake and the highest range of mountains. If a teacher, whose annual income is $12.00 per week, spends $20.50 per week, will he save money or run in debt, and how much in one year? A merchant married his daughter on New Year's day, and gave her one dollar towards her portion, promising to double the amount on the first day of every month for one year; what was the amount received ?

The elderly person who had been teaching in the county for fifteen years was asked, " Do you know the authors of the arithmetics used in the schools ?"

"Titus Bennett, Greenleaf, and John Rose," he replied. The last named was a teacher in Salem county, N. J., and his arithmetic one of the best in use.

"Where is Mecca, and for what is it noted?" "How many continents are there?" "Two," replied the student; "the eastern and western." "What does the eastern contain?" "Europe, Asia and Africa." "How old was Methuselah when he died?" "Never saw his age recorded in school-books," replied the old gentleman. "How long was Noah building the ark?" etc.

"What is multiplication?" was next asked. "Multiplication shows what any number amounts to when multiplied by another number; or, it is a compendious way of adding numbers.

TWO EXAMPLES.

<table>
<tr><td>Short way explained.</td><td></td></tr>
<tr><td>93</td><td>93</td></tr>
<tr><td>68</td><td>68</td></tr>
<tr><td>——</td><td>——</td></tr>
<tr><td>6324</td><td>744</td></tr>
<tr><td></td><td>558</td></tr>
<tr><td></td><td>——</td></tr>
<tr><td></td><td>6324</td></tr>
</table>

"Take the first example. Say 8 times 3 are 24; set down both figures and carry 1 to the next line; 7 times 9 are 63; put down both figures and you have the product, 6324. This rule applies to whole and fractional numbers, and the calculations are much quicker than the old method."

"And you attended the grammar classes?" inquired the superintendent of another candidate.

" Yes, sir."

" Ah! What is a noun, verb, adverb, pronoun? What is the adjective personal pronoun of 1st person, of 2nd and 3rd person? Repeat the general rules? Please parse the following: 'The master will give two books; all men have two eyes apiece; most insects have six feet, some nine, others ten, others twelve ; birds migrate twice in the year; happy is the teacher whom all scholars love.' "

The examiner was getting out another book to continue the examination, when in comes a boy and says : " Is Mr. S. in here? 'cause if he is, the stage is waiting at the door, and Mr. Lloyd wants him to come right away, for he carries the mail and driving to meet the boat."

" Yes," I hastily put in, " that's so."

Conscious that I had been found ignorant of many facts, dates in history and questions in school books which others retained in their memory, and being brought up in the country, I arose at once, and with a profound bow started for the door.

" Hold on," said the superintendent, as he grasped the pen and filled out a license, remarking at the same time, " I shall expect to hear a good account from Little Jordan District before the end of your quarter." Five minutes later I entered the stage coach, and while the spirited leaders galloped through the ancient village of Mullica Hill I was sitting on the top seat with the driver perfectly satisfied, a restful air pervading my heart, while in my pocket reposed the license of a teacher of public school, to continue in force for another year. The business of teaching in those days was in the hands of but few men, and their services were in constant demand. Although the compensation was small, yet single-handed and alone they surmounted many barriers and arose step by step to distinction.

The greatest number of scholars in daily attendance during the second year of teaching was sixty-five, and the smallest number seven. One day in January I walked three miles through a storm of wind and rain, only to find seven scholars, four boys and three girls. When about half way a sudden squall of wind turned my umbrella inside out, and carried it away. I was very wet and cold. After waiting a moment and no additions coming, I said, "We might as well leave here; there will be no school to-day." A bright little girl responded: "I have come through two miles of rain to recite my geography." We saw our duty at once, and replied, "Yes, Mary, you are entitled to all the instruction I am able to give."

Being somewhat gifted in vocal and instrumental music (the German flute and other instruments), we called the little company to order by saying: Let us commence the morning exercises by singing in chorus hymn 284.

> "Little drops of water,
> Little grains of sand,
> Make the mighty ocean,
> And the beauteous land.

"And the little moments,
    Humble though they be,
Make the mighty ages
    Of eternity.

"So our little errors,
    Lead the soul away
From the paths of virtue,
    Oft in sin to stray.

"Little deeds of kindness,
    Little words of love,
Make our earth an Eden,
    Like the heaven above."

The experience of a teacher is varied and amusing in many respects. School districts, as well as schoolboys and girls, change with the progress of civilization. One evening I took my hat, intending to call upon a friend, when I observed a carriage driving up to the boarding house, and a young man requested my company that evening to attend a public school exhibition. My mind was at once relieved from all gloomy thoughts, and as the country roads were good, and the distance only ten miles, I resolved to accompany him immediately. Arriving at the place, the exhibition had commenced, and a bright-looking lad was reciting extracts from " Washington's Farewell Address." The house was crowded to overflowing, and at first we could get no further than the door. Next, two girls and two boys commenced a dialogue, " The Man who didn't take the Newspapers ;" composition, " The Industrious Scholar ;" instrumental, violin and flute; dialogue, " Mrs. Caudle's Lecture ;"

recitation, "Our Schooldays Revived;" singing, "National Anthem;" recitation, "The Boy who played Truant;" recitation, "Our Native Land;" composition, "Free Trade and Sailors' Rights;" dialogue by four boys, "Protection to American Industry;" dialogue, "Isn't Deacon Jones' Wife a little hard of hearing?" Next on the programme two Union girls sang a war song on the platform, and away back in the house two Confederates responded with "Away down in Dixie." "My True Love is a Soldier" was then sung by a young lady, and in the stillness that followed a person representing a wounded soldier hobbled up to meet his sweetheart, and started the air of "Home, Sweet Home," which was eagerly caught up by the audience, and as the war was then going on the story of itself was very affecting and beautiful. A bright little boy next recited, in a clear voice, the following lines:

> "I would not die in spring time
>   When worms begin to crawl,
> When cabbage plants are springing up,
>   And frogs begin to squall;
> 'Tis then the girls are full of charms,
>   And smile upon the men;
> When lamb and peas are in their prime,
>   I would not perish then.

> "I would not die in summer,
>   When trees are filled with fruit,
> And every sportsman has a gun,
>   The little birds to shoot;

The girls then wear the bloomer dress,
  And half distract the men :
It is the time to shriek it out,
  I would not perish then.

"I would not die in autumn,
  When new mown hay smells sweet,
And little pigs are rooting round
  For something nice to eat ;
'Tis then the huntsman's wild halloo
  Is heard along the glen,
And quails and oysters fatten up,
  I would not perish then.

" I would not die in winter,
  For one might freeze to death ;
When blustering Boreas sweeps around
  And almost takes one's breath,
When sleigh bells jingle, horses snort,
  And buckwheat cakes are tall ;
In fact, this is a right good woild,
  My friends, I would not die at all."

Next a middle-aged person related his experience, " The
Days when I went Gypsying," and " How I Courted
Sukey Smith." In the midst of the applause which followed the stovepipe fell upon the floor, and the smoke
began to fill the house. It was soon righted, however,
and quietness reigned supreme. I had often assisted in
preparing exhibitions of this kind myself, and in my
own school house they eventually became popular and
were highly appreciated by the country people. When
the teacher informed his audience that it gave him great
pleasure to introduce Mr. Swing, from Salem county,
sensitive and modest I arose, and very innocently com-

menced by saying, Mr. President, ladies and gentlemen, if the trustees will insure the stovepipe from falling down a second time I will endeavor to make a few remarks, and pausing a moment for breath, the children laughed; then the audience took it up as if the incident had only increased their pleasure. A moment later my tongue seemed loose again, and timidity and bashfulness vanished away.

I like these country schools. My happiest memories are of the years that I walked two miles to one of them and carried my dinner in a satchel.

During the spring of 1863, about two months after the incident related in a former chapter, it was my good fortune, with sixteen others from the same township, to be drafted to serve in the army of the United States "for a period of three years, or during the war." Before this occurred I had thought of resigning my commission and going out as teacher to New Mexico, Sumatra, Borneo, Japan—anywhere in creation to run away from myself. Then I thought of the lonely island of Juan Fernandez—in mid ocean—and the house where Alexander Selkirk exclaimed to himself:

"I am monach of all I survey."

Now the draft has come; hit the schoolmaster, they said, and it is too late. Looking over the list of drafted persons, some people said: "This is a good hit;" while others expressed their sympathy and remarked that Salem county had aleady sent its full quota of soldiers to the front, and the services of those remaining were needed at home. Another person remarked: " I would prefer going to war at any time rather than teaching a country school." Putting on a bland and spring-like expression, we visited the largest cities looking for substitutes; the most exciting, though not the most desirable, place being at a recruiting office, among soldiers, sutlers, sailors, and the army and navy headquarters. In the process of time I had found substitues for myself and others at a cost of five hundred and fifty dollars each; returned from the war and was for a time the hero of the hour. Trustees and people received me, and as I had sung patriotic songs with their children they seemed more social and agreeable than ever before. But when I reached the schoolhouse I heard an unearthly sound within, a somewhat unhappy blending of voices. Shade of the inharmonious, what does it mean? and upon entering found the children singing a solo. Nailed to my writing desk was a beautiful flag upon which was inscribed the following patriotic lines:

OUR COUNTRY'S FLAG.

Hail glorious flag! we cherish thee,
Unblemished standard of the free!
A nation's pride, a nation's boast—
Thou art guarded by our country's host
    Of heroes firm and brave.
Then fling our banner to the air,
Columbia's stars are glittering there;
And let it wave majestic, grand,
O'er all the cities of our land,
    And ocean's stormy wave.

25

Some years later the writer was invited to address a school exhibition and reunion of teachers and scholars at the same place. After complimenting the children for their improvement in learning oratory and musical attainments, I said: It is very pleasant to recall our successes. The soldier loves to fight his battles over; he warms up, his eye sparkles, he becomes eloquent. What can loosen the tongue of a retired merchant like a request to give an account of his early life and struggles, of how he worked his way to the proud position which he now occupies? We have heard them many a time, and never grew weary of listening. The aged minister shows it more clearly and revels in it more constantly than either the soldier or the merchant. These fathers in the conference forget the present and sometimes consume the time. When one of them spoke at great length a young minister went to Bishop Janes and asked him if there was no way to shorten their speeches. "No," said he, "these old men have earned the right to be heard as long as they live;" and so they have, if they have done their work well.

To recall vanished joys is not entirely unpleasant. It is not easy to explain how it is that pleasure can be found in lingering over broken pictures and hopes that never can be realized, and happiness that is gone forever. Yet of the fact there is no doubt; most persons know it by experience, and it is attested by the poets truest to human nature:

Long, long be my heart with such memories filled,
Like the vase in which roses have once been distilled ;
You may break, you may ruin, the vase if you will,
The scent of the roses will hang round it still.

The "district" schoolhouse of forty years ago has gone out with the old "oaken bucket," but its memories were embalmed and surrounded with a charm which not even the model schools of to-day can give. Our school report says there has been an average attendance of forty-five, larger than on any previous winter; thirty boys have not been absent more than three times and several have not missed a single day.

"I remember being asked rather anxiously by a little girl whether twice two was four in France and Germany also. I gave her great comfort by assuring her that it was, not only in France and Germany, but also in the heavens and the earth and the sea, and in all times and seasons." Daniel Webster once said that he would not undertake to say what were the mathematics of heaven. But the Yankees have made great advances since the time of Daniel.

Luther said: "If a man is not handsome at twenty, strong at thirty, learned at forty and rich at fifty, he never will be handsome, strong, learned or rich in this world."

The reading of good books are very important to children for this reading forms a very important feature in the formation of our character and life. If you will notice the books and newspapers on the centre table of wealthy men, you may form some estimate of the people living in the house. As the result of my own observations, those who have access to newspapers at home, when compared with those who have not, are much better readers, better spellers, and define words with care and accuracy. They are better grammarians for the newspaper has made them familiar with many varieties of style, from the comic advertisement to the most finished oratory of the statesman.

Some years ago a gentleman from New Jersey, Dr. Charles Swing, was traveling on a steamboat on the Ohio river, and made the acquaintance of another traveler who seemed to be very polite and courteous; they took staterooms together on the boat. Later in the day the doctor concluded that this agreeable stranger was becoming very meddlesome and inquisitive, and after all he might be nothing but a gambler or an imposter. Obtaining an interview with the clerk of the boat, he requested another stateroom. The rooms were all full, said the clerk. Then the doctor concluded to sit up all night and let the stranger occupy the apartment alone. Going into the room for some article in the evening he observed the man quietly reading the Bible, then all suspicion and fear vanished away; he was afriad no longer. In the society of a good old man reading his Bible there is nothing to fear.

We recollect just here an incident which occurred in the winter of 1853 while the writer was stationed in one of the counties of this state. Upon our school register were inscribed the names of sixty-five children, large and small, all the way up from six to twenty years of age. In our quiet room at the boarding house we sometimes looked over the lessons and studies for the following day, being young in years and having but little experience in the management of children or the trials of a teacher's life. Upon one occasion it was nearly midnight when we retired to rest; a deep snow lay upon the ground and the weather was extremely cold. In a few moments we heard the loud barking of the dog and some person walking over the frozen snow. The messenger approached the house and began knocking at the front door. With the exception of the writer the people in the dwelling were all asleep, and no one answered the call; presently we raised the sash in the window above and inquired, " Who is wanted?" " We want the school teacher," said the lad; " Grandfather Connley is very sick, and he requests you to come immediately and write his will." Accompanying the messenger to a large farm house in the country, we found a venerable looking man, past eighty years of age, and apparently very near the close of life. Having recently come in possession of a large amount of property, he was anxious to make a will and remember his children, grandchildren and relatives in a handsome way. The entire balance of the night being spent in the arrangement and writing of this document, then with trembling hand the signatures were attached. Said he, " Teacher, I wish you to remain with us for breakfast, then my grandson will take you to the schoolhouse in the sleigh." After complying with this latter request, he said, " I feel so much better since the will is written. My earthly work is almost finished; \

can depart in peace." A few weeks later this aged pilgrim, who had been for so many years a successful navigator of the land and the sea, quietly passed away, having completed his earthly work.

Life is not to be measured by years but by results; and many a man has crowded into a quarter of a century —labor, discovery, observation and conclusions—what might well have occupied the whole hundred years. It is enough if we economize the days, and we are sometimes permitted to put the study and labor of a hundred hours into one of them. Upon the tombstone of Capt. Connley it is written that he was a loving husband, a tender father, an ingenious navigator and serviceable to mankind.

At another place it was my pleasure to renew the acquaintance of Professor D——, a venerable looking man upon whom I had often called on agricultural, political and educational errands in my boyhood. Have you been teaching many years? I inquired. "Yes," he replied, " for more than half a century, and still engaged in active work." During a cold and stormy day in midwinter he was taken suddenly with apoplexy, and fell from his chair; was taken home in a carriage and soon after expired. The following afternoon, at the hour of recess, a strange boy entered my own school house and exclaimed, " I shall go to school no longer. The master at New London is dead."

This incident recalls the memory of Professor A——, another man of good memory and excellent education. He frequently wrote articles for newspapers, and deliv-

ered lectures on education, astronomy and political economy. Had taught many years in the Eastern States;
the last fifteen in Burlington, Gloucester and Salem
counties. He was usually dressed in the fashion of the
Quakers. He was known all over the country, and by
some of the boys was nicknamed "Old Straight Jacket,"
"The Star Gazer," &c.

Going home upon one occasion he informed his
daughter that there was another difficulty brewing in the
village. The trustees had visited his school, complained
of its management, and quarreled among themselves.
He said he believed there was no perfect place or perfect
people on this earth; felt weary, disappointed with life,
and ready to die.

That night one of the trustees dreamed that the gates
of heaven opened to his enraptured vision, and standing
on the shores of immortality he saw the Quaker schoolmaster beckoning him to come, for he had found a country, he said, "where all is perfect harmony and perfect
peace." In the morning he informed his neighbor of
his wonderful dream, and proposed calling upon the
teacher at once, when, to their surprise and astonishment
they learned that he was dead.

LIVE FOR SOMETHING.

Live for something, be not idle—
 Look about thee for employ !
Sit not down to useless dreaming—
 Labor is the sweetest joy.

Folded hands are ever weary,
  Selfish hearts are never gay,
Life for thee hath many duties—
  Active be, then, while you may.

Scatter blessings in thy pathway !
  Gentle words and cheering smiles,
Better are than gold and silver,
  With their grief-dispelling wiles.
As the pleasant sunshine falleth,
  Ever on the grateful earth,
So let sympathy and kindness
  Gladden well the darkened hearth.

It is related that Eastman made an enormous fortune in Poughkeepsie with a business college. At the time of the war he was eking out a living as the proprietor of a small school. Under the draft law, scholars were exempt from military service, and Eastman soon found his school so full that he had to move into more commodious quarters. The secret of the plan to evade conscription leaked out, and within six months Eastman rented every vacant room in the town and filled it with "scholars." Illiteracy spread with alarming rapidity, and middle-aged men who had been considered fairly educated merchants suddenly forgot how to read and write or to do their sums, and found it necessary to attend Professor Eastman's business college. The professor prospered accordingly, and even when the war deprived him of his "scholars" his business was firmly established.

The true method of strengthening the memory is to cultivate a habit of close and careful attention. What is read, heard or seen should not be dismissed instantaneously, but should be, as it were, revolved in the mind for a moment. This may at first prove a little irksome, and may give a certain appearance of sluggish apprehension, but it will not long be so, and the gain will be found incalculable. Robert Houdin, the great French conjurer and magician, gives an interesting account of the origin of the " second sight," which he invented and which was brought to such a pitch of perfection by the late professor. He says that as he and his son walked along the streets they would look at windows crowded with toys or jewelry. Then they would each write down as many articles as they could recollect having seen, and, going back, would verify their lists. Very soon, he says, his son could with one comprehensive glance take in every article in a large, well-furnished window. It is needless to insist upon the extreme value of a good and trustworthy memory. Petty annoyances, as well as serious inconveniences, are the results of forgetfulness, and most forgetfulness is the result, not of any organic defect or morbid condition, but of simple heedlessness, and the habit of " letting things in at one ear and out the other."

We are very apt to remember the errors and mistakes of ourselves or others much more vividly than their excellences or the average current of experience. How the recollections of an awkward blunder in company, or a careless, ill-advised remark will send a chill of shame and regret through the system. A faithful horse may carry his rider a hundred miles without a misstep, but a round stone concealed in the sand may betray the step of the horse and bring him to his knees, causing the rider to give him a bad name as a saddle horse, forgetting the million steps securely taken, and remembering only the one failure, and even in that case overlooking entirely the adequate cause of the misstep. And this is a good analogue of human character or conduct. One may live half a century a model of correct deportment, and a single act of impropriety be recorded as more than an offset to all that was commendable.

A southern negro, an ex-slave, hired a field from his old master to cultivate, he to receive one-third and the master two-thirds of the crop. The old negro was honest, but not up in arithmetic. The field yielded two loads, both of which he put in his master's crib and reported to the astonished landlord: "Dar is no third, sah; de land am too poor to produce de third, sah."

An old farmer being asked why his boys stayed at home when others did not, replied that it was owing to the fact that he always tried to make home pleasant for them. He furnished them with attractive and useful reading, and when night came and the day's labor was ended, instead of running with other boys to the railway station and adjoining towns, they gathered around the great lamp, and became absorbed in their books and papers. His boys were still at home when the oldest was twenty-one, while others had sought city life and city dissipations as soon as they were seventeen or eighteen.

I once read of an individual who, after being in a trance for several days, forgot all he ever knew, though once he was an able preacher. He had to re-learn his letters, and spell out words and sentences. Just think of it; you and I can read fast, as our eye moves over the page. We do not have to spell a word, so long have we practiced. Now, what an affliction it would be should we lose at once our ability to read. God be thanked because we have eyes to see, and knowledge to enable us, and books to read. That minister, as day after day he taxed his brain to learn to spell and read, was made to feel what a blessing he had lost. An aged colored man once said to his master, " I'd give anything, massa, if I had it, to know how to read the good book." His master replied: " Sambo, you are too old a dog to learn new tricks." But Sambo did learn to read the good book. He spent all his leisure time in learning, first his letters, then in spelling, then in putting words together in sentences, until one day he took his Bible in his hands, fell upon his knees, and said, " I do bress God I can read." And he lived years to read and derive comfort from the word of God.

How much enjoyment comes to us every day from being able to read. Then let us call to mind the kindness of those who taught us when we were young, and carefully improve our privilege in reading such books as will make us wiser and better.

Another important lesson in the education of children is obedience. " Obey your parents in all things," is the divine command. This virtue is commendable, not only in children and youth, but often admired in old age. On Sunday last the Rev. Mr. Brown told a little anecdote of General Grant which is worth repeating. He said that while he was pastor of the First M. E. church at Long Branch Grant returned from his famous tour around the world, and notified him that he should attend his church on a certain Sabbath. The preacher also said that in conversation the general told him that he always made it a practice to attend church once on Sunday, generally in the morning.

Well, the day came, and one of the best seats on the centre aisle was reserved for the general. He came into church surrounded by his family, and having just returned from his trip his hair and beard were both very long. Of course the church was well filled with people who craned their necks to get a glimpse of the great man.

On the following Sunday Grant came again, but this time he was alone and his hair and beard had both been cut close. He quietly took a seat in the pew reserved for him. The sexton saw him, but did not recognize him, and stepping up, said: " My dear sir, I am sorry to bother you, but really this pew is reserved for General Grant, and you will have to take a seat on the other side."

Grant said not a word, but got up and stepped across the aisle and sat down in a pew on the other side. In a few moments the preacher entered and seeing the general not in the pew reserved for him, called the sexton and inquired about it. " Good gracious," said the sexton, "I did not know him. I thought that was an intruder, and I ordered him out of Grant's pew."

The abashed sexton at once stepped down to where Grant was sitting, made profuse apologies for his stupidity and requested the general to return to the pew reserved for him, which the latter did as quietly as before, without a word one way or the other.

IN CONCLUSION.

I remember the days of my boyhood and the early instruction of my father, who accomplished something in his day and time for the cause of truth and education.   Living as he did about two miles away from the church of his choice, we usually geared out the team of horses on Sabbath morning for the church.   Occasionally the country roads were bad and the weather cold and stormy, then he would say, "Boys, you need not run out the carriage to-day; we will read the books and newspapers and learn something at home."

> "To serve the present age
> My calling to fulfill,
> O, may it all my powers engage
> To do my Master's will."

We remember just here an incident which occurred near the commencement of the late war.   A countryman from the green hills of Vermont, attracted by the sound of fife and drum, and the excitement of military life, applied at a recruiting office to enlist for the war. Looking upon the American eagle and the star-spangled banner as it floated in the breeze, he read the inscription,

"Victory or Death." He said, "I love my country and my native land, and long to fight in my country's defence, but do not like these words, 'Victory or Death.' If you will enlist me in the service I will go in for victory or cripple!" As advocates of education and national reform, let us, like the good soldier, go in for victory or cripple. Let us record anew in our memory that we are not living in the world for ourselves alone, but are living so as to enjoy hereafter a higher and grander destiny. Let us remember that there is plenty of water in springs, river and ocean, and to the industrious and persevering man there is no such word as fail. Then let us fight manfully the battles of this present life; let us be true to ourselves, true to the living and true to the dead.